Contents

Luke and Laura: A Love Story

Laura and I didn't meet in the way people normally do. She picked me out as a partner when the substitute dancing teacher told us to pair off and dance to the rock and roll records she played on the record player connected to the public address system. I was still peeling off my oil soaked machine shop boots, as directed by the teacher, when Laura seized my right hand. I wouldn't have picked her because, at the time, I preferred the looks of tall blonde girls, and Laura had shoulder-length black hair.

She grabbed my hands and held them so hard it hurt. She started whipping me around so fast, the other kids had to clear a path for us. At first I thought she was just plain nuts, a psycho in tight jeans and a white blouse. The other kids were dancing like normal, without holding hands like they did on the TV shows for teenagers. Some of the other kids stopped and watched us, but we kept up the frenzied, crazy hand-holding dance style. I kept at it just for the iconoclastic hell of it. But Laura was really into the emotion of it and either watched our feet or my face. Her hair whipped behind her like a dervish. Between the brief lulls between dances she fiercely squeezed my hands, smiled, finally and told me her name. We were sweating and her gardenia perfume seemed to blossom in the air. She didn't ask my name.

Our dancing debut happened in the Spring of 1969 in a old fashioned dancing school with a wooden floor on the second story of a building near Chicago's Logan Square. The big auditorium had been used by labor leaders in the 1880s and 1890s to hold union meetings. It had hosted a radio show with a live audience in the 1920s, then it served as a banquet hall before the dance school was established during the Korean War.

How did I wind up in dance class? Goddamn Judge Kelly put me there. I had been in front of his bench three times. Once for peeing on the sidewalk in front of the Plaza Art burlesque theater on North Avenue, once for public intoxication across the street from Lane Technical High School, and once for fighting with some Puerto Rican kids at the corner of North and Wells in Old Town. The last time I had to appear before the judge, I accused the cop, a Puerto Rican named Oscar Soto, who had busted me all three times, of playing favorites.

"Why didn't he bust the Puerto Rican kids?" I demanded.

"Because you attacked them..." Oscar was perfunctorily cut off.

"Out of order." Old Judge Kelly gave Oscar a dirty look over the tops of his bifocals. Oscar hated my guts after that. He respected authority.

Judge Kelly wasn't a bad guy. He was a New Deal liberal, so he believed that I was a product of my urban industrial working class upbringing or lack thereof. Consequently, when my mother told him that I was out-of-control, and that the high school counselor had recommended "dance therapy" for my sociopathic and anti-social behavior, he readily agreed. Not because the old guy actually thought dancing would improve me, but because he quickly detected that I loathed the idea. The deal: successfully complete the dancing curriculum or find myself in the State School for Boys in St. Charles, Illinois.

So, when this beautiful dark haired girl grabbed my hand and started bopping to the music and dancing like a demon, I had to follow her frenetic lead or have my shoulders pulled of their sockets.

A lot of the other kids laughed, but as Laura pounded the floor record after record, song after song, I got tired, and the other kids stopped laughing. I began to wonder if a lunatic had permanently attached herself to me. My feet began to ache. Then, I gradually relaxed, because our ferocious dancing alienated the other kids. I loved flaunting conventions anyway, from wearing sideburns, long hair in the back, and a black leather jacket to skipping school and getting drunk.

If our intense dancing freaked out the other kids, so be it. I started bopping harder than Laura, and eventually wrenched my hands free and began flailing my arms like a lunatic. I knew Judge Kelly would disapprove. Our radically interpretive dancing continued for the duration of the class.

When we finished, Laura asked me to walk her to the L terminal at Logan Square. We had Cokes at the Terminal Restaurant under the tracks. Sweetest Coke I ever drank. She worked there, so we got the Cokes free. She gave me her phone number, but was perturbed when I told her I didn't have one.

Hell, at the time, I didn't even have an address, I had been kicked out of the house by my father, another staunch believer in authority, titles, judges, and the law. I had been crashing from day to day at the apartments of some guys I knew, students at the University of Illinois.

When I escorted her to the terminal, she grabbed my head and kissed me hard right on the lips. Then she went through the turnstile and flounced up the stairs to the trains. So ended, what, up to that moment, had been the most stunning day of my life.

I got back into my car, a black Plymouth Fury convertible with a big ass 383 motor. I drove over to Wicker Park to see if I could buy some dope wholesale from the dealers who waited in the tiny park. I retailed the marijuana to the college kids for extra bucks and a place to crash for the night.

Lately, I had been having problems with this goofy old man who liked to yell at me and chase me out of the park. He was a little guy with a pot belly, and people on the street said his name was Nelson. The drunks in the Milwaukee Avenue bars called him "the Swede." I think he lived on Evergreen Street, because that's where I encountered him the most often.

"Get the hell out of our neighborhood you goddamned dope dealer." He pissed me off, because I was just a middle man. The dealers were the guys in the park selling wholesale. Whatever his name, he was fucking up my business.

I knew I would never return home. My father had it in his mind that he was going to stick me into the machine shop program at Lane Tech. He had signed me up, but I solved that problem by ditching school altogether. He had threatened me with the Army if I dropped out, so there was no going back. No fucking way was I going to Vietnam. I don't know how he figured he had the moral high ground in telling me how to run my life. He worked as a screw machine set-up man at some big factory on the Northwest Side that everybody called Bastard and Blessing. Nobody knew the real name of the place.

I had managed to get a night job with the Black Cat Cab Company despite the fact that I was underage. They operated out of Logan Square, too. I thought that if I could make steady marijuana sales out of the cab, that I could make enough bread to get an apartment and get a life. All I had to do was avoid Judge Kelly, Officer Soto, the Swede, and my father.

A couple months later in the Terminal Restaurant Laura said, "Let's move in together. We can pool the money. You can finish high school, and I'm going to the University of Illinois in the Fall for a nursing degree."

In the background I could smell bacon and eggs sizzling on the grill. It was 2 A.M. but the Terminal Restaurant was open 24 hours. Laura looked severe in her white restaurant uniform, a short skirt and a button down blouse. She tied her hair back when she worked. I hated that.

Our conversation was punctuated every so often by a grizzled old man wearing a White Sox baseball cap. He would raise his empty coffee cup and say, "Miss?" He looked like a terminal alcoholic or junkie, thin, wearing ragged jeans and dirty t-shirt. And Laura would walk down the long, formica counter and fill his cup.

I had noticed during my visits to the restaurant that Laura didn't make much in tips. She didn't chum around enough with the customers. She was all business. She took the order, delivered the order, then delivered the check.

The day after we met, I phoned her and she asked me to pick her up at her address in Uptown. Uptown was a permanent slum on the North Side lake front. My father had once told me, "Don't trust nobody who lives in Uptown. They're all bad news." But after several weeks of dating Laura, I decided I could safely ignore my father's judgement of the good people of Uptown.

"So, what do you think?"

"About what?"

"Luke. Wake-the-fuck-up. What did I just ask you about?"

"Oh, moving-in together, right?"

Laura placed her hands on her hips and stared at me with a frown on her face.

Laura's father had died of black lung the previous winter. Her family had just moved from southeastern Ohio. Her father wanted to try to get a factory job in Chicago, but he passed out in the street while looking for work. He went into a coma and died a day later in the hospital.

Her mother had quickly found a boyfriend and moved with him to a northwest suburb, Carpentersville, just three months after taking up residence in Chicago. Curiously, he was a carpenter.

Laura accompanied her mother and three little brothers, but returned to the city a week later because she felt her "stepfather" had been hitting on her. Laura moved into a tiny apartment with a girl she had met while briefly attending Senn High School, Irma Maldonado.

I hated Irma from the git-go. She was a brainless, stuck-up bitch who dressed like a hooker in day-glo mini dresses, and tube tops.

"Luke?"

"Yeah. Why not? We can do that."

"You don't have to be so fucking enthusiastic."

"No, baby, I want to do it. Let's go look for an apartment tomorrow."

"You gotta lose the dope dealing first, if you want to live with me."

"Laura, I keep telling you, I'm going to quit dealing - after I make a bankroll for us. We need enough to live on while I finish off high school, then get through at least a year of college. You need a car, too."

"I don't need a car. I can take the bus and train to school. If we both work part time, we'll have enough."

"Laura, I want some real bread, ok? I'm tired of being poor."

She leaned across the counter and gently took my hands. I could look deep into her cleavage where the warm scent of gardenias wafted up. "Listen, I'm afraid. I'm worried you're in over your head. People get murdered every day in Chicago over drugs. I see it in the newspapers all the time."

There was something about Laura that just plain got to me. Some people call it chemistry. I call it magic. Yeah, I had that magic feeling for her. Where she was ying, I was yang. We just matched up like a salt and pepper set.

"Laura, I'm not going to get shot. I know what I'm doing. And I'm not going to be doing it much longer. I'm just waiting for the right deal. When it comes, I'll see it, and I'll be down road - but with some money for a change." I hadn't mentioned the big deal I was cooking, because it wasn't wise to talk about business to anyone. If they thought you might have a few bucks on you, they would shoot you.

Laura turned loose of my hands and straightened up. Down the counter we heard the plaintive call, "Miss?"

I watched Laura's slinky butt move down the counter. We had only been dating for a week when we made love for the first time. I didn't tell Laura, but it was the first time period for me. We walked out into the park along the lake near Belmont Harbor. She had planned on having a little picnic. It was a warm breezy day. Then a big storm blew-in from the southwest. I mean it went from sunny to black, low-flying clouds in a heartbeat. The waves on the lake picked up immediately, and I had lived in Chicago long enough to know when to start looking for shelter. So did all the other people in the park, who headed for the tunnel under Lake Shore Drive. I watched small boats putting into the harbor at full speed. But Laura refused to leave, she wanted to watch the storm unfold over the skyscrapers down the lake front in the Loop.

In a few minutes, the wind was at hurricane strength, the rain came slashing in horizontal in sheets, and we were soaked. Lightening hit all around us in the lake waters. I was scared shitless. Then she started peeling off her clothing and told me she wanted to make love under the tree that was partially sheltering us.

I honestly didn't know where to start with a woman's body, but I sure learned in a hurry. We did it on the ground in back of the tree, the wind howling, and thunder breaking directly overhead. We were putting our clothing back on as the first brave souls emerged from the tunnel. Laura pointed out over the lake. Far off, on the horizon, I watched a funnel cloud touch down on the lake, then whip around in a lazy serpentine motion.

After that, I couldn't keep my hands off her. And she knew it. But she couldn't seem to keep her hands off me either, although I think her motive was real love and mine was mainly lust. It was gradually becoming clear to me, that she was probably a better person than me. More honest, more loving, probably more mature, and definitely more idealistic. But, as the days went by, I felt those qualities rubbing off on me.

As Laura returned up the counter to me, little Irma came prancing into the restaurant. Her hair looked wild, like she had just been electrocuted and her lipstick was running slanticular to her lips.

"Hi, baby." Irma reached over the counter and hugged Laura.

"Hi, Irma." Laura squeezed Irma's shoulder after the hug.

I never said much about Irma to Laura because I knew they were such good friends. But I had my suspicions about the girl. Irma didn't have a job, but she always had money including her half of the rent money for the apartment. She was always going to parties. I knew she was one of the big consumers at the end of my business food chain. I couldn't help but watch her tight little skirt slide thigh-ward as she settled on one of the round counter stools next to me. She caught my glance and tried to yank her skirt down, but that was a hopeless task.

Sometimes in my more paranoid moments I wondered about both of them. Laura seemed to be an accomplished lover, but when I asked her about former boyfriends, she said I was the first. She said she couldn't have one when she lived with her mother because she was so strict. I still wondered about all that whenever I saw Irma.

"What are you guys doing?"

"Practicing my ice skating." I couldn't resist being sarcastic with that little pinhead.

"Huh?"

"Luke is just being sarcastic, because I won't move in with him."

"Why not? I thought you guys loved each other?"

Laura smiled at me, folded her arms in front of her, and leaned back against a cooler. "Hey, I'm not going to give up the business until I'm ready too." I folded my arms as I sat on the round counter stool.

"You like getting up too close to the edge, too much," said Laura.

At that moment, Officer Soto walked in the door. He looked the old man over as he strolled up the aisle. He smiled big time at Irma who smiled back. Then he said to me, "Hello, ratbrain. Isn't it time you slithered back down your rat hole?"

I gathered up my stuff and left without a word.

The Sears store on Lawrence Avenue was packed with people for the Autumn clothing sale. It was a Friday night and everybody had just received their paychecks.

"What about this one?" Laura was looking inside a big, new white washing machine.

"I think it's better because its got more cycles. You can wash delicate clothes or jeans."

We were in the process of furnishing a house I had rented down on Grand Avenue. It wasn't the best neighborhood, and a lot of the Ukranians who lived there were moving out because of the rising crime, but I thought it was a deal because we got two bedrooms and a garage.

I had consummated two little deals with my new business partners from Independence Avenue in South Lawndale, and I had plenty of money to put up for the deposit and the furniture and appliances. Laura was still trying to get me to quit the business, but things were just getting too lucrative. I had way more money in my savings account than I was letting on. I would have been more honest about the amount if she would have let me alone about the business. But if she knew the total amount, she'd make me quit, she as hell.

The only inkling she got of my new set-up was Irma asking me one time why was I driving over to the West Side ghetto all the time now? "The cab company stuck me in the West Side garage. I got some new customers, " I explained. If I would have said, "New suppliers," she would have shut me down, then and there.

"Where were you, watching me drive over to the West Side?"

"Around."

Yeah, like around a street corner, on the edge of the ghetto, I thought to myself.

I gave Laura enough money to get enrolled at the university. I told her I was signing back up for school, but I lied. Why the hell should I go back to school, when I could make a good living with my business? When I bought her the Cadillac, she had a fit. I lied and said I was making payments, but I had bought it straight up for cash. After that I knew I had to cool it with the spending or she would catch on. I wound up driving the Caddy, a big black Fleetwood. My father loved it. I told him I was a supervisor at the cab company. He bought it. What did he know about cab companies? He set-up screw machines.

Unfortunately, I had less time to visit Laura at the restaurant. I wanted to tell her to quit, but I couldn't let on I had that much money. Instead, I found myself spending a lot of time at a cafe, Floyd's Fifth, on Fifth Avenue near Marshall High School. It was located in an African American neighborhood, and only one other middle aged white guy, named Tony, hung in the place with me. He was always well dressed with a sports coat, and he drove a Caddy, too. I was pretty sure he was Mafia, but we seemed to be running non-conflicting businesses, so things were cool with us.

Tony asked me one day, "Travelling a little light for these parts aren't we?"

"What do you mean?"

Tony carefully folded back his sports coat revealing a shoulder holster containing a 9 millimeter pistol. "You're travelling too light, buddy. You know what I mean?" He smiled at me.

I thought, no way was I going to carry a gun. My wits were good enough. Wits and runaway. That's how I did business. No need for artillery.

In the empty lot next to our house, the landlord was dumping old cars, and weeds grew up between the wrecks. The building on the other side was boarded up, but sometimes late at night we could hear the junkies cooking up in there. Sometimes we could see their camp fire flicker against the brick walls. As the weather got colder, the big oak tree in the backyard shed it leaves. The furnace didn't work too well and the landlord didn't want to fix it. I paid some repair guys to get it working right.

Three Mexican families lived in the old greystone across the street from us. Nobody in the whole clan seemed to be able to speak any English. But they were friendly enough, we nodded to each other in the mornings and evenings going and coming from work.

Laura and I didn't have a lot of time at night together because she was always studying. When she asked why I wasn't, I explained I had set up school for the Spring. I watched TV and made popcorn. She spread out her textbooks and studied on the used dining room table we had bought. When she finished, usually around ten P.M., we would cuddle up on the new Sears sofa. Sometimes we fell asleep in each other's arms while we watched the Johnny Carson Show. Outside we could hear the leaves rustling in the wind.

A couple of times during the Winter months, I thought a couple of the ex-cons in the daily hang-out bunch at Floyd's, Mack and Carlos, were getting a little too interested in my business, so I quit using the place and started doing the trades right on the streets. Everybody else was doing it that way, too. I got so I could spot undercover cop cars better than radar could. But gangs were getting involved in the traffic, and I could see that my days in the trade were numbered anyway.

One Spring evening we were leaving the house, to go talk to my parents about getting married. I didn't want to do it, but Laura insisted. Laura looked beautiful coming down the front steps in a mint green summer dress. I was too busy looking at her to see Mack and Carlos come up. My first inkling of the hell that was to follow came when I saw Laura's face form a frown. She was looking down the sidewalk beyond me. All she said was, "Luke?"

I turned to see what she was looking at only to be confronted with a .357 magnum leveled just a foot away from my nose.

"You get back in that house," said Mack, the really scary one. Carlos, who usually said little but went through life with a half-witted grin stood a little in back of Mack, and he was holding a .45 auto on us. If I had been alone, I probably would have made a break for it right in the street. But I didn't want anything to happen to Laura. So, I didn't argue and went right back up the steps with Mack's gun barrel poking me in the back.

In the front room Mack demanded, "Where's the money, man?"

I handed him my wallet. And I told Laura to get hers out of her mint green purse. She instantly complied. Carlos grabbed them both and handed the fifty bucks or so to Mack who never took his eyes off us.

"What's this shit, man? You ain't got nothin' but 50 bucks here. I said, where's the money?" Our looted wallets now littered the front room floor with their contents.

"It's in the bank. I keep my money in the bank. That's all I got on me."

"What?" Mack seemed genuinely perplexed. I definitely didn't want to cross him, but it was the truth. I only kept a few bucks out for spending money. Mack looked around the house for a minute while Carlos held his gun on us. Mack came back and said, "Alright, tie 'em up. We're gonna find that money."

That's when it really started getting bad. Carlos tied me up first with duct tape, then he did the same to Laura. We were bound like mummies laying face down in the front room completely trussed up. Then they tore the house apart looking for a stash of money that wasn't there. After a while Mack went out to the Caddy and tore through it, too. After 45 minutes, and completely frustrated he returned to the house and savagely yanked me into the kitchen. I couldn't see Laura anymore.

"Now you tell me where the hell that money is, or I'm gonna hurt you." He didn't even sound angry, just totally frustrated.

"I'm telling you its in the bank, man. The account book is in that roll top desk in the little room off the back of the house. Take it, take my Ids, and go check it out of the bank."

"What, you think I'm stupid, man? The bank gonna know I ain't you." Then he started kicking me. First he kicked my shins until they were aching and black and blue, then he started kicking my arms, hands, and fingers. Before that session was over, I was crying and screaming to him the money was in the bank.

I don't know how long that went on, it seemed like an hour. Then he said, "All right. You ain't gonna talk. Let's see if the woman wants to talk to me." When I started screaming, Carlos wrapped duct tape around my mouth and head.

In the next room I could hear the thuds of Mack's blows on Laura and her whimpering even though I had duct tape on my ears, too. I began struggling with all my might against my adhesive bonds. After some time Mack said, "Ok, they ain't talking. We gonna have to get rid of them."

Carlos said, "Let's do the woman first."

"Man, you sick. This is our damn occupation. We is thieves, man. We don't do none of that sicko stuff."

"Oh, I didn't know that," said Carlos.

"Man, just grab the other end and get going. You want people going around the 'hood saying you is a sicko?"

"No..." answered Carlos. I heard the front door open and slam. In a minute they were back for me.

Mack said, "Last chance, sucker. You talkin' or what?" I forcefully nodded my head, "Yes."

"Ok, that more like it." He started peeling the duct tape off my mouth. But when he heard me utter the word "bank" it went right back on. "Yeah, I know, its in the goddamned bank. You know what, you a smart man. You knows I'm gonna kill you anyway, but you ain't letting have that money. Something in that I gotta admire." They proceeded to unceremoniously carry me to the Caddy and dump me into the trunk with Laura where we lay face to face.

I was horrified when I saw her. Her nice new dress was torn and splattered with her blood. Her face was cut up in places and it looked like he had concentrated on beating her in the face. I must have looked bad, too, because I could see it in her eyes. She had worked the duct tape partially off her mouth, and in a muffled kind of way she asked me if I was OK? I nodded energetically, yeah, don't worry about me.

As the car took off, she worked her way over to my face and tried to peel the tape off my face. She'd get a little of it peeled back, then we'd hit a bad bump, or they made a hard turn, or accelerated or stopped and we rolled back and forth without restraint. But Laura kept working on me until I could sort of talk back. I could tell they were going down an expressway by the road noises outside.

"Honey, are you ok?" asked Laura.

"I'm sorry. You have no idea how sorry I am about this."

"It's ok. I love you."

"I'm sorry. I'm sorry. I should have listened to you."

"It's ok. Don't worry about me. I love you."

You would think our last conversation would have had more content, but we were both exhausted and terrified, and our ending was coming up soon and certain. During that long ride over the area expressways I did ask her, "Did you have any other lovers?"

"Luke. I keep telling you, no. Why would I lie? We're gonna die."

"I just wonder because of Irma?"

"Irma?"

"Yeah. I think she's a hooker. And you were living with her."

"I *know* she's a hooker. You think I was a hooker?"

"No... but you were living with her."

"So, she's a hooker. That's the only way she could survive. She doesn't have a family either. She was abused as a kid. I love Irma. Don't be so judgmental about people."

When the car finally lurched to a stop, I could tell we were on a gravel road. Not many of those around Chicago. The trunk lid flew open and we could see a starry sky above us, and the narrow gravel causeway we had just traveled over with black bodies of water on both sides. We could see the full moon twinkling on the surface. I immediately recognized Wolf Lake. My father had often taken us fishing in the region down by the steel mills and Gary, Indiana.

First they hefted Laura out and dumped her with a thud in the driveway, then me. We were lying back to back. I could see another car, that Mack and Carlos obviously hadn't seen, parked off the main road where their headlights would not have found it. As my eyes focused in the dust our bodies had kicked up, I saw it was an unmarked Chicago Police car.

"Throw the woman in first, Carlos, she lighter. I'm gonna have a smoke."

I watched the driver's side door of the police car open, and the interior dome light shone down on a topless, but otherwise clothed Irma Maldonado, performing a sex act on a man in a suit who was fully clothed except for his pants zipper. I observed in fascination as the man athletically raised himself from the seat, yanked the zipper shut, and in one flowing motion, shoved Irma down, shut the door, and pulled his .45 auto on Carlos and Mack.

"ALL RIGHT, YOU DIRT BAGS. FREEZE." It was officer Soto.

Soto sorted out all the evening's action in about two sentences. He ordered them unbind us. He rebound them. When Irma asked permission to get out of the car, he yelled at her to stay put.

"Alright, you white trash. I never want to see you in Chicago again. You understand me? He waved the .45 in the direction of Laura and myself.

"You'll never see me again, officer, " I bellowed obediently.

And he never did. Laura and I hiked out to the Interstate then hitched a ride into Gary. The blast furnaces painted the night sky red above us. We wired her mother for money and took the bus to Madison, Wisconsin where we knew no one and have lived ever since. Soto obviously couldn't take those two in because of his compromised situation. He probably untied them after a while and gave them the same lecture we got.

And, I finally figured out who "the Swede" was when I picked up a copy of *Walk on the Wildside* by Nelson Algren for my freshman English class at the University of Wisconsin.

Otis and Andre

I met Andre for the first time in a run-down commercial building on Chicago's Exchange Avenue that had been converted by a local community group into a makeshift school. They ran a variety of social programs from the building including a program, that tutored high school dropouts for the high school equivalency examination. It was an unofficial program put together by some folks who had been in the Black Panther Party back in the 1960s. I knew one of the founders from "the old days," and I had been recruited as a teacher despite the fact that I was white and the school was located in the vast African American ghetto on Chicago's South Side.

I had a teaching degree and full state certification, but had never managed a classroom. As a member of an extremely sectarian Marxist-Leninist vanguard group, I had been sent into Chicago factories to "organize the revolution" upon my graduation from college. It seemed plausible at the time because I worked my way through college laboring in machine shops. That was the logical consequence of my entire family's long sojourn in Chicago factories. Of course, any organizing project seemed plausible to the members of the generation of 1968.

Anyway, my Panther buddy, Cedric, whom I hadn't spoken to in 20 years, phoned me up one evening and asked me to volunteer. I told him I was concerned about my safety in the neighborhood.

"Peter MacNaughton is scared to come into a black neighborhood, now? What's happening, man? You turn into a sissy?"

I rode the funky old Illinois Central electric train from the Loop. The South Chicago branch runs down the middle of 71st Street like an ancient interurban electric. The train glided past the old South Shore Country Club, once the jewel of the neighborhood. Andre, my first, and, as it turned out, my only student, welcomed me that wintry Saturday morning.

I more or less jogged the long block from the station to the school's storefront. The homeless tended to cluster in the entryways of apartment buildings in the neighborhood. Young men openly sold drugs on the corner.

The South Shore neighborhood had seen successive waves of ethnic groups move southward from places like Washington Park. Originally a middle class Anglo-Saxon neighborhood, it had been overrun by the

Irish, German and Russian Jews, then middle class African Americans. It had most recently been inherited by the African American lumpenproletariat. Terrified of the neighborhood's inhabitants, I found it reassuring to have a tall, good-looking teenaged kid welcome me without reservation.

"Good morning, Mr. MacNaughton. I'm Andre Boyd. Can I get you a cup of coffee?"

Andre didn't really fit my racist preconceived notion of a poor ghetto kid who had dropped out of high school because of the Third World style poverty that existed on the South Side. He didn't have a trace of a street accent. He didn't wear garish and baggy street clothes or gang colors. And he was polite.

As I got to know him over the next few Saturday mornings that winter, I found Andre didn't really need any tutoring. His grasp of mathematics exceeded my own, and his scientific knowledge had definitely reached broader vistas than my own. In fact, during a couple of our sessions he took me upstairs to the new agency's office and taught me how to construct a database with a computer.

"So, what the hell are you doing here, Andre? You're better educated than me. You don't need a teacher."

"I made a deal with my father. If I promised to get drug rehab and take a high school equivalency class, my father agreed to pay my apartment rent. If I go to the college he wants, he'll pay me an allowance."

"What does your old man do for a living?"

"Oh, he's the deputy director of the State of Illinois transportation agency. He works in the Loop. My mother is a lawyer."

"I see. Why did you leave home?"

"I didn't. My father put me out."

"Why?"

"Because he caught me smoking marijuana. He didn't want me around my younger sisters anymore."

It turned out that Andre's family lived in the South Kenwood neighborhood near Hyde Park and the University of Chicago. It's an integrated area for middle class people. After questioning Andre at length, I unfolded a story that had more to do with authoritarianism than drugs. Andre had managed to get himself, during his senior high school year, a scholarship to the University of Chicago's business school.

Unfortunately, Andre perceived himself as an inventor, not a businessman. He wanted to attend the Illinois Institute of Technology, also on the South Side. He avidly read magazines like *Omni* and *Scientific American* and all the widget/how-to-build-a-homemade-rocket journals like *Popular Science* and *Popular Mechanics*. I had never met a kid so obviously cut out to be an engineer.

What finally emerged in our conversations, which had frankly turned to mentoring and counseling rather than tutoring, was a snapshot of the raging authoritarian father trying to obliterate any sign of independence in the son. The "drug problem" turned out to be little more than incidental experimentation.

Unfortunately, I could see Andre had no intention of picking the scholarship off the table and attending the University of Chicago. I worried about the kid, because the old man had him over the barrel. If Andre didn't cave-in to his father, his future didn't look very bright out in the South Side's streets. The kid was smart, but he wasn't street smart.

I offered to talk to his father, but we both agreed a middle-aged factory worker wouldn't make much impact. I gave Andre my phone number and address, but I had a strong intuitive feeling he'd never call if things went sour. I sensed that our gap in having a fully human relationship had more to due with age and social class than race.

Then one Friday night Cedric phoned and informed me that the "school" had been temporarily closed.

"How come?"

"Didn't get the grant money we counted on. Couldn't make the rent, man."

"Think we could raise it with private donations?"

"It's a little more complicated than that, man. As you might imagine, Pete, you weren't my first choice for a tutor. I mean, you're OK and all, but I wanted somebody black. A role model. You understand. I tried to get this black lady who teaches high school at DuSable. But she remembered me from times past, from my street and prison days. So, not only did she not want to help, she went around telling everyone that we were a "gang front." The landlord got a hold of that and canceled our ticket."

I met Otis for the first time when he responded to my newspaper ad which advertised a 1982 Ford LTD station wagon for sale. The old buggy was rusted out, but the motor and transmission were still good, so I figured $500 would be a fair price for it.

We had agreed to meet in the alley in back of my Uptown apartment building. I took an immediate dislike to the guy. A balding, middle-aged,

African American of average height, he showed up wearing black work boots, and a blue work uniform with a bank name stitched over one shirt pocket and "Otis" stitched over the other one. His frayed topcoat hung open. He was only about five foot eight, but he looked powerful. It looked like he had acquired a knife scar over the bridge of his nose.

"You MacNorton?"

"Yeah, but its MacNaughton. Call me Pete."

"This the piece of shit you sellin'?" He pointed to the Ford, peacefully rusting under the Howard Street L tracks.

"This is the 1982 Ford LTD station wagon with a good motor and transmission that I'm selling, yes."

"Look like a piece of shit, man."

"It's in good mechanical condition."

I didn't hear his response because trains roared overhead simultaneously heading north and south. We were showered in sparks, and we could smell the ozone in the frigid air. Otis, meanwhile, sidled up to the chain link fence and pissed in the snow between the Ford and the brick wall of the apartment building. At the same time, the winter sun suddenly came out and painted Otis, me and the Ford with an intricate criss cross pattern of elevated superstructure shadows.

The gloom swiftly returned and the sharp shadows vanished just as abruptly as he turned to face me. We test drove the old Ford up Broadway, over to Lake Shore Drive, then back down Lawrence Avenue.

"I don't know, man. Don't seem too hot to me. What I do if the car breaks down on me?"

"It ain't gonna break down, man. If it fucking breaks down, call me up and I'll give you a ride." Why the fuck I ever said that, I don't know. I knew it was a mistake the minute I said it.

Oddly enough, Otis seemed to feel at ease with me right away. I could tell that he sensed I was working class, too. Anyway, the lack of mutuality made me uncomfortable, because I sure as fuck didn't like him.

"OK, then, I'll give you $100 for the thing."

"Shit. Are you kiddin' me, man? I could get $800 for it. I've discounted it for the rust."

"Yeah, man. I live way the fuck down on 67th and Stony Island. I gotta drive everyday out to Austin and Lake where I works at the bank."

"Why don't you take the L? Get on at 63rd Street, take it to the Loop, then take the Lake Street L right to the bank's doorstep."

"Been stuck up twice on the L. They got me coming down the steps at 63rd and Stony one time. Got me up on the Loop platform one time, too. I carry this now, when I rides the L." He opened his oily blue coat and revealed a handgun and holster under his armpit. I got a heavy intuitive flash that this fucker wouldn't hesitate to use it. Suddenly, I felt vulnerable in the gloom under the L with this guy.

I agreed to sell the Ford for $250 after prolonged negotiations along with the proviso that I would personally give him a lift if the car broke down on him within the next three months. He unwrapped the bills off a big wad – he had obviously brought the full $500 just in case he had met his match at negotiating. He caught me eyeballing the money.

"I gots a good job, man. I been the janitor at the bank for twenty years. Gonna buy me a building next year. Rent all the units out, never repair nothin', and collect my money."

"City's been crackin' down on that shit. You gotta keep the building in good repair, now."

"Naw, I'm pays off the alderman."

A week later, a day after a blizzard, I got the phone call at 5 A.M. from Otis. " Hey, man. Your car won't start. I gots to go to work."

"Oh, shit, man. The sun ain't even up yet. What do you mean, 'my car?' Motherfucker is definitely your car."

"Man, you said you was gonna give me a ride if this pig broke down."

"I can't give you a ride. Take the L." I felt shitty as soon as I said that.

"What! Man, all you white motherfuckers be the same. If you sold the motherfucker to a white man, you'd be givin' that motherfucker a ride. None of you motherfuckers any good, man."

"Fuck you." I hung up.

But when I finally woke up and got out of bed, the conversation bothered me. As I prepared to go to work at 7 A.M. the phone rang again. It was Otis again.

"MacNorton?"

"MacNaughton. Hey, man. I'm sorry. You just called too fucking early in the…"

Otis cut me off. "You oughtta be sorry, man. In fact, you the sorriest assed motherfucker I know." Otis sounded positively cheerful. "Hey, man, I'm just fucking with you. OK? Hey, MacNorton, you still there?"

"Yeah, I'm here Otis."

"Come on and get me, man. I'm down at 11th and State."

"Cops got you, huh?" He had just given me the address of Chicago police headquarters.

"No, man. I took the L like you told me. Only this fucking kid tried to stick me up. Motherfucker pulled a screw driver on me."

"Oh, shit, man. I'm sorry. I should have given you that ride. I'm sorry, man. You OK?"

"Yeah, I be fine, man. The little motherfucker who tried to stick me up ain't doing too good though. I busted a cap on that little mother-fucker."

"Oh, no. You shot him?"

"Damn right. I capped him."

"Oh shit, man. I'm sorry. I'll come down right away."

When I arrived at police headquarters, they parked me in the long row of chairs in the waiting area in the main lobby. I felt really shitty. I had promised the man a ride, and then I reneged on my word. And, sure as shit, the guy gets into a jam as a result. Waiting for Otis I resolved to drive the man anywhere in northeastern Illinois. After a half-hour or so, the cops escorted him out of an elevator to the main receiving desk.

"Hey, my man, MacNorton." Otis sounded jovial.

"Otis, I'm sorry about this, man."

"Hey, its OK, man. The bank done gave me the day off with pay. Shit, I'm making out on this deal. Only thing, the police gonna keep my gun." Sure enough, the cops frowned significantly at Otis. It looked to me like a "don't push your luck" frown. They obviously didn't like Otis any more than I did.

The cops shoved a "discharge" form in front of Otis to sign. Looking over his shoulder, I read through the police report of the shooting inci-dent. It said Otis had killed, in self-defense, "one Andre Boyd, a human being."

Telemarketing Blues

Bev feared her divorce had trapped her into a never ending cycle of poverty. She understood now that her downhill slide had commenced when her husband Arnold had lost his job with a "major accounting agency." College sweethearts, they had been happily married over twenty years. They had raised three children, Kelly, Karl, and Arnold Junior to their teenaged years. Starting out in an apartment building in Chicago's Northwest suburbs they had worked their way to a modest home in Arlington Heights, then to their "dream home" in Barrington Hills, an exclusive suburb replete with many farmettes which sported stables. They had lived the American dream.

Then Arnold was abruptly "downsized." After two years of unemployment, they had been forced to sell the house and rent a modest brick bungalow in the old village core of Palatine. After three years of unemployment Arnold's drinking had reached an unacceptable level for Bev. When she pointed out his disheveled appearance and suggested it might impair his job search. He said, "They don't want any pot bellied grey beards." He snarled at her to "go get a job if it was so easy." So, she did.

She had never worked since their marriage. Prior to that she had worked as a retail clerk in a cosmetics department in a Loop department store. She proudly found a job at the local K-Mart store working in the jewelry and watch department. When Arnold pointed out that it was a minimum wage job and would have no appreciable impact on their financial situation, she tartly replied that at least she wasn't a bum like some people.

Within six months they had divorced. She kept the aging Nissan. Arnold kept the now rusty Lincoln. They had sold most of the furniture and electronic goodies by then anyway, so there wasn't much more to divvy up. Arnold Junior, the oldest, elected to go with his father. Then Kurt acted like he wanted to go with the men, too, but she finally talked him out of it, saying that Arnold Junior would be back soon.

And she was correct in her assessment. Arnold had always acted far too sternly with the boy, and that tendency had been exaggerated by their currently reduced circumstances. Before two weeks had elapsed, Arnold Junior had returned to her. Her ex-husband then disappeared, but three months later she began receiving very small court mandated child support checks. She realized that he had found some kind of minimum wage job, too. The envelopes were postmarked from the Chicago's north side. Arnold Junior said he thought his father was working as a security guard, because it had become the focus of his late night ravings during his worsening drinking bouts.

It bothered Bev to think that her husband felt that he had to leave because he could only get a minimum wage job. His pride hadn't permit him to remain with her and the children because of his employment. After all, he had earned a Masters Degree in Business and CPA certification. Guys like him weren't supposed to be unemployed. Bev knew that his 54 years worked against him as it did her, too. She was 47. Arnold's pride made her sad because any job would have been temporarily acceptable to her, even minimum wage, provided that he kept looking for professional level work. However, she couldn't permit her divorce to take up the spotlight of her attention. She had to focus on her own deteriorating financial situation. Even with all three kids working part time jobs she couldn't make the monthly rent on their house.

The operative emotions she encountered when she found her meager furniture and belongs on the sidewalk and in the snow in front of her house were humiliation and anger. She found Kelly sitting in one of the kitchen chairs next to the curb. The sheriff had nailed an eviction notice to the door. Kelly informed her that the landlord had already changed the locks. She also informed her mother that her brothers had been so embarrassed they had gone to the public library to wait in the warmth. Despite having picked up an additional weekend job working at a local convenience store she simply could not afford the rent on a house. She turned down a job as a cleaning woman because the work looked too athletic for her age. She ruled out prostitution for the same reason.

They moved southeasterly again, following the Chicago and Northwestern rail line toward Chicago. She found a two bedroom apartment that she could afford in a massive apartment complex near O'Hare Airport. They all hated the area. Technically suburban, the area had a menacing urban look to it. The neighborhood was criss-crossed by expressways and shadowed by skyscrapers. Their building was filled with Mexicans, Middle Easterners, Filipinos, and Europeans including Irish and Polish right off the boat.

The kids hated it. Kelly had nightmares about the long interior hallway they had to traverse to reach the apartment. All of the children hated their new high school. Bev was apologetic, but it was the best she could do. For a brief period she accepted welfare and aid to dependent children. The women she had met in the basement where everyone did their laundry were happy to explain were and how to apply. A young white girl, Sarah, drove over with her to the welfare office located on the nearby Northwest side of Chicago and showed her the ropes. Bev hated all the legal red tape.

Then she found a job. She responded to a newspaper advertisement, a sales position, which required someone who spoke fluent English and communicated well with people. She telephoned the listed number as directed and spoke with Dick Richhead, the owner of the company. She sold herself hard, bringing up her Bachelors Degree in English and her recent retail sales experience. Later she realized the only thing Dick had been looking for was fluency in English. Shortly afterwards, when she left for a face to face interview, she discovered the office building that housed the company, Pumping Sunshine, was well within walking distance of her apartment. Unfortunately, no sidewalks existed and the embankment of the Northwest Tollway provided an insurmountable obstacle. The only way to reach the tall glass walled building was by automobile, and it took half an hour via a serpentine route.

Inside the modern building Bev felt better. She liked the atrium and the flourishing tropical plants. She took the elevator to the 15th floor as directed and quickly located the office door marked Pumping Sunshine, a wholly owned subsidiary of Blue Sky, Inc. And, she was surprised to discover that she wasn't really being interviewed. The woman who had been introduced as her supervisor, a young, slim, nervous woman but well attired, perfunctorily asked her to fill out her employment papers. Her name was Athena Wells. She chain smoked cigarettes. Bev later learned that Athena's father was English and her mother Greek.

"Could you tell me what the salary is?"

"I thought Dick covered that with you. Base pay is seven dollars an hour. Depending on how well you do on each shift, you can earn almost double that. It's commission based, didn't Dick tell you?"

"Noooo. Can you tell me what I'll be selling?"

"Whoa. He didn't tell you shit about the job did he?"

"Well, he said it would be inside sales..."

"Inside sales, my ass. You're going to be selling magazine subscriptions to people. You have to call them, make a scripted pitch, close them, and move on to the next one. We rotate shifts once a week. One week you work days. The next you work evenings. You gotta make your daily, weekly, and monthly quotas. If you don't, you're gone. Simple as that. You want the job or what?"

"Yes."

Bev found the money a respite from minimum wages, but she hadn't expected selling magazine subscriptions to be a pressure packed job. Two women quit in the middle of the shift her first evening on the job. She didn't like the idea of being monitored on another line by Athena either. And, she found it difficult to make her quotas. People hung up on her half way through her scripted pitch. When she tried to deviate from the script, Athena called her over immediately after the call and reprimanded her. When she arose to use the bathroom, Athena told her that she could only leave her cubicle during breaks or lunch period. She had said, "Ok," but made her way to the bathroom anyway.

After her first dreary week of evenings spent on the 15th floor, she had already had enough. Her headset left her ears numb after eight hours of pinching. Her wrists ached from typing the information gathered after each call into her dumb computer terminal, and her bladder was usually full. Two more women had quit. It was impossible to socialize with anyone at work. The only social time available was in the parking lot or on the elevator. With the alarming volume of turnover of her co-workers, she realized the job would be socially atomizing.

She persevered through the winter, generally making quota or a little above. Athena gave them group "motivational" talks that only seemed to further demotivate and demoralize people. Everyone appeared to be frightened to speak up to complain about the working conditions or the idiotic scripts they were forced to cheerfully present to the hapless customers. Bev grew mightily tired of the men who shouted obscenities at her over the telephone. What did they think? She enjoyed calling people away from their dinners or favorite TV programs in order to be pitched a magazine subscription? Why didn't they show a little common decency? She was just doing a damn job. She didn't own the company or come up with the idea of dunning people in their homes. As long as it was legal why take it out on her?

The most annoying aspect of her job, Bev had to ring a little bell, the kind they put in retail establishments, to call a person out of a back room. The bell enabled Athena to listen in on the successful sales presentation and confirm the kill. Sometimes Athena walked the aisles between the cubicles reminding the women tethered to the telephones and computers that she hadn't heard that bell in a while. Sometimes Athena would divide the "killing floor" as she called it into two teams to create additional competition. Bev grew to hate Athena.

By Spring Bev had seen almost a complete turnover in the women employed by Pumping Sunshine. She had managed to make most of her quotas, but she rarely earned more than the base rate. Going below your quotas, of course, meant termination. She had seen a number of women terminated by Athena. Only the strong survived until termination. Because Athena would ride them every hour, every day, until they buckled under the stress and voluntarily quit. Athena seemed to pride herself on her toughness. She had developed the ability to listen, poker faced, to all the hard luck stories. She faced with equanimity the sudden, ugly, explosive scenes which occurred when women quit in the middle of a shift showering Sunshine and Athena in a merciless rain of expletives.

Bev came to understand that the favorite method of quitting was simply not showing up for work anymore. The second most favored method was feigning illness in the middle of a shift, departing, and never returning. And the third, least favored method, which was chosen by some of the emotionally volcanic women, was the social explosion at work, which enabled them to shout obscenities at Athena. Athena serenely supervised through it all. Even the rumored threats Bev heard repeated in the elevators from discharged telemarketers didn't seem to faze Athena.

In the Spring Bev felt depressed. Kelly continued to do poorly in high school. Arnold Junior tried returning to his father once again, and Kurt simply remained morose. Bev didn't have any friends anymore. Her rotating schedule took a toll on her remaining budding friendships with women in her apartment building. Geographically she felt atomized by her neighborhood and her work life could be described as tedium punctuated by terror.

She sought other work and even got a few interviews. But when she came face to face with employers, she suspected, that like Arnold, she was just one more "pot bellied grey beard." Then the Nissan finally broke down, and she found herself saddled with more bills. She feared being in debt the rest of her life. As her motivation seemed to drain off with the fine Spring weather, she routinely fell short of quota, and found Athena stalking her more and more frequently. More and more frequently Athena made sarcastic remarks, "Planning on selling anything, tonight sweetie or are you just gonna fill up the chair again?"

Completely demoralized, Bev struggled to make quota. After two successive evenings below quota, Athena summoned Bev into her office at the end of the shift.

"You were below quota again tonight."

"It was a bad list, Athena. It was a bad area code. How many people in New York City want to buy a magazine about fishing?"

"I've sold that magazine to plenty of people in New York. I just don't think you've got what it takes to be in telemarketing. Your numbers have been slipping for quite some time."

Then the cold realization struck Bev. Athena had already written her off, this wasn't a pep talk, it was the beginning of protracted harassment to force her to quit. Somewhere a Blue Sky computer had spit out her name as "unproductive" and had targeted her for termination.

"I'll bring the numbers up tomorrow."

"You better. The company can't carry you forever, you know." Athena gave her a cutesy look through the cigarette smoke.

Bev visited the gun shop with some trepidation. She had never owned, loaded, or discharged a firearm in her life. But times and people change. Athena had given her an ultimatum. "Meet your monthly quotas in the upcoming week or you're fired." A clearly impossible task, because she had fallen so far behind, Bev had decided on another option.

The bald headed tattooed man behind the counter had a name tag pinned to his t-shirt. It proclaimed his name, Daryl.

"Daryl, I'd like to look at a used handgun that a lady could use for self-defense."

"Well the boss makes me wear this here." The middle-aged man pointed to the nametag. "But my true name is Duke.

Bev felt immediately attracted to Duke's earnest demeanor and warm smile. "I've got an asshole for a boss, too."

Duke deftly walked her through the small caliber firearms, professionally describing each piece and demonstrating the loading, safety features, and aspects of each weapon. She settled on a .25 automatic that fit her budget. Duke talked her into buying an extra clip and two boxes of bullets. When they discovered that Bev didn't have an Illinois firearms card, Duke cavalierly purchased the firearm and ammo in his own name and accepted cash from Bev to complete the illegal transaction. Duke prided himself on his judgment of people. He felt convinced that Bev was a good citizen despite the fact that he had just met her.

He also supplied Bev with the necessary forms for her to apply for the Illinois gun card.

Bev staked out the parking lot after each shift, timing Athena and observing where she typically parked her automobile. Bev assumed she would be fired on Friday, Athena's favorite day for "cleaning house," as she was fond of putting it.

Thursday evening Bev quietly awaited Athena. She had pulled her rusty Nissan next to Athena's sleek new sports car. When Athena came clipping down the sidewalk, Bev started her engine then got out to confront the young woman. She looked startled when Bev accosted her.

Bev casually pulled the .25 auto out of her purse and pointed it at Athena's face. Bev had taken care to make sure the chamber and her clip were empty.

"What's this?" Athena sounded unsteady. In the moonlight she could see the glint of the stainless steel frame of the automatic handgun. Bev blocked her access to her automobile.

"I just thought that I'd shoot you before you fired me." Bev responded cheerfully.

"What? " Athena's usual low gravelly voice broke into an uncharacteristic soprano. "What?" She repeated with even less energy.

"Yeah. I'm going to shoot you." Bev snapped back the slide of her little gun. It sounded convincingly ominous despite the fact that it wasn't loaded.

"Please.... I wasn't going to fire you.... " Athena put her hands up in front of her plainly shaken face to shield herself from the incoming bullets. Athena had grown used to people whining or throwing shit fits when she fired them. Bev's calm steely determination completely unnerved her.

Athena began tentatively stepping backwards while simultaneously crouching into a fetal ball. Her hands remained over her face in a futile attempt to hide in the sinister void of the vast parking lot. "Don't... please..."

"Why not? You got it coming, and you know it."

Athena involuntarily began dry sobbing. She did know it. But she also continued her instinctive backpedaling even as she crouched low toward the sidewalk. In a minute Athena found herself fleeing headlong back up the walk toward the massive shape of the office building, looming in the darkness.

Bev removed the empty clip and drove home. While she waited for the police to arrive, she prepared the next day's meals for her children. She wrote an elaborate note for Arnold Junior explaining the situation. Finally, she sat down and watched late night TV infomercials. When she finally went to bed in the early hours of the morning, she was convinced that her plan to apply for social security mental disability had gone awry. Although bitterly disappointed that no police had showed up at her apartment, she finally transited into sleep.

Friday she reported to work at the usual time, prepared for anything, although she did leave her .25 at home. The women crowded off the elevator onto the 15th floor but were uncharacteristically greeted by the owner, Dick Richhead. He escorted them all into a conference room where he introduced their new supervisor, Meredith Sharkey. Like Athena, she was fashionably dressed, young, and a cigarette smoker.

Bev, now the senior telemarketer, asked, "Where's Athena?"

"Athena checked herself into a mental health center last night. She really wasn't cut out for this business," said Dick as he departed turning the group over to Meredith.

Meredith took a deep breath and said, "Ok, ladies. We need to get a few ground rules straight. If you don't make your daily, weekly, or monthly quotas, you're outta here.

After work Bev met Duke for dinner and drinks at a local lounge.

Crime Clubbers

June listened intently to the commercial playing on her dilapidated radio. The radio announcer repeated the offer a second time; "Anyone with information leading to the conviction of the perpetrators who stole ten cases of soda pop with a total value of $71 from the McKinley Park Field House can collect $1000 in reward money. Call Crime Clubbers."

June had once worked as a quality control technician at one of the big steel mills in South Chicago. She had been unemployed since the mammoth factory had closed. At age 51 she knew her prospects for another full time job were very dim. She had been divorced for many years. Her oldest son had died in Vietnam, the other lived in Los Angeles. He installed cable TV for a living and had three kids. He often urged his mother to join him in California, but she insisted her home was in Chicago.

She had patched together a precarious living by working various part time retail clerking jobs at gas stations and convenient food stores but usually wound up quitting after being unjustly accused of stealing. She had never stolen anything from anyone. Three times she had a gun stuck in her face. The street thugs seemed to be becoming increasingly crazed and vicious.

She had quit her last gig after the owner had grabbed her while she worked in the back of the store during the bleary hours after midnight. She had managed to fight her way free, but the old bald-headed bastard had refused to give her the wages she had been owed.

Now, she barely made the rent on a tiny apartment on South Western Avenue. They were located just south of the new Midway L. Sarah, the 19 year-old who shared the apartment, often said she was going to take the L to the airport one day and just fly away.

June had picked Sarah up in an Archer Avenue bar one Friday night. The homeless girl had run away from her young construction worker husband, Bill. His favorite activity seemed to be getting loaded, coming home, then beating the hell out of Sarah. Sarah used to say that Bill's boss mentally kicked the shit out of Bill, Bill turned around and kicked the shit out of her, and when Bill wasn't around, she kicked Bill's un-housebroken dog in revenge.

They split the rent and enjoyed each other's company. Their vast age divide never seemed to be a problem. They easily forged an affectionate mother/daughter relationship. June got things done. Sarah contented herself with following. June handled practical matters, Sarah was the dreamer.

"Juney, turn that radio down, will ya?"

"Hey, kid. I got a money making idea for us. I want you to call your new cop boyfriend and ask him some questions." Sarah's boyfriend was a married cop named Randy Steel.

"Randy?"

"Yes.

"Randy, honey, if somebody stole less than a hundred dollars what would the judge do to them?"

"I dunno. Probably give him a $100 fine, make them pay the damages, and make 'em pay court costs. If they pled guilty and had a clean record, the whole bill would be about $250. Assuming they were white people, and they were cooperative."

After June confessed and was convicted of stealing ten cases of soda pop based on Sarah's testimony, they split the remaining $750 they had received from Crime Clubbers.

June and Sarah

I had been sitting around in a Archer Avenue tavern for about an hour eyeballing a very pretty young woman. I was waiting for my old graduate school buddy from the University of Illinois at Chicago, but he never showed up. He had called me up, out of the blue, and offered to turn over a bunch of old photos of anti-Vietnam war marches and radical meetings in which we had participated during the late 1960s.

I had the night off from my evening shift in the dog food factory courtesy of Screwyablue Corporation. They had written me up for absenteeism and given me three days off. I always marveled at the totalitarian genius of modern corporations. A guy takes too many days off because he can't stand the work, so how is he punished? More days off, of course. The logic worked for me.

Because it was a summer week night, the tavern wasn't crowded. The place smelled like a giant ashtray. The rug leading from the door to the bar displayed a long diagonal worn-out spot. And the silver Christmas tinsel that hung year-round over the bar reflected the light from the lurid green neon sign in the window. The place seemed like a typical, shopworn, Chicago neighborhood bar.

Anyway, I eventually worked my way over to the pretty young blonde, and asked her if she wanted to hear any special songs on the jukebox.

"Sure," and in a friendly voice she named a half dozen country and western songs and artists. I hated country and western music. I prided myself on my extensive knowledge of the Chicago blues scene. But the bar seemed to be mainly populated by Mexicans, Eastern European white working class types, and hillbilly's, hence the curious music menu offered on the jukebox. Tex-Mex, polkas, and country and western.

I played the songs she had requested then returned to the bar in an attempt to further the conversation. I figured I didn't have much chance with her because I was middle-aged, balding, and pot bellied. But if you don't try, you don't have any chance. However, she acted very friendly. While we chatted, I kept trying to steal looks down her low-cut, pink blouse. She wore matching pink and white shorts. I didn't care for her prolifically pierced ears and nose.

"My name is Peter MacNaughton." We shook hands.

"My name is Sarah."

"So, what do you do for fun, Sarah?" I tried to keep from staring at her legs.

She laughed. "Well lately, I testified against my best friend in court so we could make $750 bucks." Her rising intonation transformed the statement into a question.

I laughed. "Sounds like fun. How'd you do that?"

"Well, my roommate, June, heard this Crime Clubber report on the radio. They were offering a reward of 1000 bucks for anyone with information about the robbery of soda pop from the McKinley Park Field House.

"How much pop did you rip off?"

"We didn't rip if off. We don't know who took it. But it was worth $71."

"You're shitting me. Somebody offered a reward of a 1000 bucks for $71 worth of pop?"

"Yep. So, June turned herself in, and I testified against her.

"On a crime she didn't commit?"

"Yep."

I bought her another beer. In Chicago you never know what kind of person you're gonna meet in a tavern in a strange neighborhood. I mentally measured the absurdity of her story against the larger backdrop of the ongoing spectacular social decay going on all around me in the Psychotic Atomik Empire. She seemed sincere, and I really didn't think she was lying.

"So, your friend is in jail now?"

"Juney? Oh, no. She got supervision, a $100 fine, $71 in damages, and court costs. We had $750 left over for us. You know, I tell some people that story, and they just don't get it."

I still didn't know if she was bullshitting me or had just told me one of the most hilarious true-life stories I had ever heard. "Ah ha. So, how about we head over to the casino in Joliet. Have some fun."

"Oh." She patted my shirt sleeve. "I've got a husband, Bill. He's a construction worker. I've got a boyfriend, too. Randy. He's a cop."

"OH." I pulled my arm away. At that point I was sure I had been trying to pick up a lunatic.

"No. Noooh." She laughed and tugged at my sleeve. I'm separated from my husband. I'd divorce him if I had enough money or knew where-the-fuck he was living. I'm just going with Randy now."

"Ah ha."

She bought me a beer. "Listen, I've got a nice girlfriend, June. She's supposed to meet me here. I'll set you up with her. You'll like her. She's more your age, and she's pretty."

So, we sat and drank for another half hour listening to idiotic country and western tunes while I awaited June's appearance with anticipation. Unfortunately, Randy showed up first.

I knew he was a Chicago cop the moment he lumbered through the door. He was a big motherfucker, well over six foot. Ugly, too. He sported the typical closely coifed military, corporate, cop hair style. He immediately insinuated himself between Sarah and I at the bar and without looking at me, said to her, "Who's the asshole?"

"Randy, be polite. This is Peter."

"Hello," I offered while still pulling my bar stool away from the couple. "Can I buy you a beer?"

"Yeah, whatever." He responded never looking in my direction. "I gotta talk to you about June. I was just over to your apartment, and she wasn't there. Do you know where she is?" He had grabbed her arm.

"Why? What's the problem?" Sarah managed to twist her arm free. "Goddamnit, Randy. Don't be wrestling with me." She squirmed on her bar stool. The old Polish bartender brought up three fresh beers. I knew he was Polish because he wore a button that proclaimed, "It's Fun to Be Polish."

"Did you know your little buddy was wanted?" He grabbed her arm afresh, this time with enough force to hang onto it despite Sarah's wholesale writhing on the bar stool. If I had been a hero, or unusually stupid, I would have told the big asshole to knock it off. But I wasn't a hero, and I definitely wasn't stupid, so I shut-the-fuck-up and surreptitiously tried to wriggle my bar stool away from the two of them.

"Where you going?" The monster demanded, finally turning his total ominous attention in my direction.

"Huh? No where?"

Still clutching Sarah, who writhed like a snake trying to break his grip on her wrist, he said to me, "Are you on probation?" I watched pain etch Sarah's face into contortions.

"No. I'm cool."

"Are you on parole?"

"No."

"Let's see some ID."

I didn't think he had any business asking for my identification, but what the hell was I gonna do? Call the cops? I hastily pulled my wallet and showed him my driver's license and Screwyablue corporate ID card.

"Whatta ya doin' in this neighborhood? I don't know you. You live on the North Side. What the hell are you doin' here?"

"I was supposed to meet an old buddy of mine."

"Well, where is he?"

"He didn't show up."

"Yeah, right. You're just another North Side commie or queer. Or you're in here to buy drugs from someone. I don't want you hanging around her. You understand me?"

"Yessir, I do." I gathered up my IDs and got off my bar stool. I knew if he found out I actually was a Marxist he'd pulverize me.

"I just left."

Sarah finally pulled loose from Randy's gargantuan grip by yanking free with all her weight. She hurt her wrist doing it and squealed in pain. "You don't have to leave, Peter." I saw tears in her eyes apparently brought on from the pain in her wrist. "GET OUTTA HERE, YOU ASSHOLE," she yelled into Randy's chest. I tried to head for the door but Randy had stepped back and blocked my exit. He obviously thought that he had gone too far in a public place. Everybody in the place was watching the two of them.

Sarah groaned and held her wrist. The bartender brought her some ice cubes covered in a white bar rag. Randy looked concerned.

"I'm sorry if I hurt you. But I gotta tell you June has an outstanding warrant."

"What are you talking about?" Sarah sounded angry, exasperated. Tears slipped down her face while she applied the ice to her wrist.

"I'm trying to tell ya. She murdered her husband. She shot him. Then she put him into his car and set him on fire. She's wanted." Randy shoved the warrant into Sarah's hands. She read it over.

"I don't care. I don't believe it. Juney's a good person." Sarah allowed the warrant to fall to the floor.

"Well, Juney should have thought twice before she pulled that scheme to get the reward money from Crime Clubbers. The computer kicked out her prior warrants today." Randy picked up the warrant and placed it on the bar. He glanced at me, plainly expressing disgust, then finally said, "I'll stop by the apartment latter when I get off duty.

"I don't want to see you," Sarah replied.

"I'll see you later. You better tell me where June is, if you know. Otherwise you're harboring a fugitive. You'll go to jail, too." Then like a gunfighter from a western, he backed out of the tavern facing us down. Before disappearing out the door he pointed to me with a final admonition, "I don't wanna see you here ever again."

"No problem. You got it."

"Don't listen to him," Sarah said. I didn't respond and watched Randy through the front window. I intended to depart the minute he pulled away in his unmarked squad car. "Help me with this... please." I turned around and Sarah held up her limp wrist imploring me to assist her in taping the white bar rag packed with ice cubes to her tortured and injured flesh.

I couldn't resist helping her. So, I straightened her arm out on the bar, then clamped the lumpy rag to her arm with some surgical tape that had magically appeared on the bar. While I was engaged in my medical volunteer work, I continued with my other ongoing project of trying to look down Sarah's blouse. As I finished, Sarah abruptly jumped off her bar stool and yelled, "Juney!" to a very petite and very worn looking woman in her 50s. I guessed June was less than five feet tall. Sarah embraced her and started crying anew. Naturally, I was disappointed that June was probably ten years older than myself. And she showed a lot of extra wear for every year, too.

"What happened to you?" asked June while she examined Sarah's wrist.

"Randy grabbed me.. he didn't mean it."

"Again? Why do you put up with it? Tell him to get lost. Tell him you're gonna report him to his superiors at the station. First you let Bill beat the crap outta you, and now this jerk. Randy's no good for you kid. He's married. He's got kids. He's not gonna leave his wife. You know that."

Sarah responded by crying. June embraced her and rubbed her upper arms and shoulders like a mother would. June patted Sarah's head like she was a little girl while Sarah hugged June like she was her mother. June ordered a mixed drink and glanced over at me.

"Hi," I volunteered. "I'm the doctor," I pointed to the improvised wrist wrappings.

"Thanks."

"His name is Peter. He's my friend." Sarah sounded exactly like a child.

"Buy you a drink, Peter?" June offered.

Now I felt embarrassed. I didn't want to take up with June. If Sarah was too young for me, then June was definitely too old. "Sure." I felt confused. "But I gotta go then." I pointed out the door in the direction that Randy had zoomed off into.

"Oh, that asshole? Don't let him bother you. Everybody hates his guts," said June.

A chorus of assenting views was suddenly voiced by a variety of people in the bar. Most of them contained obscenities. "Yeah, he's a red rosy prick" was my favorite.

"I'm June," she extended her free hand to shake. She still stroked Sarah's hair. Sarah, delighting in the attention, looked up at me.

"Peter. Peter MacNaughton. So, you're the evil mastermind of the soda scheme?"

June laughed. "Yeah, that's me. What the hell, we made 750 bucks on the deal."

"Randy says you killed your husband." Sarah disengaged herself and handed June the warrant Randy had left behind. June put on a pair of eyeglasses that definitely weren't fashionable. Sarah and I both sucked on our beers as June carefully and slowly read through the legal document.

Finally she said, "Shit. Getting convicted on the soda burglary kicked this up didn't it?"

"Yeah," said Sarah. See looked at June expectantly. She wanted an explanation. Instead of leaving, which I knew was the intelligent thing to do, I found myself riveted by my curiosity. I wanted to hear her explanation, too. June didn't look like a murderer. She seemed tough, intelligent, and sensitive to other human's needs. Not the kind of profile that fit shooting somebody then setting their corpse on fire as the warrant alleged.

"You wanna know if I did this honey?"

"I know you didn't," responded Sarah.

"Well, honey, I did do it. I waited for my oldman to fall asleep in his drunken stupor. And when that vicious, stupid man finally fell asleep, I done shot him with his own pistol. And it wasn't nothing I done on impulse neither, honey. I planned it. I'm proud I planned it. I drug him out to his car and set it on fire. Only thing I didn't do right was I didn't use gasoline, I used kerosene 'cause we had a whole barrel of it in the garage for our heaters."

Sarah stared at June.

"Honey, that man beat me every day of my life. I did everything I could to get away. Every time he found out my plans he'd beat me double. Twice, I just up and left the house while he was at work over at U.S. Steel on Ewing Street and 71st. Twice he done caught up with me and beat the tar outta me. I did what I had to do."

Sarah embraced June again. "Ya see, honey. When I tell you about getting away from somebody who's abusive, I know what I'm talking about."

"What are you going to do?" Sarah asked.

"What am I gonna do? Better ask what you're gonna do. I'll tell you what to do. You go hop on the L tonight, don't go home, and ride down to the end of the line down at Midway Airport. Buy a ticket to anywhere. Get the hell outta here."

"I don't have very much money," Sarah sobbed returning to her child-like sounding voice again.

"Just go, honey. I know what I'm talking about."

"I gotta go back to the apartment and get my clothes."

"You don't have any clothes worth going back for."

"I got my money there."

"I'll go back for our stuff. You take the L to the airport, and I'll meet you there later. We'll fly together."

It all made so much sense to me that I dredged up $36 out of my own pockets. "Here's my contribution." An older Mexican man stepped up and handed Sarah some greenbacks, too. His comment; "I knowed your husband, Bill. He was no good, too. You're a good girl. Get the hell outta here while you still can." The old Polish gent behind the bar stepped up and proudly sliced off five twenty dollar bills. Before returning to the other end of the bar, he looked at me and said, "You're always welcome here."

I drove Sarah over to the Western Avenue L stop that night. I accompanied her up to the platform and we waited for a westbound train. "Thanks alot for everything, Peter. I really appreciate it. Do you think Juney's a bad person? I can't believe she'd kill anybody."

"No, I gotta say June seems like a good person. It's too bad about her husband. Sometimes weird things happen in life, kid. You gotta defend yourself."

"I think Juney is ok, too."

A westbound train coasted into the station very quietly. The L ran over a solid earth roadbed at that point and the electric motors didn't make much noise. I waved goodbye to Sarah for the first and last time.

The next day I read a curious item in the newspaper. An off-duty police officer, one Randy Steel, illegally broke into a southwest side apartment. Apparently someone had been waiting for him. He had been ambushed and stabbed in the back. The police couldn't locate the tenants because the building was abandoned, and they had been squatters. No one on that street or in that neighborhood would cooperate with the police. The police were following leads that the officer had been shaking down gang members for money in exchange for looking-the-other-way when open drug dealing occurred. The article concluded; "police announced there were no leads in the killing." Crime Clubbers was offering $1000 for information leading to the arrest and conviction of the perpetrators.

I knew Sarah had made it to the airport with their money and clothes.

Fast Food Blues

Bill Cooper slammed his gas pedal to the floor and went torquing out of the driveway of his suburban Chicago construction site. He burned rubber far down the street. His boss had been riding him all morning. First, he had criticized his cuts on some tricky floor boards for the suburban house they were erecting. Then he had bitched about Bill bringing up material in the wrong order off the flat bed trucks to the curb. Finally, he had ordered Bill to tear out most of a wall he had spent the best part of the morning sweating-his-ass-off framing. Bill felt like the old baboon was always looking over his shoulder now. He hated the close surveillance. And he was going into the third week of it, with an infinity of similar weeks unfolding for the entire summer and fall.

At 11 A.M. everyone was already baking out on the Illinois prairie. The foreman, a stubborn, red-faced man with white hair and grey beard had berated Bill every step of the way on the construction project so far. Bill really couldn't argue with him, because the old bastard was always correct. Bill just felt that the guy wasn't being fair because he had only spent a little over three years in the trade. He knew he had a lot to learn. He just wanted the grizzled boss to chill out a little.

He realized the stress had been causing him to drink more, and he resolved not to drink on his lunch break today. He sped toward a suburban strip mall looking for fast food. His wife, Sarah, had already left him. It ratcheted his anger up a notch just thinking about that whole scene. Technically, at 19 Sarah was still a teenager. *There's a world of difference between 23 and 19.*

When he thought about Sarah he wanted to cry. He had heard she had been running around with guys in the Archer Avenue bars. *She said I beat her. I might have slapped her around a little, but fucking everybody gets slapped around don 't they. I never hurt her.*

"Hell, my mother slapped me around." He said aloud while trying to fathom what had been happening to his life.

"Sarah... I'm so sorry."

He suddenly realized he had been driving 20 miles over the speed limit in congested lunch time traffic and abruptly slowed down his sleek two door late-model automobile. He was unfamiliar with the Elgin suburban area. He had grown up and gone to high school on Chicago's south west side. However, construction work took him far afield in Chicago's greater metropolitan area. *She was a bitch anyway. She wasn't even nice to the fucking dog.* To top it off the air conditioning had broken down in his automobile. He didn't look forward to the repair bill. "Sarah, I love you."

An older gentleman wearing a suit and tie and driving a Cadillac pulled directly in front of Bill causing him to slam on the brakes. Without any acknowledgement of an apology the well dressed white-haired man proceeded down the two lane suburban road.

Enraged, Bill stomped on the accelerator pedal, then swerved into the oncoming lane to pass the Cadillac. He was forced to swerve back just as rapidly by oncoming traffic which he hadn't noticed. Furious, he tailgated the Cadillac at 50 M.P.H. He could feel his sweat drenched t-shirt clinging to him.

When the old gent finally noticed Bill in his rear view mirror, he instinctively stepped on his brake pedal in response. This reaction caused Bill to slam on his brakes again, nearly causing him to lurch into the ditch. When he finally found a break in the oncoming traffic, Bill screamed obscenities through his open window while he passed going 72 M.P.H. in a 40 M.P.H. zone. He felt infuriated when he realized that the old man had his air conditioning on and his windows rolled up. The old motherfucker never heard a word he had screamed, but Bill did derive a bit of satisfaction from the fact that he had seemed to intimidate the old fuck a little. The old guy had his hands clamped on the steering wheel and steadfastly kept his gaze locked forward, refusing to glance in Bill's direction.

Bill had to slam the brakes on yet again to avoid overshooting his destination, the drive-in lane of Hamburger Heaven.

Luisia Gomez didn't care that the lazy white teenagers in her new fast food crew called her "Louey." All she knew was that she had finally been promoted to manager of her own suburban store after working her way up through the ranks. She was still in the midst of moving her belongings out of her parent's house on the near northwest side of the city. Luisia figured that after a few years she could afford to buy one of the modest suburban houses in the Elgin area. Then she would have accomplished two of her main goals in life, making a career for herself, and getting-the-hell out of a crime intensive neighborhood in Chicago.

She had languished as an assistant manager for many years, held back because she was Mexican and a woman. She worked an infinity of double and split shifts and weekends. She filled-in when others quit or called in sick. She had taken all the management training courses and passed all of them. She took every transfer including the ones that put her into the worst neighborhoods in the city. She had put up with men managers, white, black, and Mexican hitting on her and trying to get her to go to bed with them. And that had held up her career, too. But she didn't take shit from anyone, and she wasn't going to do anything wrong. She had cried many times, but she never quit.

When some black women on the east coast had filed a gender discrimination suit against her gigantic fast food company, she had been secretly delighted. The resulting out-of-court settlement had caused chaos in the company as the big shot white managers in company headquarters trashed the company looking for promotable women. *And, of course, you assholes had to promote me, because I hung in there.*

Luisia's mother had complained about the lack of public transportation in Luisia's new suburban neighborhood. Luisia told her mother that she should learn to drive a car. Her mother also told her that she should have more "feelings" for other people, but Luisia thought she could safely ignore that advice. It was obvious to her that nobody gave a shit anyone except themselves. This wasn't Mexico, she was fond of telling her mother, "this is the United States of America."

Bill Cooper ordered two double cheeseburgers with no onions at the drive-through window. He was annoyed at the Spanish accented voice that took his order. He couldn't understand what the young woman said in response due to all the traffic noise and the poor quality of the loud speakers. He waited for an acknowledgement of his order but only got a blast of static instead. Grimly, he pulled ahead to the drive-through window.

Inside, Luisia cheerfully processed the order for the two double cheeseburgers. Initially, she had some staff problems with the kids she had "inherited" with the new store. But she had quickly weeded out the malingerers, the lazies, and the louts. She had caused a considerable amount of turnover, rapidly hiring and firing until she had swiftly built up several efficient crews. But now she was satisfied that the product could be distributed to the customers in a business like manner. She liked to take a turn "at the window" from time to time during the rush periods just to show the kids how effectively the window could be worked.

When the cheeseburger voice arrived at the window, she enthusiastically asked for the money, then briskly shoved the two cheeseburgers out the window to the waiting customer. She felt very cheerful that day because she knew she was hitting all the goal numbers in terms of quality of meals and rapidity of serves.

Then she heard the honking. She glanced back out the window to discover that the cheeseburger man hadn't moved on. He looked pissed. *Oh, oh. I forgot the fries.* When she opened the window to deal with the irate customer, two cheeseburgers came flying through. One hit her in the face. She had to put up with a lot of swearing over the years, but she had never actually been struck before.

"Gimme my fuckin' money back. I told you assholes I don't want no ONIONS.

"I'm sorry sir, please pull your vehicle up into the lot." Luisia felt humiliated, but she was still willing to work out a deal. Her concern was for the line of automobiles piling up in back of the cheeseburger asshole.

"FUCK YOU. I'm not moving. GIMME MY FUCKIN' MONEY BACK."

"Sir, I don't have to listen to this. If you don't move your car up, I'll have to call the police.

"THE POLICE? I'M THE ONE WHO SHOULD CALL THE COPS. YOU CHEATED ME"

Now the whole crew had stopped working, the kids leaning toward the window listening to the exchange. Exasperated, Luisia closed the window and angrily told them to get back to their stations. Outside she heard squealing tires as the cheeseburger man roared into a parking space in the front lot. She put her best girl on "the window" and moved to the front counter to meet the cheeseburger asshole.

He stormed through the front door, shoved aside several women and their children and leaned far over the counter. Humiliation slowly turned to fear for Luisia. She couldn't understand how anybody could work themselves into such a rage over a couple of cheeseburgers.

She watched his intensely distorted face as he said with exaggerated slowness, "Give me my fucking money back." She slowly edged over to the cash register, fearing the lunatic would lunge over the shiny stainless steel counter at her. Her hand was shaking when she got there. "GIMMETHEFUCKINGMONEY !"

"Sir," her voice choked and crackled with emotion, "You can't talk like that in here...

He plunged over the counter and hurt her hand when he slammed his hand into the cash register. Luisia and her crew members flowed away from the cash register. Proudly, she kept her head and grabbed the telephone. She dialed the police while the lunatic smashed away at the cash register.

"YOU'RE CALLING THE POLICE ON ME?"

She stood her ground although her crew scattered back into the kitchen. She warded off the fresh attack with her foot and leg, but the lunatic did manage to bang her on her head once with the telephone. She slumped to the floor crying. The lunatic stared at her ferociously for a moment, then seemed to slightly re-gather his wits, and then fled by leaping over the counter and out the front doors. Her best girl completed the call to the police. A young woman who had been carefully selected by Luisia, she proved her mettle by keeping her head, getting the license plates of the cheeseburger lunatic, and quickly writing down a physical description of the perpetrator.

The cops caught up with him a few blocks away in one of those dreary residential subdivisions where all the houses look the same with the interminable curving streets that seem to go nowhere. Bored children on summer vacation from grade school looked on curiously while the police made him lay face down on the hot asphalt pavement as they cuffed and searched him.

Inside the stuffy jail he marveled at all the charges the police had brought against him. If he had read the charges in a newspaper, he would have called for hanging the fellow. Assault. Battery. Retail theft. Disorderly conduct. Resisting police. He hoped he hadn't hurt the Mexican girl when he had batted her with the telephone.

Fucked again. Fucked again. Wake up Billy. Wake up, man.

Four months later, at the Kane County court house, Bill Cooper spied Luisia Gomez while they both cooled their heels in the court room lobby. They were both dressed up. Bill wore an out-of-style three piece suit, white shirt, and skinny black tie. Luisia wore a clingy black mini-dress, black panty hose, and heels. She had done up her hair. She stood with arms crossed severely while her large black and silver purse weighed her down. Her clothes probably would have looked more appropriate in a night club, and his more at home in a museum.

He cautiously approached the young woman. When she finally realized who he was, her first instinct told her to run, but she wasn't comfortable moving very fast in heels, so she froze.

"I want to apologize to you for what happened."

"OK." She stared straight ahead, avoiding eye contact.

"No, I mean it. I'm really sorry."

"OK. Apology accepted. But that ain't gonna get you off. I'm still testifying against you today." Luisia fumbled in her purse for a cigarette.

"I understand. I don't have a problem with that. I got it coming. I just wanted you to know that the episode changed me. I'm sorry for what I did to you. I had more inner turmoil going on that I realized, and I just snapped that day."

Luisa nodded her head. She could feel her arms shiver. She glanced up and down the cool tiled corridor, looking for the state's attorney people and lawyers. She began slowly walking toward the center of the building, an echoing expanse of floor under the court house dome. Bill Cooper shadowed her.

"I'm sorry you got all those problems." She placed the cigarette between her lips.

"I don't think you can smoke in here. "

"Oh, yeah. Right." She put the cigarette back in her purse.

"No, I'm better now. That's what I'm trying to tell you. I already feel like I've been through my trial and came out a better man."

"That's good." Her heels clicked loudly under the dome, the sounds reverberating throughout the building. The noise embarrassed her. She wasn't used to wearing heels or making that much noise. She couldn't seem to lose him, either. He followed her like a dog.

"So, are you married?"

For the first time she made eye contact. "Who? Me?"

"Yeah."

"No, I ain't married."

"You got a boyfriend?"

"No. No boyfriend." She realized the moment she said those words that she should have said that yeah, she had a husband and a boyfriend. But his question had startled her. And, after looking into his face, she realized he was sincere.

"I'd like to volunteer as a candidate, then."

She laughed in his face while making full eye contact. She finally felt like she had regained command of her nerves. "Are you kiddin' me? After you throw two cheeseburgers at me, then bop me in the head with a telephone, you got the balls to tell me you wanna be my freakin' boyfriend?"

"Yeah." He smiled.

"You know I've had a lot of guys hit on me. You just want to get out of this." She pointed to the court room. "I'm still gonna testify against you."

"Hey, I told you that's OK. That's the right thing to do. I'm not trying to get out of anything. I was wrong. I apologized. And I'm sincerely sorry about any pain and suffering I caused you. Now, I'm just trying to move on with my life."

"Well, move on without me. What about you? You got a girlfriend?"

"No. I'm divorced."

"I'm not surprised. What happened there?"

"My wife left me."

"Yeah. Why?"

"Because she was too young to get married in the first place. She's very immature. And I beat the crap out of her."

"You must beat the crap out of everybody you disagree with. I got first hand experience with that." She laughed, but didn't like the nervous tickle in her voice. She was surprised by his honesty.

"Where you from anyway?"

"Chicago."

"Yeah, where abouts?"

"Northwest Side over by Kedzie and Lawrence. You know where that's at?"

"Sure. I'm from the city, too. I'm from the Beverly neighborhood."

"Where's that?"

"South Side. By Archer Avenue."

She didn't know the city, especially the South Side, well, but nodded her head like she knew where it was located.

"Hey, there's the lawyers." He pointed to two clumps of people at the far end of the hallway, on one side the Kane County prosecutors, and, standing with a policeman, his lawyer. "We better get down there."

She turned immediately and listened to her heels clacking toward the court room. He tagged along at her side and said, "How's about going out with me tonight? My lawyer says I'm not going to get any jail time out of this. Just probation and a fine. I gotta keep going to classes about domestic violence and anger management, but I enjoy that. I'd go to them even if the judge doesn't send me."

"What do you do for a living?" She looked straight ahead facing the lawyers as she asked the question while steadily closing the distance between them.

"Carpenter. I'm a carpenter."

At the trial, Luisia described the attack as she had in the police reports and the hearings, but when it came time to identify the culprit, she failed to ID Bill, and instead named a plain clothes policeman, who was about the same height as the perpetrator. The case was thrown out, and the prosecutors made noises about prosecuting Luisia, but left her alone.

At work she was promoted to regional manager. And a year later, on the Spring night when they got engaged, Luisia pulled out what looked like a stub nosed, .38 caliber handgun from her clunky black and silver purse and told Bill, "I believe you have changed, but if you ever lay hands on me again, I'm gonna wait 'til you fall asleep, then I'm gonna stick this up your asshole and pull the trigger."

Looking stunned, Bill said, "I don't think we should keep a gun around the house."

"You're right." First she kissed him, then she took the "gun" and lit a cigarette.

The Bomb Threat

As we basked in the warm June sunshine on the steps of Chicago's Art Institute, I asked my young friend Dean if he had managed to cajole our boss, Athena Wells, into permitting him to take-off the upcoming Friday.

"She told me if I take that day off, that she'll fire me. I positively absolutely will not be given that day off. Believe me, I have tried every angle. The woman is a complete bitch."

We were waiting for Dean's fiancée, Veronica Powers, to join us for lunch in the restaurant on the other side of Michigan Avenue. Dean wanted me to meet Veronica, a student at the Art Institute, and he had also pledged to help me pick out some computer parts. Dean Crystal was a computer wizard.

We worked together at Pumping Sunshine, Inc., a telemarketing firm located in a tall glass office building out on the edge of the city, near the airport. I had been fired from my manufacturing job again, but felt confident the union would get my job back for me. To keep from starving, I took what I considered to be a fill-in job at Pumping Sunshine. The job felt like one more checker in my already checkered career which consisted of graduate student, cab driver, factory worker, fried chicken chucker, factory worker, and now telemarketer.

Everyone we worked with, however, seemed to be in the same state of flux. Pumping Sunshine served as; a fill-in for people waiting to get the results of the postal service exam, a place to park between college semesters, or as something to do while you looked for a real job. Or, as in Dean's case, it provided work for a full-time computer science student who was trying to finish his degree.

Between firings for "being unproductive and not meeting quota" and voluntary departures, the whole workforce seemed to turn over once every three months. I had managed to limp along for four months without getting fired by Athena Wells, our legendary boss.

"Just call-in sick next Friday," I suggested as we watched the Saturday afternoon traffic crawl down Michigan Avenue. I loved the way the Loop skyscrapers created acoustical canyons. You could hear the eerie echoes of automobile horns or the rumble of the L from the other side of the Loop. The skyscrapers did funny things with the sunlight, too. And like the shady side of a mountain, they created pools of cool air on a warm day. The totally artificial environment created an ambiance in the Loop not found anywhere else in the great city.

"She'd fire me. I already made the mistake of asking for the day off. She's marked the day in her computer." Dean sounded completely fatalistic, like a man who had come to accept his unavoidable fate. "Veronica's gonna be pissed about it. We were going to go to some art exhibit in Milwaukee that Friday. She already bought the tickets."

As he said that, a lovely young woman dressed in red shorts came prancing down the monumental steps in our direction. We both got up, and Dean embraced her. He introduced me, "This is Peter MacNaughton, my buddy from work." As I shook hands with Veronica I couldn't help noticing her fiery t-shirt which proclaimed, "Shoot a stockbroker, save the environment." One of her fellow art students had depicted a gang of women armed with shotguns, including very elderly women, chasing a gaggle of suits and ties. The t-shirt was hilarious, but I knew I wasn't going to like Veronica because she was too much like me.

"Let's eat," she proclaimed and pointed to the restaurant across the street.

My first impression, of course, proved to be true. I couldn't stand Veronica. Dean had constructed a perfect triangle for himself. Dean and I hit it off despite the fact that I was middle aged because we were psychologically opposite types. He loved Veronica and vice versa because they were opposites. But Veronica and I... it was too much like looking in the mirror. I just couldn't enjoy socializing with the woman. I saw an introvert trying to act like an extrovert. I felt sorry for her, too, because she was just too damn sensitive to be suited to the daily brutal grind in the Psychotic Atomik Empire. And I felt jealous of her, because I had never been able to take advantage of my artistic or creative side as she clearly intended to do with a degree from the Art Institute. When I looked at Veronica, it made me realize how anti-social and aloof I must appear to most people. On the other hand, she made me want to do better.

When I glanced into her brown eyes from time to time from the other side of our lunch table, I saw intelligence and compassion for humanity. Conversely and ironically, I also saw unlimited ruthlessness and retribution against personal enemies.

"I have to get back to the studio. It was nice meeting you, Peter. You're going to swing by and pick me up on Friday morning, right?" She asked Dean.

"Uh... I meant to tell you. I can't get the day off. That bitch Athena won't give it to me."

"Don't call women 'bitches.' It's sexist, and I don't like it."

"I consider myself to be a feminist. And I gotta tell ya. Athena is a power skirt," I volunteered.

Veronica bestowed a belabored and artificial smile in my direction that seemed to say, "You don't know what you're talking about, so you had better shut up·"

"He's right, honey. She's completely unreasonable. I've worked there two months and never taken a day off. She's pissed at me because I don't make her quotas."

"Well, tell her you'll make quota this week if she gives you Friday off. I can't cancel the trip now. I already bought the tickets. I can't get a refund."

"I can't make quota because she's got me selling fishing magazines into a list of phone numbers in Manhattan. She gives me all the bad lists. I don't have a chance."

Ignoring her previous facial expression, I chimed-in, "You don't know Athena. When we start a shift, we can't get out of our cubicle without permission. She's denied bathroom permission to people until they made their quota for that hour."

"Well, then.., tell her you're going to quit if she doesn't give you the day off."

We both laughed in Veronika's face. The idea of approaching the fashionably dressed and chain smoking Athena with such a threat seemed ludicrous.

"She'd just tell me not to let the door hit me in the ass on the way out," said Dean. "When you make quota, the job can pay twice the minimum wage, honey. There's a line of job applicants in the 15th floor lobby every day."

"She won't want to lose an educated person. You said Peter had a Master's Degree."

We both laughed again. "The only requirement is fluency in English," said Dean.

"And a very thick skin," I added.

"They can't take a lot of turnover in people," Veronica persisted.

"Honey, on average, two people quit every day. We see fresh faces on every shift."

"You have to get Friday off. You're smart. Figure out something." And with that Veronica excused herself and flounced back across Michigan Avenue leaving Dean and I at the table.

Dean leaned back and savored his coffee. He looked at me and said simply, "I'm screwed. If I take the day off, I'm fired. And I need that job. It's a shitty job, but it's still a job. You know how hard it is to find a job?"

I laughed. "I'm working the same one you are, partner. If it were easy, we'd both be somewhere else."

"And if I don't take the day off, Veronica is gonna be pissed. You can see that."

"Better to keep the job until you can graduate. Veronica will get over it," I counseled with my middle aged wisdom.

Dean, typically not the type to get emotional, abruptly slammed down his coffee cup splattering both of us, "But goddamnit, I just can't stand getting beat by that woman." He referred to the ongoing duel of wits in which he had been engaged with Athena Wells since the day he had been hired by the owner of the company, old Dick Richhead.

We all suspected that young Athena slept with the boss because she was fashionably slender and ostentatiously eager to be successful. She drove a used BMW while the boss drove a Porsche. Athena had been occupied with other activities the day the boss hired Dean. She would have never hired Dean because she instantly sensed his natural disrespect for authority and traditional ways of doing things. Because above all, Dean was an inventor and an engineer of doing-things-better. So, right from the start, Athena wanted to get rid of Dean. I saw it all.

The first time Athena handed him one of her idiotic scripts, which we had to slavishly follow in our sales presentations, Dean pointed out all her mistakes. She made him use it verbatim anyway.

When Athena handed Dean a list of phone numbers in Phoenix to sell a Southwestern magazine, Dean said the idea was stupid and demanded a list of numbers in a Midwestern city.

"Nobody in the Southwest wants to read about it. They're already there, they don't have to read about it."

Athena made him call through the list anyway. When he continued to complain, she assigned coffee making duties to him. He salted the coffee, quickly bringing an end to that humiliation.

She assigned him a telephone survey which only paid minimum wage because no sales were involved. He had to phone Iowa farmers and ask them what they liked about a certain brand of tractor. He fabricated a bunch of fake answers rather than make all the phone calls. Athena didn't suspect anything until the customer vehemently complained about all the "it doesn't start very well in the winter because it's a diesel" responses. Apparently their tractor sported a gasoline engine.

Athena then took to publicly criticizing Dean. In front of the others she told him he socialized in the office too much, and she scolded him for making too many personal phone calls (to Veronica). Dean, of course, always had something witty and sarcastic to say in response. Mocking her, he would obsequiously snap his arm back across his chest and thumping himself would say, "To hear is to obey." When she turned her back, he enthusiastically gave her the Nazi salute.

From Monday to Thursday Dean tried every ploy in the book to get the day off on Friday. Monday morning he informed Athena that he had a doctor's appointment on Friday morning. She said fine, she'd have a special project ready for him Friday afternoon. Failure to report on time for said special project duty would result in termination.

On Tuesday he tried to tell her that he had a dental appointment on Friday afternoon. His molar was suddenly bothering him. She countered with an immediate complimentary appointment with a dentist friend of her's on the 14th floor.

On Wednesday he announced that his grandmother had died, and he planned to attend the funeral on Friday. Athena laughed in his face. She told him if he couldn't produce a newspaper obituary, not to bother to report to work on Monday.

Thursday morning he asked to see Athena in her office. When he returned to the "killing floor" as Athena referred to our forest of cubicles, I asked him about his latest ploy. "What did you tell her? "I whispered.

"I just begged to have the day off. I told her flat-out about the tickets."

Curious if the truth had any effect on Athena's limited well of compassion for fellow humans, I said, "What'd she say?"

"She said, 'no.' If I take the day off, I'm fired."

Friday morning started out as regular as the alarm clock in the infinity of days of my working life. Athena held her traditional morning motivational meeting that typically demoralized and demotivated everyone. She handed out her moronic scripts and lists for the day, then returned to her glass walled office while we settled into our cubicles for the morning offensive against the hapless individuals unfortunate enough to pick up their telephones.

However, I had only dialed one number before Athena came rushing up and down the aisles. As she moved closer to me, I watched my co-workers rapidly peel off their headsets and head for the lobby and the stairwell. I assumed it was a fire drill because nobody headed for the elevators. When she reached me, she repeated her mantra, "Bomb threat. Down the stairs. NOW. Bring your purse and car keys. Leave everything else.

The parking lot was full of cops. I never realized the FBI had a field office in our building. I thought they were located downtown. The employees from all the various offices in the building milled about in the parking lot for about 45 minutes. It was a sunny day and the sudden break in routine appeared to be welcomed by all. I found Dean sitting under a little ornamental sapling on one of the carefully landscaped tree banks. He beamed a carefully controlled smile at me.

Eventually the cops came around and told us all to go home. It would take most of the day to completely search the building. Apparently the bomb threat had been called-in against the FBI. Dean drove off the moment they made the announcement.

I hoped Veronica didn't get caught.

A Metafictional Mystery:

or

The Bullshit Story

Two pilgrims, a writer and a college professor, on their way to Las Vegas discovered across the armrest of their airliner seats that they shared an abiding interest in American literature, although they quickly fell to quarreling over what constituted "great literature."

Professor Frick insisted that all great literature had been written in the realist/mimetic vein and that postmodernism represented a decline in artistic method and the decay of a great tradition. The writer, Frack, countered by offering to tell Frick a metafictional mystery which would be up to par with any literary standard.

"Alright, my friend, go ahead. But no fiction that frankly comments on itself can possibly be as entertaining or as morally useful as a fictional work that lacks self-awareness. It's the difference between neurosis and art."

"Well, try this one, Professor Frick. A number of years ago in Chicago I had a very strange encounter while waiting for a ride. I had attended a party in the Loop and lost track of time. Consequently at 3 A.M. I found I had missed the last diesel commuter train bound for the northwest side of the city where I lived. So, I phoned my wife and she agreed to pick me up at the Logan Square L terminal. In those days the O'Hare airport L ended there. I normally avoided taking the L because I feared getting mugged.

When I arrived at the end-of-the-line, I found the Terminal Restaurant was still open. So, I decided to have some coffee at the counter while I waited. Besides the old Chinese cook, the only other person in the place was a gaunt-looking young woman. I watched her stare into space while she sipped her coffee and drummed her fingers on the formica counter-top.

I seated myself two revolving stools away from the woman, and I paid for my coffee, leaving the change on the countertop. I noticed the old cook and counterman never turned his back to the woman. Alarmed, I kept glancing over in the woman's direction to see what was up. Dark circles under her eyes suggested that she was probably a heroin addict. Eventually, she noticed my surveillance, and aggressively stared back at me. I had to quit eyeballing her then.

She wore her raven hair very short in a punk hairdo. I couldn't help but notice her skin-tight, black jeans and very snug black t-shirt. She didn't appear to be wearing a bra. She looked like a typical late night loser. Maybe a prostitute. The only anomaly I detected was an expensive looking business briefcase near her combat-boot shod feet.

To help kill time I leaned away from her direction to turn a revolving display rack located on the counter. As I looked over the sunglasses and various pills for staying awake and headaches, I thought I saw, out of the corner of my eye, the girl lean over and swipe some of my change.

I was careful not to startle her as I slowly eased back onto my stool. Sure enough, it looked like some of my change had disappeared. She ordered a donut and shoved some change in the cook's direction. I thought to myself I wasn't going to make a Federal case out of some missing change.

Disdaining the idea of removing my remaining change from the counter, I stepped outside and bought a newspaper from an automatic vending machine. When I returned from my brief hiatus, I found more change missing and the young woman sitting one stool closer to me. She was munching on a fresh donut. The cook stood with his back to the grill, but avoided eye contact with me. I knew he knew what was going on, too. Most managers would have raised hell over a petty theft going on right under their nose. They would have called the cops or thrown her out. The fact that this guy didn't made me wonder if the cook knew her and feared violence.

I shook my head in disbelief. Never had I encountered a bolder thief. For a moment I entertained the idea of asking her if she needed a few bucks. Then I decided to follow the cook's lead. I intended to ignore her. It's very easy to get shot or cut-up in Chicago at that time of the morning.

However, my wife, the eternal procrastinator, and possibly the pokiest person on the planet, failed to materialize. By then it was nearly 4 A.M. I ordered another coffee while I leisurely read the *Chicago Sun Times*. Naturally, I left the fresh change on the counter. I regarded it as a challenge. I wanted to see what would happen.

After a couple of minutes, sure as hell, I saw the lithe arm and hand sneaking in my direction again. I decided enough was enough. Out of the corner of my eye I saw the cook watching the theft unfold. As I pretended to read the newspaper, I watched her hand creep ever-so-slowly toward my change. I noticed she made a point of staring directly ahead of her into space as if her arm and hand were directed by an intelligence independent of her.

Her hand had nearly reached my money when I abruptly heard my wife honking the horn out in the street. Involuntarily, my attention shifted toward the street. As I turned back to the counter, I saw her hand headed swiftly back in her direction with a large portion of my change.

When I threw my newspaper in the air, the cook ducked into the back room, and the young woman dove for the floor, away from me, apparently thinking I intended to assault her. My change rattled over the floor and counter. Without thinking, I grabbed her briefcase off the floor where it had been resting against her stool.

I fled out the door without looking back. I jumped into the car and told my wife to gun it out of there. Uncharacteristically, she did. She told me latter she had seen my newspaper fluttering in the air, and the others diving for safety. She thought somebody had pulled a gun on me. Anyway, she drove me home without incident. I opened the briefcase and examined the contents on the way home.

"So..."

"So, what?"

The airliner bumped through a pocket of turbulence.

"So, what was in the briefcase?" demanded Frick.

"Oh. It was full of bullshit, just like this story."

What Did You Learn in School Today?

After her successful job interview, Jesse Flowers wondered if the rest of her life would be spent accelerating down a continuous spiral to hell. First, her 40 year-old husband ran off with a young woman, then he instituted divorce proceedings against her, then he convinced her that she didn't need a lawyer, then he fought for custody of the kids with his lawyer and won, and then managed to keep possession of their home in the bargain. Jesse wound up with a meager cash settlement. Taking her only two pieces of furniture, a futon and her grandmother's cedar chest, she settled into an efficiency apartment where she pondered the complexities of men's midlife crises. She spent her first night alone in her two room domicile crying.

She was dazed and stunned. She began seeing a counselor just to have someone to talk to. Normally, she would have cried on her best friend's shoulder, but Kathy was married to Steve who worked for the same electronic company as her ex-husband. When Steve was transferred to Texas, Kathy had followed reluctantly. Kathy's entire family lived in the Chicago area. She welcomed the counselor's succor, but, pragmatically, she realized at age 38, she had to move on. The counselor urged her to grieve, but with her small amount of cash dwindling away, she knew the first order of business should be finding a job. Despite the mantle of emotional distress that seemed to have settled on her shoulders, she took a small measure of pride in her emerging survival instincts. She set up a checking account, a tiny savings account, and she managed to get her utilities set up and running. These were all things that were new to her. She had married right out of high school and her husband had always handled everything. Including decisively dumping her.

Driving home in what had always been her family's "spare" car, a rusty, twelve-year-old, sub-compact model, Jesse wondered if accepting the secretarial job at the recruiting agency had been a very intelligent thing to do.

She liked the modern 20 story glass building in Schaumburg that housed the agency on the twentieth floor. She liked the Woodfield Mall area where the building was located. She liked Athena Wells, the well dressed young woman who interviewed her first, although she instinctively realized that Athena didn't like her. She liked the big open office with all the computers and the friendly people and the bustling atmosphere of big business being done over the telephone.

But she didn't like the owner, Frank Braverman, who been the second person to interview her, despite the fact that Frank really seemed to like her. And that was the rub. Literally. Frank had patiently listened to her story, although her counselor had specifically told her not to "bring her problems to the interview.

After hearing her story, Frank had spent most of the afternoon telling her his story. His liberal parents from the Hyde Park area of Chicago, his radical days in Madison, Wisconsin as a university student, his sudden inspiration to go into the search and recruiting business, and his ongoing roaring success in the business. He droned on about his new Loop office. His expansion plans into other "marketing platforms" in the Midwest. On and on.

When Frank discovered that she lacked computer skills, he immediately offered to send her to school, company paid, to get the skills. He also urged her to begin taking classes for a bachelor's degree. "There's unlimited opportunity here, Jesse. But you need to get the skills and education necessary to step up to a recruiter's desk."

As he wove an imaginary verbal tapestry of her future, Frank arose from his high-backed, leather swivel chair and began stalking back and forth across the wide carpet in his private office. As if the chair mentally constrained him, he paced faster and faster while continuing on and on into Jesse's future with the company. She slowly realized Frank spent most of his time in the future wrestling with large issues only visible to himself. Eventually, however, he did work his way around to the back of Jesse's chair, which she found uncomfortable, as she tried to squirm around to face him. At one point in his description of possible branches in Jesse's future career path, Frank looked down at her fidgeting and said, "Relax. Your shoulders look like they're bunched up in knots." And, so saying, he reached down from behind her and began massaging her shoulders.

She didn't know how to respond to the massage. Confusion reigned while her mind lost Frank's conversation thread entirely. She wasn't sure if Frank was just being friendly, or if he was just one more lech. Her counselor had told her repeatedly, "You're still an attractive woman, and when you get through with your grieving period, you should resume dating again." Kathy had often complained that Jesse had aged far less than herself.

After mulling it for a few minutes, she decided that a shoulder massage was probably inappropriate during a job interview. "Frank, I don't need a massage. I'm interested in hearing about the benefits."

Frank dug his fingers deep into her shoulder muscles one last time and gave her one last squeeze. Letting go and striding back to his desk where he pulled a file from a cabinet he said, "Oh, I thought Athena went over that with you?"

The interminable interview concluded with her accepting the job, then setting her start day and filling out all the paper work with Athena.

"Well, welcome aboard. I'm sure you'll do well. Frank really seems to like you." Athena said.

"Yeah. He goes a little overboard sometimes, though, wouldn't you say?"

"What?"

"Shoulder messages?" Jesse ventured.

"Oh. He's just being friendly."

"I hope he doesn't get swarmy."

"You're lucky he likes you. Frank is loaded. And he's good looking, too. He works out every day. He can get swarmy with me any time he wants."

Jesse proceeded to sign up for evening business and computer classes at company expense. She liked staying busy and away from her grief. The classes also gave her a convenient excuse to avoid seeing Frank in the evenings as well. He frequently suggested late dinners to her and was disappointed when he learned she had to attend class. Jesse had learned in the interim that office gossip had already pegged him as having an affair with another woman in the office, Clarissa Raintree. The information bugged her, because Clarissa was a married woman with two kids. After her experience with an adulterous mate, she just didn't like the idea of married people fooling around.

The days in the office went by quickly because she was busy from the moment she arrived at the office in the morning to the time she departed in the evening. Frank hadn't been fooling about his business volume. She was constantly dealing with correspondence, sending fares, and calling job candidates to set up plane rides. And everyday, Frank managed to work his way behind her chair and massage her shoulders. Only, as time went on, the massages worked their way South, down her arms and towards her breasts.

She realized it was only a matter of time before Frank arrived at his destination. She tried shaking his hands off her shoulders. She repeatedly asked him to stop - and he would - for a few days. She did everything she could to dissuade and discourage him. But her resistance only seemed to make him more determined.

She cast around for another job, but she eventually realized that Frank was paying her well above scale. She needed the job, and she had been taking ruthless advantage of his free education offer. During her first nine months on the job, she had completed all the computer classes she would probably ever need. She had begun taking undergraduate courses toward a bachelor's degree. To pay for the courses on her own would have been prohibitively expensive. Everyday, as if to rub it in, Frank would always ask her as he commenced the massage, "Well, what did we learn in school today?" That annoyed the hell out of her.

So, she and Frank continued to do the massage lambada. One day she came to work early and moved her desk so that her chair backed up against a bookcase. When Athena arrived, she made her put it back. "What's the matter with you? The researchers have to get to those books. You can't put your desk there."

When the semesters changed, Jesse noticed that the school offered a wide variety of self-defense classes. She signed up for her business classes, then began an investigation of the martial arts offerings. She talked to several instructors and quickly realized some of them lived in another world. They talked about their "dojos," or schools, the way some people discuss their nationality. She discarded the swift-striking art of karate because she thought, at her age, that she'd wreck her elbows and knees. She thought the kung fu instructor was a spooky sadist. The tae kwon do instructor, an enthusiastic young Korean, showed her some of the spin-ning tornado kicks that reminded her of a Bruce Lee movie. It looked spectacular, but she doubted it was really effective self-defense. She visited a jujitsu dojo and the display they put on looked like it could hold its own against Chicago street fighting, but it was far too violent for her.

She finally settled on a judo class taught by a woman, Charlene, whom she guessed to be about 60 years old. The collection of chokes, pins, and throws all involved using the opponent's weight against him, and it seemed the most appropriate for her.

As the new semester unfolded, Jesse learned the chokes and throws from Charlene who routinely threw burly truck drivers and part time police trainees on their asses. In the office, Frank continued, everyday, asking her what she had learned in school. Meanwhile, he continued heading ever southward in his massages.

Thoroughly fed-up, Jesse eyeballed a want ad for an executive assistant with a suburban cab company. She applied for the job and the interview went ok. She had to go through the rigmarole of getting bonded because the job involved handling money. The old boss told her he'd call if he decided to hire her. In judo class Jesse began gaining some self-confidence back. She felt her self-esteem rise, as she, too, began throwing burly truck drivers and part time police trainees onto their asses. She quit her counselor. She was done crying over her situation.

One day, she confided in Charlene regarding her problem with Frank. Charlene told Jesse to clearly tell Frank to "fuck off." Then she made Jesse sit on a chair in the middle of a big judo mat, then had every member of the class approach her from behind and put their hands on Jesse's shoulders. Charlene instructed Jesse to "Grab a handful of ears, honey. Wherever you throw those ears, your opponent will follow." Her first several attempts to throw ears around resulted in tipping the chair and her opponent over onto herself. She got bruised, but eventually she began flipping her classmates over her shoulders with ease.

The next day, at the office, she walked into Frank's private office. "Frank, I've got something I have to talk to you about."

"Can it wait? I'm busy here. I'm expecting a very important phone call." He said without making eye contact with her.

"No, it can't. This will only take a minute."

Frank finally looked up from his desk. "Ok. What?"

"Frank, I want you to quit rubbing my shoulders."

"That's it?"

"Yes."

"Sure. I'm sorry. I didn't know it bugged you. I won't do it again. Is that it?" He resumed staring at his telephone and fidgeting with his expensive suspenders.

"Frank, I mean it."

"I hear you. It won't happen again." And the phone rang. Frank waved her out of the office. Some big shot from one of his client corporations. Jesse left. She felt that she had fulfilled Charlene's edict.

For more than a week Frank kept his hands to himself when handing her work or discussing her work. One night the cab company called Jesse and told her she had the job if she wanted it. Jesse told the old man she needed a couple of days to think about it.

The next day, while Frank dictated a letter to her, she felt his hands land on her shoulders. She vigorously shook them off. In a few minutes they returned. "Frank, I thought you were going to knock it off." She shook the hands off again. A few minutes later they renewed their progress, and this time Jesse was too busy getting Frank's thoughts on paper to shake the hands off. When he said, "What did you learn in school today?" he reached all the way down and briefly cupped her breasts in his hands.

Reaching back and grabbing two generous handfuls of ears, Jesse said, "I learned to never take any shit from assholes like you," and she flung those ears hard onto the carpet.

The Birthday Party

Jesse Flowers wondered if accepting her new telemarketing job might turn out to be the second biggest mistake of her life since she had gotten divorced. Maybe the third if you counted the "battery" charge her last boss had threatened her with. In the past year her husband had left her for a younger woman and legally seized her son and daughter and her suburban Chicago home. In her distraught state she had taken a job, the first one she had held since her early 20s, with a executive recruiting company despite the fact that she thought the boss only hired her to hit on her. Taking that job had definitely been mistake number one.

She had patiently suffered his advances because the job had provided free tuition for any courses she choose to take at the nearby community college. She also used every means at her disposal to get her boss to stop including directly appealing to him to knock it off. Nothing she did had any effect on him.

She didn't understand why he had singled her out, because at the age of 39, there were plenty of younger, prettier women in the office, who seemed to remain unmolested. When she appealed to the woman office manager, a fashionably dressed younger woman, she had laughed at Jesse and suggested getting attention from a rich and "connected" guy like their boss wasn't such a bad thing. In fact, she told Jesse she wished he'd hit on her.

Then she took a judo course and things took an inevitable turn toward violence. The last time he tried to grope her he found himself flung ass over tea kettle across the room. Which led to the battery charge that he latter dropped.

But that lead to being out of a job without references. She had applied at a local cab company for an "office manager" position, but they had already filled it when she arrived to fill out an employment application.

That unfortunate turn of events led her to her third mistake. She found herself taking a telemarketing job at Pumping Sunshine, a wholly owned subsidiary of Blue Sky, Inc. It was located in a tall, glass office building out on the edge of the city, next to the expressway and near the airport. At first she couldn't understand the casual way she had been hired on the spot without any reference checking.

After three days on the job she fully understood. The company experienced rapid and total turnover of the work force. The employees had to raise their hands to take potty breaks. Every call had been carefully scripted and was closely monitored. They had to keep telephone head sets on at all times. People quit everyday. Sometimes they just didn't show up the next day. Others quit in the middle of the shift. They had to hire new blood every day. She had managed to find work with a 20th century sweatshop.

But the work and the idiotic way it was conducted didn't bother her. She was glad to be working, and glad for the bonuses they paid when she occasionally sold something. Alaric Meinhoff bothered her. And bothered her. And bothered her.

He frequently sat uncomfortably close to her, ostensibly to listen to her calls. There was no reason for it, because he had the electronic means to cut into her conversations from his office. She dreaded the frequent occasions when Alaric summoned her into his office. She hated being in the claustrophobic room alone with him. Instead of remaining behind his desk, he always came out and sat right next to her.

"You don't have to come over here. You can stay at your desk." A desk upon which sat a photograph of his pretty young wife.

"Don't get nervous. Nobody's going to hurt you."

The vision of her last boss sailing through the air caused her to laugh. The look of utter surprise on his face had been permanently welded into her memory. That boss had been a big guy, like Alaric, too. Maybe six foot three. Maybe 250 pounds. The internal joke she enjoyed was the fact that she was barely five foot one and a hundred and ten pounds.

"What's so funny?" He smiled as he pulled up a chair and sat so close to her that he sat on her dress.

"Do you mind?" She pulled away, yanking her dress along with her.

"You know if you'd date me, there'd probably be raise in it for you."

"No way."

"I really like blondes."

Jesse made a mental note to dye her hair brunette. The same color as Alaric wife's hair.

Later that day she had indicated on a sign up sheet that her address and phone number were correct. It was a routine payroll check. They had to constantly verify addresses and phones because of the turnover. She noted Alaric's phone number on the list. And his nearby address.

She couldn't understand it. Alaric was probably only 22 or 23 years old. She couldn't understand why he choose to hit on her instead of some of the younger women in the office who were nearer his own age. One morning she came in early and complained to the owner, Dick Richhead. But he didn't seem to understand her complaints.

That morning Alaric came up from behind and put his hands on her shoulders as she finished a phone call.

"Will you please keep your hands to yourself." She said that loud enough to get the attention of the people in the cubicles next to her.

"Take it easy. Don't get your underwear in a bunch. I like you."

She turned back to the cubicle and punched up another phone number.

"Dick told me you complained."

She stoically started her telemarketing sales pitch. An angry man's voice on the other end of the line cursed her and hung up.

"Ok, what did we do wrong there?"

She swung around so violently to confront Alaric that she made him wince.

"Hey. Take it easy. It's my birthday. Give me a break." He put up his big ham bone hands in mock defense.

She swung around again to ring up another number.

"I love your blonde hair." His face was so close to her ear that she could feel her hairs move from his breath. She thought about putting her elbow into his nose. Hard enough to break it. She restrained herself. The cops hadn't been very understanding about her story when they had arrested her at the search firm. They had only reluctantly cut her loose after her boss used his connections to drop the charges.

Then an idea materialized in her mind from the place with no time and no space. She smiled her most fetching smile at him.

"Your birthday, huh?"

"Yeah." He brightened up at the smile. It was the first encouraging sign he had encountered during his long siege.

"You should get something special on your birthday." She smiled again. Then she winked at him.

"You're right. I should. I deserve it."

"Maybe we can fix you up. Why don't you come over to my apartment tonight?" She scribbled her address on a slip of paper.

"What time?"

"Oh, about nine or so."

"That's too late. Let's just go over there after work."

"Patience, birthday boy." She patted him on his bulky knee. That seemed to mollify him.

"Why so late?"

"I've got things to plan. I'll have to go out and shop for something appropriate for the occasion."

"What are you talking about?"

After glancing from side to side to make sure her co-workers were busy, she gingerly pulled her blouse back just enough to reveal the top of her brassiere. "Lingerie, silly," she whispered.

"Oh. OK."

She winked again. Alaric departed and didn't bother her for the balance of the day. As soon as she got off work, she set to work on her plans. They kept her busy until 8:30 that evening. Anticipating that Alaric would show up early, she slipped out of her dress in her small combination living room/dining area. She put on a new, silky Chinese style robe over her new brassiere, panties, garter belts, and thigh high stockings. The silky, new red underwear matched her new, skyscraper high-heels.

As she had assumed, Alaric showed up at 8:45. He had been out drinking with his young buddies, and he wanted to go to work on Jesse immediately. With difficulty she managed to fend him off. He kept grabbing for her but she managed to keep the robe on. With great difficulty she managed to get him seated on her sofa. But he wanted to get up and grope her.

Finally, she pulled back and said, "If you're a good boy, I'll give you one hell of a surprise. And, so saying, she removed the robe herself. She handed him a stiff mixed drink. He swilled it down while ogling her. She handed him another, already pre-mixed. As he pounded the second one down she went into her exotic dancer act, strutting her stuff in front of him.

"What's the surprise?"

She picked up her dress and stepped into it.

"Hey, what are you doing?"

"I'm putting it back on, so you can take it off." She handed him the third pre-mixed drink. "Now, it's your turn, big boy."

"What?"

"Take your clothes off. Get comfortable. I'll be in there waiting for you." She pointed to the bedroom door. "But make sure you're ready when you come in, otherwise, I'll get turned off and won't want to do it." And with that she slipped into the bedroom and closed the door.

Obligingly, Alaric rapidly stripped, gulped down the third drink, and busily made himself erect. When he entered the bedroom, the entire office staff, as well as his wife, shouted, "Surprise."

Jesse really didn't mind it when Dick fired them both the next day, because she noticed the cab company was running their ad for "office manager" again.

Liberated In the Name Of the People

The first time I heard Jessie Flowers ask old Ben Snell for a raise, I knew she was from the land of the lost, because Ben was the tightest, meanest man I knew. I called him Ben "Smell" behind his back. I wouldn't dare say it to his face, because no-nonsense Ben was the type who could cheerfully hack you to pieces verbally or literally, then sit down to a hearty breakfast.

Ben, of course, responded to Jessie, "No, you have to put some time in here first. You have to earn your money. You wouldn't enjoy the raise, if you didn't earn it."

Jessie thought he was kidding. "Ok, I've been here six months now. You said you would give me a raise after I worked here for six months."

"I said I'd review your compensation package after six months. There's nothing automatic about it. And I have reviewed it. You need to put some work and effort into things."

"What? " Her inflection indicated that she was catching on. "I've redone your whole computer system and all your books."

"And I've paid you handsomely for your efforts."

"You're not kidding?"

"No, I'm not kidding. Put some more effort into it and we'll talk again."

Jessie looked crushed then determined as she strode back to her desk in the tiny back room of the cab company office. Ben, a 60 year old lech, tried to pat her on the fanny. But she made certain that she circumnavigated his desk in the out-of-range zone. I watched the whole scenario unfold through the "driver's window" where I stood in the hallway holding my day's trip sheet and receipts.

That was the second time I worked for Ben. He ran a 30 cab operation out of an industrial suburb on Chicago's far northwest side. I had just been fired from a "telemarketing" company, Pumping Sunshine, a Division of Blue Sky, Inc. I had phoned people from the 15th floor of a nearby, glass-box, office building and tried to sell magazine subscriptions. We had to follow sales scripts that had been psychologically engineered and call into carefully crafted geographical lists that included selling farm implement magazines to the unfortunate citizens of Manhattan.

Naturally, with such inspired brain work going into the project, people turned over in the job at a ferocious rate. My number finally came up due to "poor production." I suggested I would have had more success if they had tried to hawk New York subway maps in Iowa. I harvested blank stares all around in response.

Anyway, I was just one more middle-aged human wreck on America's employment reefs. I was waiting to go back to my union factory job where I had been fired for "poor work performance," although union activism had been the real reason. I took the telemarketing job to keep from starving while the grievance procedure slowly ground forward. Now I found myself back driving a cab, something I hadn't done since I had been a graduate student at the University of Illinois in Chicago back in the early seventies.

I liked Ben's operation better than the two main Chicago cab companies where I had also worked briefly because he had acquired state of Illinois licenses to haul packages. We hauled passengers, too. But a typical ride found me hauling three separate small boxes and maybe a passenger simultaneously. That enabled me to legally "pull the flag" four times on the same trip. On a good day it was a lucrative racket. Most of my "fares" went into the other northwest side industrial suburbs or into the closely adjacent O'Hare Airport. The whole area had a twilight zone feel about it. The urban planners called it an "edge city." Criss-crossed by expressways, dotted by modernistic glass office buildings and high rise hotels, the area had no coherent business district or residential center.

"Mr. MacNaughton, I presume you know that you will be driving tomorrow?"

"Mr. Snell, you know I don't drive on Saturdays."

Ben quickly dropped the repartee, "This is not a discussion. I can't get anybody else. You're elected. See you tomorrow morning at 7 A.M."

"OoooKay," I responded. I figured I'd blow-in whenever I woke up. Ben would chew me out and then forget about it. Ben's only saving grace appeared to be a boundless capacity for forgiveness. I hated working on Saturdays. It was my day to trash through used bookstores, walk along the lake front in the summer, and listen to Junior Wells play the blues in the evening.

Jessie and I dated a few times during her protracted battle with Ben over her raise. I found her physically appealing, but she was a down-to-earth-type who didn't appreciate the big picture or my intuitive black humor. Jessie had recently been divorced by her husband. And that had jangled her more than most. I think she went out with me more for the companionship and as a way of getting her mind off the split-up.

She didn't handle her divorce very well. Although her husband ran off with a younger woman, he managed to keep their suburban house in Grim Piss Hollow as well as custody of their two kids. He worked for Motorola as an engineering section boss. Jessie failed to get her own lawyer, so she got skinned bigtime.

She found herself at age 39 and a half on the high seas without a paddle. When we stopped at bars after work, she complained that she had never had a life. Wistful and bitter by turns, she regretted never trying anything. Her whole life had consisted of being the wife of an suburban Imperial Corporate Citizen and raising children. She didn't seem stable to me. The loss of her children seemed to be especially devastating.

One night, when we stopped at one of the scuzzy Mannheim Road night clubs, she asked me where I had acquired a small calculator that I used to tally up our food and bar bill. "This? I didn't 'acquire it,' I liberated it in the name of people." Her lifeless look told me she hadn't understood what I meant.

"It looks just like the ones we use at work."

"That's because it is one of the ones we use at work."

"You stole it?"

"I didn't steal it. I liberated it in the name of the people. I reached around the side of the driver's window when Ben wasn't looking and ripped it off."

"Do you think that's right?"

"RIGHT? Do you think what he pays us is right? He's rich. He's got a mansion in Barrington Hills. I live in an apartment. Did you get the raise he promised you, yet?"

"No."

"And you probably never will. When you finally get fed-up and quit, he'll hire somebody else for the same money."

"Oh, I'll get the raise."

"Ok," I answered trying to sound neutral because I didn't want to turn the conversation into a verbal competition. Jessie loved doing that. Her natural love of competitive games wore me out. During the weeks we went out together the idea slowly materialized that we were absolute, polar opposites in personality.

She smiled. "I like that, 'liberated in the name of the people.'"

At the office Jessie kept up a steady siege on Ben. Every day she brought up the raise. Everyday Ben brought up office procedures that Jessie was unfamiliar with. She learned the procedure then asked anew for the raise. And everyday Ben found another procedure she needed training in. It felt like a uphill turtle race to me. One turtle would pull ahead, then the other would stubbornly catch up. Then the other turtle got out in front.

One night Jessie quickly got a snootfull at a local watering hole. I hadn't been in the place before and found most of the customers were kids in their 20s. So the place was loud and kinetic. Jessie liked it. In fact she liked it so much she took off her blouse while dancing with one of the young studs to the belligerent, electronically-generated disco music. She gyrated in her high heels like an accomplished stripper. She had discarded her bra, too, before I could collect her off the dance floor. A chorus of cat-calls rained down on me charging me with being an "old fart." My prevailing feeling at the point was that Jessie was too young and too shallow for me.

I bundled Jessie back to her apartment, and she uncharacteristically invited me in. I unceremoniously dumped her on her futon and prepared to depart.

"Don't go. I haven't shown you my photos yet."

Evilly thinking the drunken woman was going to show me intimate photographs of herself, I stopped and sat on a cedar chest, the only other piece of furniture in her two room efficiency apartment. She stumbled over to a cardboard box and pulled out some photographs, some framed, some plain. She handed them to me.

Apparently she wanted the photographs to verbalize what she couldn't. They were what I think are called black and white "gelatin" photos, the style with the soft glowing light. They were artistically stunning views of my city neighborhood, Uptown. The elevated provided the backdrop for some of them. Some were studies of empty alleys. Others included portraits of some poverty stricken people.

"I know the neighborhood, but who are the people? Just random people you shot in the street?"

"No, silly. Those are my relatives." She sat next to me on the cedar chest and pointed out grandparents, cousins, and uncles. I felt very close to Jessie then, sitting on the cedar chest for the next hour or so, looking at her photos. The photos were amazing. Sensational. I decided I should return to the drawing boards on my understanding of human nature. I had definitely missed depths in Jessie's personality that I hadn't thought existed. I felt great when her black nylons inadvertently rubbed against my leg.

"Listen, kid. You need a broader life. You should go to art school. You got real talent. If you don't change and keep up the way you have been, your shadow personality is gonna keep crawling out of your unconscious like it did at the bar tonight."

"I can't go to school. I don't have any money."

The next day Jessie went after Ben again. I knew her struggle was hopeless. Ben prided himself on his stubbornness. One night after work she informed me that Ben had blocked her access to the books with a password. Apparently during her constant complaining she had said something that had made him wary. When I pressed her to rack her memory about what she had said, she offered, "Maybe what bugged him was when I said I was going to go into the computer and give myself a raise."

"That would spook the old boy."

"If I could figure out his password, I would give myself a raise. You were right, he's never going to give me one.

So then we went through a couple of weeks of password guessing. Jessie tried everything. She tried using Ben's wife's name. His dog's name. His wife's maiden name (which took quite a bit of sleuthing to retrieve.)

"Does Ben have any nicknames?"

"Ben Smell."

"No. You know. Does his wife have any cute nickname for him?"

"Are you kidding?"

"Ben? The ex-Marine. Mr. Respect Authority? What would you call him, Mr. Softie?" Then one night the password erupted from the place with no time and space. It burst out of my unconscious with so much psychic force it woke me from a sound sleep.

At that juncture, I decided that I had misjudged Jessie, and wanted to move-on from just friends. However, the next night, when I arrived at her apartment unannounced, I found a young man there with her.

"Oh, Peter. What do you want?" She asked, meeting me at the door with a towel wrapped around her. The young man lay under a blanket on the futon.

"Uh,... I just wanted to drop off some information about Chicago's Art Institute for you." I hastily shoved the student information packet I had obtained into her hands.

"Thanks." She looked at me with a quizzical look on her face. I quickly turned to depart, but abruptly turned around in the long sterile hallway.

"I know the password."

"What?"

"I'm pretty sure, anyway."

"What is it?" Jessie was so excited she stepped out of her apartment into the hallway despite her condition of undress.

I took a few days off from work to get a new perspective on life. I knew Pen would be pissed, but he would forgive me. When I returned, I found the building locked up and all the cabs parked. Untypically, none of the other drivers were hanging around either. I thought Ben must have finally had a heart attack. I phoned him at his home.

"No, I'm fine. Where the hell you been anyway? Take a goddamn vacation?"

"Give me a break, Ben. So what gives? How come the office is closed?"

"I think that goddamn girl ran off with all my money."

"What?"

"Yeah, Jessie, the bookkeeper. I think she found out the password and looted the place."

"You think?"

"HOW THE HELL DO I KNOW?" Ben roared at me. "I can't get into the goddamn computer. Somebody changed the password. I can't run the business because it's all locked up inside the damn computer. I was better off when I kept the books on the back of a paper bag."

It took a real good computer consultant about week a hack into Ben's computer. The first consultant took a week and got nowhere. So, the cops suggested a young guy they knew about. The young hacker found a word processing file attached to new password. The cops, of course, had driven straight over to Jessie's apartment as soon as Ben reported the problem. She had already cleared out, but they did ascertain that she had taken a jet ride to Las Vegas.

The word processing file read; "I decided to give myself that raise. I have liberated myself in the name of the people. - Jessie. P.S.' Frugal' is sure a stupid password, Ben."

Ben and the cops were very hush-hush about the amount of money that Jessie had managed to rip-off. They were careful the local newspapers didn't get ahold of it. Ben's business resumed as if nothing had happened. Some of the drivers said Jessie had made off with a lot of money, others said the amount wasn't worth the time in jail it might cause her. The cops snooped me a couple of times in the ensuing months, looking around my apartment, asking if I had heard anything from her.

However, that Christmas I got a nice card from Jessie postmarked from Honolulu. She informed me that she was enrolled in a university art program, that her lawyer was making good progress getting her custody of her children back, and that the weather was fine.

Bomber Blues

Although I had accumulated a hefty FBI file in my 25 years of activism in the anti-war, civil rights, and labor movements, I had never been hassled personally by the FBI, which was more than I could say for my old pal, Peter Marshall, who had just informed me over the telephone, that he feared they had issued a Federal warrant for him.

"Man, I need help."

I had requested my file during the Carter administration and hadn't seen it since to determine if America's secret police had added any additional goodies to it. If a nobody like me could get a file started, who knew what they did to people if they were a real leader or mobilizer. They had tagged me with a "sedition" investigation, something you could get the death penalty for, and all I had ever done to acquire it was make a few speeches against the Vietnam War during a student strike in the 1960s. Granted, I did advocate the violent overthrow of the Psychotic Atomik Empire, but I had never taken up arms against them. I had always advocated mass, legal peaceful demonstrations. I had been busted during civil disobedience demonstrations blocking factory gates, but it was the kind of non-violent performance Ghandi would have been proud of.

When I pulled my file out, from time to time, I marveled at the repressive simplicity of it. They had stamped-in the name of the Chicago field office in the box labeled "office of origin." Under that "MacNaughton, Peter" had been typed. They had typed in capital letters, "SABOTAGE - SEDITION" in the "character of case" box.

The problem was, I was afraid of the FBI. I didn't want to tangle with them. I had always reasoned that anyone who deliberately provoked the FBI had a death wish. Look at the Black Panther Party and the COINTELPRO Program the FBI launched against them. A lot of innocent people went to jail for long stretches just for thumbing their noses at the FBI. Even if you were clean, they'd manufacture some evidence or plant drugs on you to get you convicted and put away for decades.

And if I met with Peter, as he had requested, then I would be automatically entangled with the Feds and the bombing that Peter had babbled about over the telephone. I had already read about the bombing on the front page of *The Chicago Sun Times*. It sounded like the "bomb," a pipe packed full of black powder, had fizzled. Apparently it had burned some carpeting and scorched a door, but nobody found it until the next day. From what I read, the engineering sounded strictly amateur. High school kids routinely concocted better bombs than the one used against the FBI office. It occurred to me that anybody could buy black powder for ceremonial use in specially manufactured firearms that aped 19th century technology. You had to possess a valid Illinois gun ID to purchase bona fide, modern, high-explosive gun powder used in bullet reloading.

Peter and I had been good friends at the University of Illinois back in the late 1960s and early 1970s. We had both been founding members of an independent radical student group called the Revolutionary Student Union. And we professed such similar politics at that juncture that people called us "Pete and Repeat." However, Peter's interests always ran in the direction of theory and ideas while mine flowed in the direction of organizing and working with people.

Then, I dropped out to get a good drug soaking, and Peter got recruited by the Progressive League of Revolutionary Socialist Workers (Marxist-Leninist). Apparently they didn't think their name sounded tough enough, so they appended the M-L tail to it. Typically, the meaner the name that got adopted by U.S. left groups, the crazier the politics. And the PLRSW, a scion of the Communist Party U.S.A, was no exception. Born out of the Sine-Soviet disputes of the 1950s and 1960s, the PLRSW, which incidentally was 99 percent composed of students and intellectuals, saw world working class revolution right around the historical corner.

At that point, Peter and I parted company for many years. I managed to shake the drugs, and Peter joined a large PLRSW splinter group in the late 1970s. He taught high school for some time, then got fired for union activities. He wound up working in a big chain bookstore in the Loop. I ran into him from time to time, year to year, at left demonstrations and rallies. We'd exchange phone numbers which would go unused until we would meet again a year or two later at yet another rally. I hadn't talked to Peter for over a year on the day I received his frantic phone call.

"Are you gonna help me, man, or what?" Peter demanded.

Logic demanded that I answer, "No, I don't want to get involved in your ultra-left, sectarian bullshit."

Human decency dictated to me, "This really goes against my grain. What do you want me to do?"

"Meet me at my ex-wife's apartment." He gave me an address on the southwest side of the city.

That idea really chilled me. I had expected him to ask for money. I had an anonymous money drop in mind. Go to the bank, get some cash, put it into a paper bag, and drop it in a Loop trash container. Peter walks past from the other direction and fishes it out.

"What for? What can I do for you? You can't stay here. You know as well as I do that they're gonna be watching all the known leftists."

"I don't wanna talk over the telephone. Your line might not be cool. You gonna meet with me or not?"

"OK." For a moment I wondered if this was an FBI set-up. Then I felt bad for suspecting my friend.

"Ok, then. Tonight, at 5 P.M. And bring me as much cash as you can."

"Right." Peter hung up. I thought: the annuals of history are full of cases of friends betraying friends. I considered standing him up.

I checked a transit map before departing and decided I could walk to the address from the Western Avenue stop on the Midway L. I left early to have enough time to get to the bank, then hack my way through rush hour throngs and two transfers on the L platforms. I trudged up two steep flights of well worn stairs to the elevated structure at Wilson Avenue. It looked like just another bleak, cloudy November day in Chicago. Below on Broadway, I watched discarded newspapers swirl in a gutter.

So, I rumbled toward the core of the city, the Loop, riding over the intricate hundred-year old steel lattice work supporting the speeding electric train. I tried to calm my compulsively paranoid thought process. I had always viewed the L as a means of escape, a pathway to liberation, and a passage to mysterious unknown parts of the city.

I remained watchful during the tense trip, fearful that I was being followed by the FBI. Peter's ex-wife lived in a three story apartment building in the brick bungalow belt. The neighborhood appeared to be white working class and constructed during the 1950s and 1960s.

Inside, I was greeted by Peter. No one else appeared to be around. Peter had shaved off his long beard and cut his hair to a fashionably standard length. He had always looked like a hirsute lunatic. Now, he looked like an engineer or accountant.

"I don't want to hang around. Here's the money." I handed him what I had been able to spare from my meager savings.

"Ok, thanks. I understand, man. But I gotta talk this out with some-body. Take your fucking coat off and stay long enough to help me get this untangled in my mind, will ya?"

Reluctantly, I removed my black leather coat. He sat us down at the kitchen table in the tiny, stuffy apartment. The place was clean but bland in a dreadfully, uninspired "decorated" manner. Everything was neatly picked up. Instead of sheets on the windows as Peter had trimmed his apartment, his ex-wife had installed "window treatments" whose fabric maintained a country and western motif which ran through the entire apartment's decorating. In one nook, the shelves contained various porcelain animals. The ribbed velvet pillows on the couch in the front room matched the window treatments. I thought I detected the lingering chemical smell of air freshener. I found the place mind numbing with it's 100 percent homogenized banality. But the place did smell nice, I thought I detected the scent of cinnamon.

"Man, I wasn't ready for this. We weren't a terrorist organization. Nobody in the organization made any provisions for something like this." Peter referred to the sudden, ferocious Federal onslaught against them. The morning papers had been full of accounts of arrests in the middle of the night.

"They only missed me because I spent the night with my new girl-friend, Tina."

"Ok, to the best of your knowledge what's going on?" I asked him.

"Man, the FBI trashed my apartment last night. They got a man in a suit posted in the lobby of my apartment building."

"How do you know that?"

"Because Mrs. Diaz sent word with her great grandson. He's a real tall, gawky kid. He's around 14, I guess. Naturally, they call him 'Shorty.' The kid ferreted me out in my favorite neighborhood bookstore by Wicker Park. I'm sipping cappuccino and the FBI is looking for me. Anyway, I bought a copy of the newspaper and there it is all over the front page."

"I don't know why the FBI wants to bust me. I haven't broken any laws. I didn't set off the bomb. And I got no fucking idea who did. I wonder if anyone in the organization actually did it. My only crime has been editing our very erratically produced newspaper. We usually pay for a press run of 500 issues. We're lucky when we distribute 200."

"So you don't think anyone in the group did this?"

"Man, I don't know. Some of the men and women in the organization have talked big about taking on the Feds and confronting the government. They managed to expose several modest cases of municipal and state level corruption. They managed to mobilize several hundred people on a couple of occasions for street demonstrations when they closed a child care center in the neighborhood. That was our hottest fever point. As far as I know, those are our crimes. Shit, man, as far as I know, the FBI put the damn bomb there themselves. It's another Haymarket."

"Maybe you guys got infiltrated. An agent provocateur. Maybe the Feds planted somebody and had them set off a bomb. They like to do that with some of the lumpenproletarians they keep on parole leashes. They tell them to plant a bomb and rat out their friends and in exchange they don't go back to jail."

"I'm starting to wonder about it, too. Nobody I know advocated blowing up government offices or military targets. Maybe the FBI did set us up."

"Man, I got on the L at Damen and North Avenue and didn't know whether to shit or go blind. I had no place to go. I'm up there in the breeze listening to the trains rumble over that old steel superstructure. I took a train to the Loop because riding out to O'Hare Field seemed stupid. I knew the cops had to be waiting there, because it's the main airport. Man, when the train plunged down into the subway that shrieking noise almost freaked me out."

"Yeah, I don't like it either, when the trains go into the ground."

"I found a fast food restaurant where I could hang without drawing attention. I waited until Clare (he referred to his ex-wife who was still employed by the Chicago Public Schools) had enough time to arrive at her apartment after classes."

"So, Clare knows what's going on."

"Hell," he tossed a copy of the *Chicago Sun Times* across the table to me. It landed front page up. "Doesn't everybody in the city?"

"Alright. First, you need a lawyer. I can help you with that. We got a handful of folks who take cases like this. Five or six phone calls and I'll know if we can get a movement lawyer pro bono. What's Clare's position on all this?"

"She's a good kid. I can stay here as long as I want."

"She could lose her job if they catch you here. They'd get her for harboring a Federal fugitive."

"You wanna let me stay at your apartment?"

"Ok, I get the picture."

"Clare is cool about it. She likes the excitement."

I wanted to say she wouldn't like getting arrested and losing her job, but I definitely didn't want to house Peter in my apartment, so I shut up. He was probably right about Clare, anyway. I remembered her as the type who enjoyed high drama, lots of attention, and thrills for thrills' sake. "Does Clare have a boyfriend who comes around?"

"Not that I'm aware of."

"Better talk to her and get fully aware."

"Ok." Peter wrote a note. I was glad to see that he was still meticulously methodical. He would be needing that personality trait in the coming days.

"What about your new girlfriend?"

"Tina? She's cool. She's in the organization. In fact she's one of the rising young leaders in the group. I'm proud of her. She won't tell them anything, if she gets caught."

"How old is she?"

"22 or 23, I think."

Peter was at least 45 years old. My surprise must have shown on my face.

"It's not what you think. Mrs. Diaz kind of shuffled her in my direction to mentor and things just.., developed."

I laughed, "Yeah, things can 'develop' with a 22 year-old in a hurry.

Peter maintained a poker face and doodled with his notes. "Ok. Who's this Mrs. Diaz, anyway?"

"She was active in the Puerto Rican independence movement in the 1950s. She split out of the Communist Party with the PLRSW. She architected the split from the PLRSW. She's the founder of the organization."

"Active in the 1950s? How old is she?"

"I don't know for sure. At least 90."

"She's in her 90s?"

"She'd old, but she's with-it. She's a very dignified old woman."

I mentally went over that construction, 'a very dignified old woman.' "I'll see about a lawyer. I'll see about raising a few more bucks by privately passing the hat. I'll wire the money to you in Clare's name. Don't call me, because they might tap my phone. I wouldn't go looking for Mrs. Diaz, either. Stay away from your apartment, and stay away from Tina, too."

Peter took some more notes. "This is good, man. Thanks. I usually keep my head pretty well, but this has been taxing, you know what I mean?"

"Hell, yes."

I got Peter the lawyer and did manage to raise a few more bucks from the immediate circle of our leftist acquaintances. I worried a lot. The bombing story continued to remain on the front pages of the Chicago newspapers. The TV stations and radio picked up on it, too. Typically, the press blew the story all out of proportion. After all, we were talking about some carpet burns and a scorched door. However, the FBI and authorities had no intention of letting the story die down.

I knew the lawyer was trying to figure out who, if anyone, in the organization had actually put the "bomb" in the building. They hauled-in Mrs. Diaz, and that publicity hurt them big time. Nobody wanted to see the government beat-up an elderly woman. And as Peter had predicted, she acted very dignified during her TV street interviews on her way in and out of the FBI building. The publicity cut two ways against the government; one, who in their right mind would believe the frail old woman would start a bombing campaign, and two, if she was the reputed "head" of the nefarious organization out to overthrow the government, then how dangerous could this group really be?

The attempt to psychologically beat-up Mrs. Diaz proved to be a serious mistake. Popular opinion abruptly turned in her favor. Besides, the little press conferences the elderly ex-school teacher held in the street came off quite well. They made sense. The government did seem to favor the wealthy and the big corporations against the poor and labor as she claimed. And why did the city have to close the child care center? Why pick on the poor? Despite my fears, I joined a left united front demonstration against the FBI in front of their office building.

While listening to Mrs. Diaz's daily lessons on TV it gradually became clear to everyone that the old woman was very tough, intelligent and completely opposed to terrorist methods. She hugged her great-grandson "Shorty," while she delivered her message of peace and justice. She convinced everyone that she hadn't ordered the bombing.

The authorities had to shut her up, so they toned down the investigation, quit making a big show of hauling various people in for questioning and quit talking with the press. With their main source of disinformation dried up, the media quietly dropped the story from the front pages and the nightly news.

Meanwhile, Peter continued to inhabit his underground twilight world. He couldn't surface, because he feared they had a warrant on him and might try to pin the bombing on him. His lawyer urged him to turn himself in and see what the wanted from him. When Peter put the issue to me, I counseled him to ignore the lawyer and lay low. Maybe they just wanted to go fishing with him to see if they could get enough information to either stick him or another member of the organization with the bombing.

Finally, after two weeks and nothing resolved other than the fact that he couldn't stand living with Clare another day, Peter phoned me and asked me to set-up a meeting with him and Tina. He wanted a face-to-face to plan a getaway out of town with her.

The problem, of course, was getting in touch with her without alerting the FBI. We suspected they were watching her, too. Eventually, I called her at work, the Drake Hotel where she worked as a maid, and told her that I had finished repairing her shoes and they were ready for pickup. Peter had told me to say "at the little office" which meant his favorite bookstore in Wicker

Park. She picked up on the ruse right away and agreed to "pick up her shoes" at 5 P.M. that evening.

I felt an immediate emotional and physical attraction for Tina the moment I saw her. Tall, with long, dark hair, I felt enchanted when Peter introduced her to me. I was mildly surprised when I discovered she used makeup. I vacantly wondered if those kind of issues were still being vehemently discussed within the women's movement. She wore heels with her tight and short maid's skirt, too. Peter told me later that she was more "left" than "feminist." I thought Mrs. Diaz seemed both "left" and "feminist." Peter and Tina embraced, then we all sat at a table in the tiny area in the rear of the bookstore designated as a "coffee bar."

"Peter, I've been so worried about you."

"We gotta get out of town. Peter MacNaughton, here, will help us."

"I can't leave my family, Peter. All my friends live in Chicago."

"Look, they're gonna tear up the landscape until they find whoever it was that bombed them. They're gonna try to pin it on one of us. We gotta get outta here."

"Well, they can pin on it me because I did it."

"What?" I said, in a completely involuntary reflex. Peter sat there stunned.

"I did it. Now, I'm going to turn myself in."

"What?" echoed Peter. "Why? What the hell were you thinking about?"

"I was mad because they closed the child care center. Both my sisters had kids in there. My one sister had to go back on welfare because she didn't have a place to leave her baby any more. A lot of my friends kept their kids there, too. The kids are the ones who are really suffering. All because we exposed some city officials. So they retaliate against the young mothers and children?"

"Why didn't you leave a note with the bomb?" I asked out of idle, idiotic curiosity.

"It got burned up with the bomb, I think."

Peter and I vacantly stared at each other.

"I'm sorry. I know it was stupid. Now I do. It got me so angry when they closed the child care center."

"Why did you go after the FBI? Why didn't you put the bomb in City Hall?" I asked. I knew it didn't matter at that point. But my psyche was spinning out all kinds of questions.

"I don't know. I wasn't thinking, I guess. What's the difference? They're all in it together."

Neither one of us had a formulation to answer that because she was correct. They were all in it together. Unfortunately, it's not a good strategy to take them all on at once.

We sat around the tiny, round table staring at our respective cups of coffee. Peter ultimately spoke up, "Man, we gotta get out of town. Help us. What should we do?"

"I know where you guys can get a car. The smart thing would be to drive to New York, send the car back with someone else, then you go underground in New York. Lots of cover in New York..."

"No," Tina interrupted me.

"There's already been too much bullshit. I'm turning myself in."

"At least talk to the lawyers first," I urged.

Tina didn't listen to anyone that day. We pleaded with her well into the evening to talk to the lawyers or just run. As unceremoniously as she had placed the bomb in the FBI building, she decided to turn herself in. She was determined to turn a crime of passion into her own martyrdom. Nothing could dissuade her. When she left the bookstore, she was sobbing. Peter and I left individually, both meditating on the excesses of idealism.

The next morning I received a phone call from Peter at 6 A.M. He sounded frantic. "Have you read the paper yet?"

"Fuck, no. You just woke me up."

"They indicted Shorty. They matched his fingerprints to the bomb fragments."

"Fragments? There weren't any fucking fragments, because there wasn't any fucking explosion. Fragments? Who's zooming who?"

"Man, just get a copy of the paper and read it."

I did. I discovered they were pinning the whole rap on a 14 year old Puerto Rican kid named Fernando "Shorty" Lopez, great-grandson of Mrs. Diaz. Tina did turn herself in, but the authorities ignored her. Apparently, she had convinced Shorty to manufacture the bomb, then she delivered it. It had been her and Shorty's little secret. But she had worn gloves that blustery November day, so only Shorty's fingerprints showed up. The authorities apparently reached the decision that Tina was trying to take the rap for Shorty. They didn't believe her confession. And, lacking any other evidence to tie her to the crime, they refused to prosecute her. They didn't want to risk a big "save Tina" movement growing up around the case. They had caught Shorty dirty, and they could prove it. Case closed.

Shorty got rapidly railroaded into a "juvenile detention center." Then, when he turned 18, they sent him down to the Marion Federal Penitentiary where he was chained to his bed for 23 hours a day with the rest of the boys. Tina was expelled from the organization, but she broke up with Peter before that. The last I heard of her she had joined a group of nuns who specialized in bringing medicine to children in Central America.

Peter and I drifted further apart chiefly because he seemed to feel that I hadn't done enough for a comrade in distress. It turned out the FBI never had a warrant on him. They only wanted to drag him in for questioning. I heard via our shared matrix of left-wing friends that he had drifted out of the organization and hadn't participated in any left activities since then.

Mrs. Diaz kept on keeping on.

Me, I was just glad I hadn't gotten tangled up with the Feds and wound up with the bomber blues.

Forklift Fighters

I worried that my first tormented day on the job in the dog food factory was also going to be my last. The forklift they had assigned to me didn't have any brakes. They had put me to work hauling skids loaded with finished cans to waiting semi trucks. I desperately wanted to keep the job because my wife had been unloading truck loads of grief on me regarding my chronic unemployment and even more chronic dope smoking. She was working as a substitute grammar school teacher, trying to get a full-time job in one of the nearby suburban Chicago school districts. We had two kids in day care and a lot of unpaid bills. And back in 1973, when this went down, everyone under 30 seemed to be unemployed, including dope-soaked former college revolutionaries like myself.

Anyway, I politely pointed out my lack of stopping ability to my foreman, a harried, middle-aged, red-faced man named Rex. I already had the word on Rex. He had written up so many people for minor rule infractions that his street name had become "Shakespeare." The first time I mentioned my lack of brakes, he said, "Then don't run it so fast. Turn off the key. It'll coast to a stop." He resumed making notations on his clipboard. I found this advice to be perfectly idiotic, but continued working up to lunchtime. Every time I accelerated, I got anxious because I had to continually be prepared to find safe gliding-to-a-stop pathways. And that wasn't easy in the hot, crowded factory.

Once, I nearly broadsided another forklift at right angles as the Mexican driver went shooting down another aisle. I found it impossible to slow down and still make the skid-loading quota assigned to me. On the dock, I nearly ran over a semi driver, a young long-haired guy with a Confederate battle flag emblazoned on his t-shirt. His string of creative obscenities followed me into the back of his truck.

At lunchtime I asked a fellow forklift driver, a black guy whose sole name seemed to be "Jones," what I should do about my lack of brakes. We sat outside with our backs against the building in a tiny pool of shade cast by an overhead awning. The bricks felt hot against the back of my damp t-shirt. Occasionally, we caught a rancid whiff of the dog food curling around the side of the factory.

"I wondered why you so tense and nervous. Man, you're sweatin'. And we got the cool and breezy jobs rolling down the aisles." He referred to the unfortunate employees who had been consigned to an even lower rung in hell - the steamy manufacturing departments where they shoved the putrid dog food into the cans and sealed them.

"I'm afraid I'm gonna have a wreck."

"You can go to the union. Dan the committeeman for us fork drivers. But he's no damn good. Everybody know that. He won't stand up to the company. Too scared for his own job. He scared of Rex, too. Man, this here union ain't worth a damn."

"I can't drive this forklift like this. I'm gonna kill somebody.

"Tells Rex."

"I already did. He told me to keep driving it."

Jones laughed. "Then I guess you gonna keep on drivin' it."

After lunch I walked over to the blockhouse shipping office. Rex had been chatting amiably with his young, red-haired secretary. He looked up from the conversation to greet me with a dour face. "Yeah?" The window air conditioner rattled like a machine in its death throes, but it kept the office quite frosty. But it was stuffy. I could plainly smell the redhead's perfume and Rex's cheap, pungent aftershave.

"That forklift doesn't have any brakes at all. I'm afraid I'm going to hurt somebody or myself." I was concerned that after hours of unrestrained sweating, I probably reeked in their stagnant icy world.

"Look, kid, you can either get back on your pony and start hauling cans or I can pull your timecard and we can get somebody in here who can. What's it gonna be?" Rex rolled his chair over to the old fashioned timeclock surrounded by racks of cards. "What's your name again?"

"MacNaughton," I said with total resignation. "Peter MacNaughton."

Rex found my card and put his hand on it, then turned to me for direction. He plainly indicated that it was all up to me. I could drive the forklift as it was, or he could pull my card and send me home to my no-longer-understanding wife.

"OK." I shuffled out of the air conditioned office feeling embarrassed and defeated. Rex and the redhead continued their conversation.

On my first forklift trip back into the warehouse I had to swerve wildly to avoid a millwright pulling a work cart in the aisle. I careened into one of the metal pillars holding up the roof. I nearly bucked off the forklift, banging my forehead on the front bars of my roll cage. The old millwright came to my aid immediately. My tongue detected the faint salty taste of blood around my upper front teeth.

"You OK?"

I looked down at the grimy, grey-haired man. I felt dazed.

"Looks like you got yourself a nice bruise." He pointed to my forehead and cheek. Obviously, an expert in industrial injuries, he opined, "It's gonna be shaped just like that bar you hit. It's already yellow and swelling. It's gonna be black and blue tomorrow. You're gonna look like a raccoon on that side of your face.

"Thanks."

"You're welcome. Now, how come you didn't stop? You almost hit me. If you hit me, mister, you better kill me, because if I'm still alive, I'm gonna come up there and pull your sorry ass off that seat and kick the shit outta you." He smiled. It was a joke. I was twice as big as him and at least 30 years younger.

"I couldn't stop. No brakes."

"No brakes? Then why the hell are you driving the truck? Take the truck down to the maintenance shop and tell Rex to check you out another machine.

"Rex told me to drive it this way.

"That asshole."

I could feel my flesh swelling on my face. I could also feel my fear turning into anger. "Where's the union steward? I'm not putting up with this shit."

"You're new here ain't ya?"

"Yeah, I'm new here. I started today."

"Better go slow. Just take it easy. The union ain't gonna help you."

"Just tell me where he's at."

"The union here just collects dues. They don't do nothin' for anybody. Just cool out and go about your business." The old millwright headed off to his cart.

"Would you please just tell me where the fuck the guy is. Please."

The millwright pointed down the aisle. "Down there, buddy, in the electrical shop. Guy named Dan. He ain't gonna do you no good, though. Rex finds out you been talking to the union, he'll fire you just for that."

"Fuck Rex."

"Whatever you say." The millwright headed off in his own direction. He wasn't smiling any more.

When I first caught sight of Dan, he looked like just one more hillbilly caught up in the industrial maw of Chicago. A skinny guy in his 60s, he sported an oily duckbill hairdo like Elvis, sideburns, and a series of tattoos that extended from his wrists to his armpits, which were all on display because he wore a leather vest over a sleeveless black t-shirt. He wore black jeans like me, held up by a big black leather belt complimented by an enormous, ornate belt buckle that proclaimed the word "Electrician". When I walked up on him, he was energetically banging the hell out of a fuse box with a big, cross peen hammer.

I introduced myself and he took the cigarette out of his mouth long enough to shake hands and announce his name as Dan Chadwick.

"What can I do for you, son?"

"I got a union problem."

He sighed and put down the hammer. "Union problem, huh?" He looked me over, sizing me up. "How long you been workin' here?"

"I started today."

"And you already done got yourself a bona fide union problem, huh?"

"That's it."

"Yeah? What's the problem?"

"I'm a forklift driver. I got no brakes on my forklift."

"Uh huh. Mention that to Rex did you?"

"Yeah."

"And he told you to drive it like it was."

"Yeah."

"And this is your first day on the job."

"Yeah." Dan shook his head the way a person does when they've been spooked by something. "So, you gonna do something?" I asked.

In response Dan sat down on a shop stool. He wiped the sweat off his face with a red handkerchief he kept in his back pocket. It was the kind all the dimestores used to carry. He pointed at a nearby work bench. "Pull up a chair and let's talk this over."

I sat on the workbench. Dan remained lost in thought. He continued to smoke, employing long, lazy, elaborate hand motions. He was quiet for so long I became concerned that he was on drugs. The silence made me uncomfortable. Finally, he spoke.

"Well, you have to consider the fact that you're on probation. Rex can fire you for any reason during your first 90 days."

"Man, that's bullshit."

"Yeah, I can't argue that. But that's the way the contract reads."

"So, if I bitch about the forklift, he'll fire me."

"Could happen."

"And the union can't do anything about that, I suppose."

"No. They fire you, and it's up to the union to get your job back. After they fire you, we go in and argue your case."

"So, what are you gonna do. Nothing?"

"Might be smartest thing to do for the next 90 days."

"Right. And I get killed on the forklift in the meantime, or wind up killing somebody else."

"Yeah, I know what you mean."

"Yeah. Right. You're familiar with the problems of forklift drivers."

"Actually, I am. I used to drive forklift. I worked my way up through the ranks to skilled trades."

That surprised me. But it made sense. Anyone who labored in the factories for a lifetime tried to work their way up the food chain.

"And, I had a very similar problem as yours."

"What was that?"

"No brakes on a forklift on my first day at work back in Ohio, in the 50s."

"Really." At first I thought he might be bullshitting me, but I had a good feeling for the guy. My intuition was telling me the guy spoke the truth. Which accounted for my problem spooking him initially.

"Yeah. It seems its taken 20 years for this story to go full circle. First day on the job in the big mill. I had this foreman, Fred. Very rough, very tough. But a forgiving guy. He told me to drive the forklift or go home. He needed the machine in service. They had an order to get out, and his boss, a creepy, soulless, engineer-type, named Frank, had told him to move the goods or else."

"We had this union steward who had been recently been appointed, his name was Sid, but everybody called him Sneaky. Or Sneaky Sid. The real steward, John, had been made to resign his post by the union, on account of the fact he was a communist. They had just passed Taft-Hartley into law. And nobody who was a communist could hold elected office."

"How the fuck can they do that? That's unconstitutional."

"Those were the real Cold War days. It was the McCarthy period. John had been elected steward by the men in every election since the CIO formed the union in the 1930s. But the government said he had to resign or go to jail."

"So, what happened with your forklift?"

"I went to Sid, and he said he couldn't do anything. I was on probation. He told me to get back to work before I got fired. So, I tried working like that, with no brakes. First thing you, know I put my forks through the side of a boxcar. Couldn't stop, and wham! Right into the train. Almost hit two laborers. They were mad as hell.

"I got off the forklift and told Fred I couldn't drive the thing like that anymore. He said that was OK with him. And he fired me right on the spot. He ordered another driver to come over and get on my machine. The driver refused saying, 'That thing ain't got any brakes.' Fred fired him, too. That guy quietly told me to stand my ground next to the fork-lift. At the time, I didn't know that guy was John, the old steward. He was a sawed-off runt of a guy, about five foot tall. I didn't realize all those craters on his face were the result of numerous impacts received on many different picket lines.

Fred went and got another guy. That guy refused, too. Fred fired him.

"Next thing you know, there's nine of us standing outside the mill gate, all fired for not driving an unsafe machine. Pretty soon here comes Sid. He tells the other eight guys they can go back to work, but I'm fired because I'm on probation. Fred is standing behind him in the parking lot.

"John steps up and says, 'None of them are going back until we all go back,' and he pointed at me. Fred scratches his head, walks back into the mill, then comes back with Frank, the superintendent. Frank has a very studied 'I'm not going to take any nonsense' look on his face. He probably used the same face to play poker. He's a college-educated prick. No offense intended." Dan nodded in my direction.

"How the hell did you know I went to college?"

"I can tell you're a college-educated man by the way you talk."

I didn't think my demeanor or vocabulary was radically different from the other guys on the shop floor, but apparently the "lifers" could nose me out of the crowd. I began to realize that Dan had some natural abilities despite his lack of education.

"So, what happened then?"

"Frank came back with the same offer - with a five-minute time limit. He offered to bring back the other eight guys, but not me. About that time some of them big, hairy, white guys and brawny black men who manned the blast furnaces started to walk out into the parking lot to see what was going on. We stood there in a line, arms crossed. You could feel the pressure building on Frank. He yelled at Fred to get the other guys back to their workstations. Fred turned around and yelled at them. But they just stood there and stared at him. More guys kept walking up as the word spread throughout the mill. I think it dawned on Frank that pretty soon, everybody in the whole steel mill was gonna be standing there in the parking lot.

"Then Frank goes, 'Do you men know,' and Frank pointed to John, 'that this man is a known communist? Your own union removed this man from a paid staff job because of his affiliations with the communist movement.'

"The men stood by. Nobody said a word. I knew what everybody was thinking. Maybe John was a communist, but that was his business. But he was our shop floor leader, and he knew all the moves. Nobody verbalized it, but they were all ready to follow him into hell, because he'd know how to successfully file a grievance and twist the devil's tail.

"'Well, what's it going to be? Are you going to follow a goddamn communist?' And let me tell you, Pete, in them days, in the 1950s, you didn't want to have nothin' to do with no communists."

"So, what happened?"

"About that time, Sid comes running out into the parking lot. We can see, right off, that he's hysterical. He yells to us that he's been on the telephone with the international union, and they told him to inform us that they didn't intend to back us up - we were on our own and would have to take the consequences."

"Yeah? How'd they take that?"

"We all just stood there. It had been a cold, cloudy November day up to that point. Then it started raining. A lot of them boys didn't have a jacket on. Some of the guys off the coke ovens weren't even wearing shirts. Nobody said nothin'. They just kept staring Frank down.

"'Well, what's it going to be? Are you all following this man?'

"The unanimous inarticulate testimony indicated, that, yeah, that's exactly what we were doin'. Finally, Frank waved his arms and hollered to Fred, 'Get these men back to work, will you?' And he stalked back to the front office. Fred yelled at us, 'What are you guys waiting for? Get back to work. Push that damn forklift over to the maintenance shop for some new brakes. "What about him?" John pointed to me.

"Yeah, yeah. Check out another forklift, troublemaker."

"And that's what Fred called me, 'troublemaker,' from then on until the day I quit."

"I'm not looking to start a wildcat strike over this. But I am afraid of driving this way."

"You don't have to worry about a wildcat because management has got the upper hand here. They've had it for years. No, we have to worry about getting fired on the spot. They've been doing that lately to intimidate the union even more."

"We?"

"Yeah, we, goddamn it," Dan raised his voice. "They fired a steward a week ago because they said he was too strident in arguing a grievance."

"They can't do that. It's against the fucking law."

"You know that. I know that. The company knows that. Meanwhile, a man is out of work until we get him his job back."

"They're gonna have to give him back pay."

"Maybe he'll get back pay. Maybe he won't. Some suit called an arbitrator decides that by flipping a coin. That steward has got two kids by his current wife and one kid by a former wife. He's got a lot of freight to pay. And the company knows it. He'll probably get his job back, but would you be 'strident' the next time you argued a grievance?"

"Ok, maybe I should just forget it. Maybe I'll get a different forklift to drive tomorrow."

"They told you I wasn't any good didn't they? That I was a company man and won't fight for people?"

Dan's utter honesty tripped me up. I had anticipated someone more self-serving. Someone duller. Instead of an illiterate opportunist I had encountered an intuitive idealist.

"Well...

"I know what they're sayin' about me. There's a sit-down job I've applied for in the purchasing department. A nice clerk job. I stir up too much shit, and I ain't gonna get it. And I'm 55 years old, Pete. I need that job. I'm gettin' too damn old to be crawling around on greasy punch presses looking for electrical problems."

"Let's just forget it," I said, genuinely convinced that dropping it was the smartest thing for all concerned.

"I'd like to drop it. I really would. It would be the intelligent thing to do. But now I can't."

"Why not?"

"Because I went and told you my story." Dan took a long drag on his cigarette. "Now, I gotta step up to the plate."

"I don't get it."

"It's my turn to do the goddamn fighting whether I like it or not." He motioned me to follow him. We stomped up to the front of the factory and Rex's blockhouse office.

"Look, I don't want to get fired over this."

"Me, neither. But if we don't get that forklift repaired, pretty soon all you guys are gonna be ridin' around with no brakes. That's not good for any of us, on wheels or on foot."

Rex gave me a ugly look when Dan motioned to him through the glass that he wanted to talk to him, then picked up the telephone. When we entered the office, Rex indicated that we should sit down. His secretary left. We sat in the battered swivel office chairs while Rex finished a long conversation about some shipping minutia. Stuffing was coming out of my chair. It was clear to me that he had initiated the phone conversation to make us wait. Dan lit another cigarette.

They were strong cigarettes. The pungent odor of tobacco overwhelmed the faint scent of redhead and Rex's raw aftershave. Apparently, smoking was Dan's deliberate response to Rex's psychological warfare.

Finally Rex hung up and demanded, "Yeah, what's up?"

"His forklift doesn't have any brakes. He can't run it like that."

"Went and complained to the union, did we?" Rex eyeballed me with contempt.

"He didn't complain to nobody. He almost ran me over. I asked him why he didn't stop, and he told me he didn't have any brakes. He also told me that he informed you of that situation this morning."

"So, he's driven all day like that. Now, all of a sudden, its unsafe?"

Dan smiled at Rex. "I don't want to file a safety grievance on this. If I file a grievance, then you and me and your boss are gonna sit around in a lot of meetings discussing it for the next six weeks. Maybe we'll have to get all the forklifts inspected. Maybe the big shots in the front office will get interested in the subject. Before you know it, we'll have a couple hundred man hours in it."

Rex turned his malevolent stare in my direction. "Had to cause a problem, huh, troublemaker?"

"I told you, I'm the one with the problem, Rex. Not the kid."

"Yeah, what's with you Dan? I thought you were a team player. Now, you're looking for problems?"

"It is my problem. He nearly ran me over."

"Let me work it out with the kid." Rex pointed to me.

"I'm representing him. Work it out with me."

"Oh, so now you're representing people."

"That's my job, Rex. I'm the union steward."

"OK, mister union steward, I gotta have that machine in service today. I got dog-food cans that gotta get loaded on trucks. He's been driving the thing all day. Why can't he finish the shift with it? Check it in for maintenance at quitting time."

I was about to say "OK" to that, but Dan sensed my eagerness and monopolized the verbal space.

"If it ain't safe, then it ain't safe. Let's get the damn thing out of service before somebody gets hurt."

"Let's finish the day with it, ship some cans, and make some money. That's the deal, take it or leave it. I don't need these kinds of problems." Rex bent his head around and stared at me.

I wanted Dan to take the deal. But I kept my mouth shut.

"You're gonna have real problems if somebody gets hurt. Especially after two people been in here telling you there was an existing safety problem. If somebody gets hurt bad, do you think the company is gonna back you up when they learn you already knew about the problem? I'd say that would be genuine trouble. The company is not gonna take liability, if they can hang it on you, Rex. You know that."

Rex glared at us.

"Look at the kid's face. He just about knocked out his teeth."

Rex studied my face for a moment. "Don't smoke in my office. Put out that cigarette. " Dan deliberately took one last puff, then crushed the cigarette out on his boot.

"OK, OK. You win. Is the fucking thing safe enough to drive to the maintenance shop?" Rex addressed me.

Dan responded, "That's all the further we're driving it today."

"Alright. Get to it. What are you waiting for?" Rex swiveled away from us and picked up the telephone again. "And you damn well better make your quota today, troublemaker." Rex said pointing to me. Dan motioned me out of the office.

Outside, back in the warmth and din of the factory, Dan winked at me. "You know how to get to the maintenance shop?"

I smiled. I thought about all those bare chested men standing in a November rain. I knew Dan was thinking about them, too.

The Doll Factory

When I first approached Marcy and Anne in the tavern on Chicago's Lincoln Avenue, I knew I had the advantage because I already knew their names, while I was a total stranger to them. I looked them over before introducing myself, to see if I wanted to try to pick one of them up, and quickly decided that either one of the them would be ok. They were both in their 30s, making them fifteen years younger that me. They were both brunettes, and they were both pretty. It was a sultry Saturday afternoon, and they were both wearing shorts while they sipped mixed drinks at the bar. I noticed a really ugly doll sitting on the bar between them.

"Marcy and Anne, I presume." When they turned to look at me, I intuited in a flash that the tall one had no interest in a pot-bellied, grey-haired middle-aged man like myself.

"Who the hell are you?" said the tall one. She blew her cigarette smoke right at my face.

"Oh, I'm Pete MacNaughton. The manager of the quick oil change place across the street asked me to tell you that it's going to take another hour and a half to get your transmission straightened out. I'm getting an oil change, so I'm waiting over here, too."

"Thank you, goodbye," said the tall one.

"Marcy, don't act like an asshole," said the short one, who by logical deduction had to be Anne. Anne smiled at me, "Would you like to join us for a drink?" She was smoking, too.

"Uh..." I nodded in Marcy's direction.

"Where are my manners? Please, by all means, join us for a drink," said Marcy.

Anne winked at me and nodded for me to sit down next to her at the bar. I thought what the hell, what did I have to loose? They looked like working class women to me judging by their casual hairstyles and clothes. The bar, a typical Chicago neighborhood watering hole, was located far enough north on Lincoln, near the big bend in the street, to be out of range of the pretentious middle class assholes who lived in Lincoln Park. I had been downwardly mobile since my university days, long enough to successfully identify people who considered themselves too good to associate with members of the urban industrial proletariat.

I ordered a drink and offered to buy them a round. Marcy declined and Anne accepted. Big surprise there.

"So, what do you ladies do for a living?"

"We're unemployed," said Anne.

Marcy turned her attention from a tennis match she had been watching on a TV over the bar and said, "Yeah, thanks to you." At first I thought her comment had been a genuine recrimination, but they both laughed. I liked the way Anne's big metal earrings shimmered when she laughed.

"I'm missing something here," I ventured.

"We're roommates, but I don't own a car," said Marcy. I thought I still detected a peevish undertone. "We both got jobs in a factory in Elk Grove, out by O'Hare Airport. Annie drove everyday. She got her ass fired, so, I had to quit, too." They laughed again, harder this time, then they both broke into a giggling fit.

"Well, now I know I'm missing something."

They had obviously had a few already. When the giggling ended, Anne said, "It was a doll factory. We thought it would be fun to work there. But they ran the place like a concentration camp."

"We could only use the potty at our appointed break times or during lunch," said Marcy.

"You were only given one smoking break in the morning, and one in the afternoon," said Anne. Judging by the way the two chain-smoked, I could tell that must have been a major drawback for them.

"We were forbidden to leave the building at lunch time," said Marcy.

"And they wanted us to work like slaves," said Anne.

"You just couldn't keep up," Marcy sneered. They both resumed the giggle fit.

"She wrote me up for not keeping up with production quotas," Anne said in explanation to me.

"Who did?"

"Marilda Meinhoff," they both sang out in unison. That provoked so much laughter, they managed to get the bartender's attention. He was sitting all the way at the other end of the bar, near the cash register and the door, quietly reading the newspaper. I could tell he was gauging the general level of drunkenness.

I liked the way Anne slapped me on the arm while she laughed. I had her pegged as the sweet, good natured one. Marcy had a lot harder edge on her. My knee accidentally touched Anne's a couple of times as she swiveled back and forth on her bar stool. I noted with satisfaction that she didn't automatically switch positions to avoid any future contact. I thought things were going pretty well.

"Ok, I'll bite. Who's Marilda Meinhoff?" I knew mentioning the name would send them into more paroxysms of laughter. They didn't disappoint me. The bartender was up on his feet now, wiping down his end of the bar. Occasionally, he cast a furtive glance at the two young women.

When she finally recovered, Anne gasped, "Our supervisor." She had laughed so violently, she had given herself a coughing fit.

"Is that one of the dolls you manufactured?" I pointed to the foot long female doll sitting on the bar.

Marcy picked the monstrosity up, leaned across Arne, and shoved the thing in my face while growling, "Hi, little boy. Wanna piece of candy?" It was a female doll that looked like a cross between a witch and a monkey. It was positively the ugliest doll I had ever seen. Anne slipped off her barstool as Marcy put her weight into her as she lifted off her chair to stretch her arm in my direction. Anne managed to land on her feet, but she wound up leaning all over me. I liked her aroma.

"I'm sorry," said Anne as she patted my arm. "Calm down Marcy." She climbed back on her barstool. The bartender stared at us. We could all read his mind. "No more alcohol for this bunch."

"Marilda used to put smiley face stickers on my time cards because I met all the production quotas," said Marcy.

"She used to put smiley face frowns on mine," said Arne.

"What's that cord on her backside?" I pointed to the doll. It looked like a fuse for an explosive.

I could tell they genuinely had trouble restraining their laughter this time. But the bartender keep eyeballing us, so they kind of sputtered out the laughter under their breath.

"You pull the cord and the doll says something," Anne informed me.

"What's it say? Mama?"

They laughed so hard they both fell off their barstools. The bartender marched down to our end of the bar and announced, "That's it. You're outta here." He pointed to the door. I knew he meant it, so I was the first one out into the sunshine. They were still laughing as they put their heads on parking meters and coughed and laughed.

"You're pathetic," Marcy said to Anne.

"Me?" The laughter continued.

"You got us thrown out of the bar.

"Me?"

"You got fired so you lost both our jobs."

"You didn't have to quit. You weren't in trouble until you messed with the doll."

"Oh, yeah. I'm gonna let some bull supervisor like Marilda Meinhoff fire my best friend."

"You messed with the doll? What did you do?" That was the big one, I discovered. When they finished that last laughing jag, they were both sitting on the curb trying to catch their breath.

"Here," Marcy offered. She handed me the gruesome doll. "Pull the string."

When I pulled the string I heard a tape cassette rumble to life deep inside the doll. The doll sang out, "Marilda Meinhoff is a fat headed authoritarian asshole who needs her big fat ass kicked."

"How the hell did you manage that?" I asked. I noted a young guy with long hair hop off a CTA bus a block south of us. He started jogging in our direction.

Anne smiled at me and said, "Marcy sneaked into the little room where they dub the cassette tapes after I got fired. They installed that message in the dolls for a week before they caught on.

The young guy with long hair bopped up to us about then. He turned out to be Anne's boyfriend. Across the street the manager of the oil change joint waved to us. Their car was ready.

"We're going out to dinner, Marcy. Can I drop you somewhere?" Anne asked. She and her boyfriend prepared to cross Lincoln Avenue.

Marcy tossed the doll to Anne, then turned to me and asked, "Are you doing anything? Do you want to go see a movie with me?"

Insubordination Blues

Butch yelled at me, "You lazy sonofabitch. Your union got your job back for you two years ago. And we're gonna get it back again for you this time. Now you got the balls to tell me you ain't got time to help your union. It's payback time, MacNaughton. Get your goddamned coat on and let's go. We need help."

"What do you need me for? Forget it, man. I'm not going."

I was sorry that Butch, my local union president, and sub-district organizer, thought I was a lazy sonofabitch. But I guessed from his uneducated, proletarian perspective, I must have looked that way. I regarded myself as a bohemian. A de-classed intellectual caught in a vortex of downward social mobility.

Butch yelled, "Look at all these damn whiskey bottles, Pete. What the hell is becoming of you? Are you turning into a damn alcoholic? It's ten o'clock in the morning, and you're just rolling out of bed."

"I'm unemployed. I can do that. It's legal."

The young Mexican woman furtively eyeballed me. Butch McGuire had brought her along. She was an intern organizer sent by the AFL-CIO. I guessed she had just recently graduated from college. I realized I hadn't made a very good impression with a sink full of dishes, my kitchen table cluttered with liquor bottles, playing cards, poker chips, empty potato chip bags, and porno magazines.

"Hey, my alarm clock broke. Look, I just don't have the time for it, ok? Besides, we don't have a chance of organizing that place. The guy who owns Push Electronics, Alexander Glashauser, he owns Parliament Electronics, too. He'll fire everybody who's pro-union. Three weeks from now we'll be sitting in the bar with a roomful of pissed off people who lost their jobs."

"We ain't even started yet, and you already got the battle fought and lost? You got time to help us. You're not working. I know. I talked to your mother. You're just laying around your trailer here, drinking every day.

He was right about that. But I was too hung over that November morning to be embarrassed about the flophouse appearance of my seedy house trailer. In fact, I was too hung over to worry about my own state of dishevelment, a two day old beard, and the greasy hair sticking out of the sides of my head. After Butch started pounding down my door, I only had enough time to pull on a pair of jeans. I was barefoot and wore a United Metalworkers t-shirt. The Chicago suburbs are not the best place to spend a winter in an old, poorly insulated trailer with a rickety propane gas heating system. It had been too cold to take a shower for nearly a week. "Are you coming or what?"

"You shouldn't treat him like that," said the girl. I liked her right away. She was tall and slim, with dark hair and green eyes. She was wearing jeans, combat boots, a heavy loose-fitting sweater, and a surplus U.S. Army fatigue coat. Butch had introduced her as Celina Rodriguez.

Frustrated she had single-handedly stopped his rodeo, Butch yelled, "How should I treat him?"

"With respect."

Butch dramatically flopped both arms down to his sides. He looked like a short, squat red faced Irishman with his grey hair severely trimmed in a crewcut. He had dressed for business that morning wearing combat boots, dress slacks and shirt, and an expensive, full-length, black leather coat.

"Yelling at people is not a good way to recruit them to join an organizing drive."

"See, she knows how to organize. If you stop for coffee first, I'll go." I was sorry I volunteered, but my idealistic streak spontaneously won out despite the fact that I didn't feel like we had a chance. Worse, a little intuitive flash just barely manifested itself; I remembered student strikes in which I had participated in the 1960s that had absolutely no chance of success, yet we had won.

"Well, lets go then, goddamn it. You know it smells like cat piss outside your front door."

That was the second time that I had been terminated at the dog food factory for insubordination. When they fired me, I thought, what the hell, the union will get my job back again, I'm on vacation. I figured it would take them about a year to get the job back. If I got my back pay, fine. If I didn't, I didn't care. I'd been divorced for years. My kids were grown. I'd given up on trying to write the Great American Novel, trying to open various businesses, and trying to find the love of my life. So, as they say, when you finally give up, you can just have fun.

Butch knew I wasn't lazy, because he'd seen me work over a lathe for decades. I had repaired just about every machine in the dog food factory. What he couldn't verbalize, was his taking exception to my attitude. And that attitude embodied total alienation from life in the Psychotic Atomik Empire. I got fired because I called my boss a "jackass." I called him a jackass because he had unnecessarily ordered me to machine a new part to replace a perfectly good part. A big dog food mixing machine had crashed, and they wanted it up and running. The kicker was, after I replaced the part, the machine still wasn't going to run because they hadn't identified the real problem. That meant I would continue to have a supervisor breathing down my neck for an abnormally long time. And that pissed me off.

I probably would have gotten away with calling him a jackass if we'd been alone, but we weren't. The big corporate boss had been standing right next to him. The big shot looked at my jackass boss, and he fired me on the spot for insubordination.

But I hadn't been insubordinate. I had simply called a spade a spade and a jackass a jackass.

So, I found myself out-of-work, but fully employed in the job of having fun. Ever wonder what those characters are like who live in house trailers on the back end of a lot of a modest working class house? Well, they're just like me, because whenever my life turned into shit, I moved back into the rusting relic that sat on the back of my mother's house lot between her home and the Chicago and Northwestern railroad embankment.

Whenever I ratcheted down to my lumpenproletarian existence, I'd make ends meet by delivering phone books, cleaning big rugs, shoveling snow or mowing lawns, and hauling klunky old appliances out of houses for people then reselling them to a legit repairman, Bad Bob, who operated a small re-sale showroom. The un-repairable ones? I'd throw them out of the back of my rusting van along unincorporated Cook County roads in desolate, secluded industrial areas near gravel pits or big factories or rail yards.

Because I didn't' have to punch the clock everyday, I had plenty of time to visit all my old low life friends I had left back in Chicago's Uptown, in the bars along the skid-row area on Wilson Avenue and Broadway. My acquaintances sold cocaine and heroine and lived big until they got shot or shoved into prison. Bad Bob was from the old neighborhood. An Italian, he had been in the Mafia, but he was busted him for selling drugs, so they told him he was out of the club. He bought a pardon from the governor, but because he wasn't with the outfit any more, he had to watch it.

Bob was a pretty good pal, the kind of guy who helped you when nobody else would. But you had to be careful around him. A Vietnam Vet, he had seen 359 continuous days of combat over there. When things got crazy, so did he. He mostly hung out at Rocky's, the local tavern which was frequented by the area factory workers including the Parliament workers. He knew everybody and everybody's business.

From time to time I'd consider selling marijuana, but I was too big of a sissy. I didn't want to wind up in prison. Bob and I visited one of our old pals in the big state prison in Joliet, Illinois. The old worn stone facade, the bars, the surly guards, and the tattooed, scarred-face inmates convinced me that was a place to avoid. I thought about bartending, but being a sissy, I didn't like fighting with drunks.

When the union got my job back, and the good times returned. I'd rent an apartment, build up my capital via overtime pay, then buy a condo. When I inevitably got sick of getting backaches from bending over the lathe, I'd get insubordinate, get fired, sell the condo, and air out the trailer again.

Whenever I thought about Alexander Glashauser, the operative emotions that emerged were fear and loathing. Fear because the guy seemed to be connected to the highest levels of the federal Republican Party and the really big national money. Loathing because of his transparent greed and neurotic obsession with controlling everything and everyone in his path. When he didn't receive the kind of press coverage he thought he deserved in one of the many elections in which he ran and was soundly beaten, he managed to get the reporters fired who had covered the story. After that episode, the video cameras always caught him from his photogenic side. When he wanted special tax relief for Push Electronics, which handled a lot of military contracts, he had the power to summon U.S. Senators from around the country to his boardroom in Illinois. He managed this by the simple expedient of contributing heavily to their re-election campaigns.

Once, when I waxed a little too vehemently against the little prick, my mother went after me. I was informed that there was good in everybody if you look for it. And we didn't live in a black and white world. I didn't argue with my elderly mother, but I was convinced that she was wrong. Glashauser was the exception that proved that rule. He had no redeeming qualities, and Technicolor wasn't the kind of world he lived in.

We met old Juan Lopez at a diner on the edge of the suburban "industrial park." The diner had been constructed out of brick in the 1950s and the building looked tired and out of date. We sat in a booth in the back for privacy. Butch and Celina Rodriguez had driven over in his Cadillac while I made a pit-stop at my mother's and got cleaned up.

I dressed for organizing; work boots, black jeans, a flannel shirt and my black leather union jacket.

When I got there, I could smell pancakes and strong coffee. Butch had already knocked back a big breakfast, but Celina and Juan were still picking at theirs because they spending more time talking than eating. I ordered the haybailer's breakfast which included virtually everything on the menu. I was profligate with the money because I knew Butch was putting it all on the union account. I could tell the waitress didn't like serving people in serial order; first Juan, then Celina and Butch, and then me. I knew Butch would fix her up with a big tip.

"This here is our inside committee," Butch pointed a butter knife at Juan.

Juan nodded and smiled at me. He had a mouthful of gold teeth and a weathered look of decades of factory work. He was wearing a blue factory uniform with his name stitched over his breast pocket. I pegged his age at around 60, about the same age as Butch. Juan still had jet black hair and sideburns. I liked him right away.

"Ready to rock and roll, huh, Juan?" I asked.

"We need the union very bad. We have lots of safety violations on our machines. And they don't pay us nothin'."

Celina inteviewed old Juan at length in Spanish. I savored the taste of my hot sausages and bacon while she went over the situation with Juan. She eventually pulled out a notebook and starting taking notes. Butch, who sat across from me, kept nodding and winking at me. I could read his mind. He thought he had an inside track and the organizing campaign would be a sure thing. I knew otherwise, because I had been a volunteer organizer for years. The likelihood of success was remote because Glashauser had so much money and power.

When she and Juan finished, she thanked him in English. He stood up and shook hands with me, then Butch, thanking us, too. Butch hung on to his hand while he brought out a union card and swung it around on the table in front of Juan.

"I need you to sign this before you go."

Juan looked at Celina and asked her in Spanish what the card was all about. She frowned at Butch, then explained to Juan that he was asking for union representation by the United Metalworkers. He looked somewhat concerned but he signed the card, thanked us all again, and departed.

"You're not supposed to shove the cards at them like that," said Celina.

"Why not? They want to join the union don't they?"

"Yes, but you should sign everyone up together at the first meeting."

"What's the difference?"

"So, they get a collective sense of power from doing it. When they all sign individually, they're all scared they're sticking their necks out."

"Don't take for Gospel everything they teach you at the AFL-CIO organizing school. I know what I'm doing. I've been at this for years. You're supposed to learn from me," said Butch. I rolled my eyes. She caught it and laughed. Butch didn't and wanted in on the joke. "What's so funny?"

"You are."

"I am. Right. That guy is no good anyways. Did you see how reluctant he was to sign that card?"

Celina looked in my direction.

"Give me a break. He's a good guy. I can feel it," I said.

"I don't think so."

Celina excused herself to use the washroom. Butch glanced in the direction she had taken, and once he was sure she was out of earshot, said, "Pretty hot stuff, huh?"

"She's too young for you Butch."

"Who says?" and he cackled like a maniac. Then the lightbulb went on. "She's too old for you, too."

I was 45, but I wondered.

"You think she's tough enough for this kind of work," I asked.

"Sure. Why not? I think it's mainly women working in there at Parliament. We're gonna need a woman organizer. Especially somebody who talks Spanish."

"She just seems so inexperienced."

"We'll break her in. She won't be a virgin when we're done." Butch smiled obscenely.

"You know sometimes you make me sick."

"Ahh, lighten up. Would you please? I not in the mood for your sensitive, bleeding heart liberal crap this morning."

"Fuck you. I'm not a liberal. I'm a revolutionary socialist."

Butch leaned across the table and affected a look of intense concentration on his face. "Fuck you, too. You're an unemployed, radical shit-stirrer.

You're a fucking communist, is what you are. Good thing communism is dead or I'd be scared."

We both laughed. And then he added, "And that's why you're so good at union organizing."

"Seriously. You think she's tough enough for this shit?"

"She's not what you think."

"What do I think?"

"You think she's some Chicano girl from Texas."

"Chicana."

"Chicana, Chicano, whatever. She's Harvard educated." Butch studied my face. "Hah. Never guessed that did you?"

"How do you know that?"

"She told me."

Celina returned. "What are you guys arguing about? I could hear you all the way across the room.

"Union strategy," Butch replied. He pulled out a big wad of flyers from beneath his coat. He had printed them on red paper. One side presented the standard AFL-CIO rap for joining a union, the other side was a union card to be filled out. "We'll hand these out in front of Parliament today."

"That's not a good idea," I said.

Butch looked at me. Then with very calm deliberate motions reached inside his coat and pulled out his cigarettes. The first one of the day. His doctor had him carefully rationed to one pack a day. "OK, I'll bite. Why is it a bad idea?"

"Because you'll tip off Glashauser that a union drive is going on. He'll call in the union buster business consultants as soon as he sees the flyers," Celina said.

"Bingo," I said sipping my strong black coffee.

Butch exhaled a lung full of smoke straight up over our heads. "So, what do we do?"

"Sneak around the factory and collect all the license plate numbers we can find. Then have the union run them through the State of Illinois. Then we call on all those folks at home. After we talk to them at home, we'll know what the issues are inside the factory. When we know the issues, we hand out a flyer calling for action on those issues. The same day we call a meeting. We form our inside committee at the meeting. Then we go from there to get two thirds signed up on cards, then ask for an election from the labor board." Celina smiled when she finished.

"You must have gotten straight A's in school," I said.

Two weeks later Celina and I waited around in the union hall for the Parliament Electronics workers to show up for their first organizing meeting. The union hall, in reality, was a rented VFW meeting room with poor lighting and ventilation. We had set up a multitude of folding steel chairs. Outside, the trees were blanketed in cold November mist and fog.

"You ever wonder why Glashauser named the place 'Parliament?'" Celina asked.

"Sounded fancy, I suppose."

"I think he had ideological reasons for it."

"Like what?"

"It sounds democratic. The longest lasting dictatorships always have lots of democratic window dressing."

"Learn that at Harvard did we?"

"It's true."

"Yeah. You're right. I can't argue it."

"Can I ask you a question Peter?"

"Sure. But you can call me Pete."

"Why do you always act distant around me?" She smiled. But I could tell she was nervous. She stood in the middle of jumble of chairs with her arms tightly folded across her chest.

"I like you Celina. But I can't figure out if you're fish or fowl."

"What?" She frowned, and her bushy eyebrows raised high.

"You're father was a farm worker in California, right? Where'd he get the money to send his daughter to Harvard? You speak perfect uninflected English. An when you're speaking Spanish it sounds very refined. It doesn't sound like the street Spanish."

She smiled. "Oh. Yeah, my father was a grape picker. My mother is white. My family, from her side, is from San Francisco. My grandfather owned a big insurance company. So, yeah, my father was very poor, and my mother's family was wealthy."

"You must have had a very strange home life."

"Not really. They got divorced before I turned one. My father died in a bar fight in Oakland. My mother raised me."

"Did she speak Spanish?"

"No. She met my father at one of the rallies for the United Farm Workers. I learned Spanish in school. My name was Collins until I went

112

to college. I changed it to my father's name my senior year. So, yeah, you're right, I'm not really part of anybody's world. I see that in you, too."

"Me? How so?"

"You're an intellectual but you work in a factory. You're neither fish nor fowl either. You play mind games with Butch. He doesn't know what you're talking about half the time. When you kid him about waiting for a phone call from the Fourth International for the day's orders, he thinks it's a joke."

"It _is_ a joke."

"Yeah, but the Fourth International really does exist doesn't it?"

"Yeah. But it's just a joke."

"Butch doesn't know that it exists."

"What Butch doesn't know, won't hurt him."

"Butch won't ever have to worry about being hurt, then."

"He's not college educated, but he's a sharp guy."

"He's a very sexist guy."

"Yeah, and nobody is going to change that. He gets the job done."

"He's not exactly diplomatic when it comes to dealing with people."

"That's because he's not a diplomat. He's a union organizer."

"Looks like you're the organizer. He relies on you to do the thinking and planning."

"Yeah, but we both do the shit work."

"He's overly judgmental. He jumps to conclusions. He knows everything. He's got a big bullshit story about everything. And he doesn't respect women. He's a pain in the ass to work with. And he's just plain dumb."

"He's not dumb. He just doesn't see the big picture. I'm telling you, he's a good guy, especially when things get tough and everybody else wants to quit."

"I don't understand what you see in him."

"You will."

Mostly Mexican women showed up for the meeting. Juan Lopez and his nephew, Fernando Garcia, were the only two Mexican men. Fernando was about Celina's age. He was classically tall, dark, and handsome. And he smiled a lot. A half-dozen young white workers showed up. They were classics, too. Long hair, tattoos, jeans, flannel shirts, and work boots made them industrially interchangeable. One middle-aged, white guy, Gene, did stand out. He was rotund and had a conservative haircut. I took one look at him, and knew he was trouble.

The organizing campaign had gone according to plan up to that point. Using Celina's detailed notes, we understood what was happening in each department in the factory. We knew how many people worked in each department, their genders, their nationalities, and whether they seemed to be pro or anti union. We knew the issues; unsafe working conditions, no say in how they did their jobs, no medical benefits, and lousy pay.

We had paid house visits to about half the workers we had identified via their license plate numbers. The overwhelming majority of the Parliament workers wanted a union to represent them. We had distributed a flyer which hammered away at the issues in front of the factory on the day of the meeting. The flyer had brought out a lot of people we hadn't been able to reach. We wanted to get everyone to sign union cards at the meeting, form an inside committee, then petition the company for an election through the labor board. We had been lucky so far, the company apparently didn't know what was happening. After we passed out the flyer, we became public knowledge, and we could expect the company to strike back.

Butch brought the meeting to order. That took some doing. None of those folks had probably ever previously attended a public meeting, let alone a union meeting. For most of them, church, the Cinco de Mayo parade, or sporting events represented their only experience of public gatherings.

"Brothers and sisters, we're here today to form the union to represent you in your dealings with the company.

"Can they fire us for joining the union?" a Mexican woman asked. Dressed in a t-shirt and jeans, she looked to be about 60.

"That's illegal. You have a right to join a labor union to represent you. That's Federal law.

"Who's gonna represent us?" Another woman asked.

"You are. You are the union. We'll send you to school to learn how to bargain for a contract and how to defend that contract with grievances. After today the company will have to follow procedures and rules when dealing with people. Everybody gets treated the same after today.

They continued to pepper Butch with questions for over an hour. But he had it down pat. I had seen the same performance a dozen times. He peppered them back with his own questions, "You folks think you got the balls to stand up to the company? You know union's aren't for sissies. You gotta have a backbone if you wanna be union. You think you got what it takes to be union?"

By the end of his performance he had some of the young kids standing on their chairs shouting in unison, "Union, union," while pumping clenched fist salutes in the air. Of course, I got the clenched fist thing going early on, while applauding points that people made. Celina applauded and yelled, too. But I could tell she was studying the Butch and Peter show. I think that's when it dawned on her that Butch wasn't just a hack. He really wanted those folks to have a better life. Butch asked for volunteers for the inside committee. Everybody except Gene put up their hands.

Butch continued to work the congregation up to a fever, "Are we gonna take the company's crap anymore?" Simultaneously they shouted, "Hell no." Then Butch demanded, "Will you all sign union cards?" They swarmed to the Celina who held the cards aloft over her head.

Gene sat back alone with his hand politely raised. Butch, not one for recognizing trouble when he saw it, called on him. Gene stood up and quietly asked, "How do we know God wants us to join this here union."

"God's in favor of unions," Butch replied.

Celina stared at Butch. She worked hard at producing a look of overdone exasperation.

"We don't know that. If God wanted us to join a union, their would already be one there.

"No. You gotta form the union." Butch answered patiently. "It's OK with God."

I could sense the steam starting to leak out of the crowd. "What do you want from us, Gene?" I demanded.

" I just think we're overlooking God's role in this.

Butch picked up on new tact. "What's it say in the Bible about unions, Gene? I bet you know the Bible backwards and forwards."

"I do. And it don't say nothing about unions."

"Well, then, it's ok" said Butch.

"No, it ain't. We should wait for a sign from God."

Now Celina was eyeballing Gene with the same look she had used on Butch. The workers paused in their signing activities. Sensing that Gene had brought us to a critical juncture, I said, "I think we should sign the cards, because we haven't received any sign that we shouldn't."

Gene was the only person who didn't sign a card.

That evening, after having yet another restaurant dinner with Butch, Celina stopped by the trailer instead of just heading back to her motel room as she usually did.

"I should take you out to the rock quarry on the edge of town." I leaned back on the side cushions around my bed. I usually slept in a bunk on the other end of my decrepit trailer. That night I had folded down the kitchen table put away or threw away all the junk, and had folded out the full bed. We were both fully clothed. Celina in jeans, socks, and a union t-shirt. My clothes paralleled hers with the exception of my mismatched socks. I had all the lights out. The only light came from the television.

"Rock quarry? What for?" I watched her languid movements from behind as she nestled down her head on her arm after having propped it up for quite some time. My portable color TV bathed us in the flickering electronic light. If I reached out, I could have touched her hair.

"Go skinny-dipping. What else?"

She indolently turned around, flashed me a wicked smile and said, "It's too cold."

An intuitive flash told me that we had reached the continental divide of our relationship. She stretched out, flexing her legs, then her back, then her arms. I watched. I sensed that it could go either way that moment. She was willing to take it in either direction. The lurid light from the TV shimmered through her hair.

"Why do you live like this?"

"Like what?"

"Like this." She opened her arms to encompass the interior of trailer. "Like a bum." She didn't sound judgmental. Just honest.

I shoved my way past her and up off the bed. She looked up at me with a look of concern. She sat up briefly, then layed back.

"I don't know. I gave up, I guess."

"I didn't mean to offend you. You have the right to live anyway you want."

"I'm not offended." I drank the last of some very strong, very bitter, fast food coffee out of a paper cup. Then I lit one of Butch's cigarettes that I had bummed.

"You don't smoke."

"Oh, yeah. In past lives I have. This is just one of the ghosts coming up."

"You talk like you're an old man."

"I'm gettin' there."

She slumped back down, with her head propped up again. She just looked at me. I stubbed out the cigarette in the coffee after a few hits.

"I live like this because I'm too chickenshit to move forward with my life anymore. I need to find something meaningful to do with myself if I want to continue to grow. Guess, I'm at that proverbial turn in the road. Only this time around, I get the feeling if I don't take the turn, I'm not getting any more chances."

Celina sat up again. She brushed her fingers against my arm. "Please hand me my beer.

"You know, kid, I get the feeling you're wondering about your job, too."

"I'm always on the road. I'm always staying in a hotel. I'm always losing union elections. I'm always saying goodbye to good people, and I know when I leave town their employer is going to fire them for standing up for themselves." She recited her words like a litany. In the faint light I watched her stare vacantly at her beer bottle.

I pulled on my workboots.

"What are you doing?"

"Puttin' on my shoes, so I can drive you back to your hotel."

We all got together again on voting day. The labor board held the election on-site at Parliament. The campaign had taken several heavy hits after the organizing meeting, but the workers faltered ahead with the help of the three of us, Butch, Celina, and myself. First, the company called in the union buster consultants. This was a Loop law firm of douchebags who lived in Lincoln Park and wealthy suburbs like Barrington Hills and Inverness. These guys played golf with Alexander Glashauser while the folks he paid minimum wage ran unsafe punch presses during the torrid summer days in his noisy factory.

First the lawyers called in the Federal Immigration agency, "La Migra," as the workers called them. A lot of our women supporters found themselves clutching one-way-tickets on the bus to Mexico. Some of their children had been born in the USA and could prove it, so they didn't have to go. Some of the spouses were legal too. The resulting havoc of split-up families served as a cautionary omen to those who hadn't made up their minds about voting for the union.

Then they fired Juan Lopez for poor job performance. Butch got him a union lawyer and pitched a bitch with the labor board over an illegal firing. Butch thought they could get it resolved in six months, maybe. Meanwhile Juan was out of a job. The union offered to put him on full time as an organizer until they resolved his case, but he turned sullen and turned down the offer. Celina, who was spending a lot of time with Juan's nephew, Fernando, tried working on him via the family, but she was unsuccessful.

They made a couple of the white kids into foremen, which took them out of the voting because now they were management. For awhile, it looked like the whole thing would come apart.

With Juan gone, our inside committee dwindled to seven really tough Mexican women. They ranged in age from 23 to 61, they were legal, and they intended to fight it out with Glashauser and Parliament until the last bullet. They helped us call on people in the evening at their homes, and they handed out the flyers that blasted the company for splitting up families.

The company managed to get the union vote pushed out into the future by filing different complaints with the labor board. Meanwhile they unleashed an unremitting anti-union terror campaign in the factory, complete with mandatory anti-union meetings, posters, bumper stickers, and rewards of overtime and secret pay raises for the weak minded and disciplinary action for anyone suspected of being pro-union. Butch filed complaints on the illegal stuff the company did, but the labor board would never get to the cases in the same decade they were filed.

On voting day, we met at Rocky's Bar and Grill after the conclusion of first shift at Parliament. We had held meetings there previously, because Rocky was an old steelworker and he welcomed the business. I didn't like it because everybody had full access to booze before, during, and after the meeting. Butch always asked Rocky to go "slow serve" until the meeting was completed.

The first guy in the door that day was Gene. He was wearing a union button. "Got the sign, huh?" I asked.

"Indeed I did, Peter.

Celina and Fernando arrived next, arm in arm. "You know Juan went against us, man?" said Fernando.

"What?" I felt personally betrayed.

"Yeah. It's true. He's got his job back with the company.

"I told you he was no fucking good," said Butch.

"What happened?" I asked.

Fernando waved Butch and myself over to the barstools where he and Celina had roosted. I thought the kid looked really good for herself that day. The other workers were drifting into the bar now, and he apparently didn't want his story to be on the public record. "You know you got a friend, Peter. His name is Bad Bob."

I looked at Butch. Any story with Bad Bob in it was bad fucking news. Somebody got shot. Somebody got cut. Somebody went to jail. "He's not actually my friend. We're just acquaintances."

"I don't think so," said Fernando.

"OK, OK. Friends, acquaintances, what's the difference," said Butch.

"Yeah, yeah. What happened?" I asked.

"Juan goes to your buddy, Bad Bob, and asks to buy a kilo of coke."

"How do you know that," I asked.

"Bad Bob told me this morning. He stopped us in the parking lot."

Celina nodded in affirmation. "He asked me if I was the union organizer helping you." She pointed to me. "I said, yeah. Then he said…"

Fernando interrupted her, "Let me tell it. It's my story."

"Go ahead," she said.

"Then he said, 'You tell that fucking MacNaughton that he owes me a big one.'"

"Owe him what?" I asked.

"He said that he knew Juan had been fired and didn't have any money. He asked Juan where he got all the money to buy a kilo of coke. Juan got smart with him. So, Bob pulled his gun and took him over to the machine shed in back of Parliament. He hung him upside down from a motor shaft and told him if he didn't say where he got the money he was going to turn on the motor. Juan was scared shitless, so he told."

"Yeah." Butch and I both hated the relaxed pace the story insisted on taking.

"He got the money from Parliament. They wanted Juan to stick the dope in your trailer.

Then they were going to call the police. They offered to give Juan his job back if he did it."

"Fuck me," was all I could verbalize.

"No, fuck them," Butch said, loud enough to get the attention of the folks at surrounding tables. "I'm taking this shit to the police.

"Whoa. You can't do that, man. You'll get Bob in trouble. That's not how I repay favors."

Butch yanked his sportscoat down hard. "Goddamn."

"So Juan. He's OK?" I asked.

"Oh, yeah. He walked around all day with a big No-Union button."

"And two shiners," added Celina.

Fernando laughed, "Yeah, Bad Bob kicked the shit out of him."

The meeting was dismal one. One of the Mexican women brought the results over to the bar after second shift had voted. We lost the election 122 to 101. We had no doubt there would be another round of reprisals in a couple of months. The union buster lawyers usually recommended waiting until the union stuff had died down completely, before firing, one by one, everyone who had participated in the organizing committee. Fernando went looking for another job the next day.

Celina was ordered to Alabama to help on another campaign. But she had caught on to the losing strategy of the AFL-CIO, which consisted of; pump up the workers, follow the rules no matter how badly they were stacked against you, watch the workers get crushed, then abandon the workers when they lost the vote. Precisely the opposite way the CIO had signed up millions of people. Mobilizing people for mass direct action scared the shit out of the bureaucrats who owned the AFL-CIO.

So, she quit. She got a job in the Loop as an administrative assistant for an environmental attorney. She and Fernando moved in together in an apartment on the near Northwest Side of Chicago in Humboldt Park.

I cleaned out my trailer, and the day I bought a newspaper to look at want ads, Butch called and informed me he had gotten my old job back. I bought Bad Bob a steak dinner in a nice restaurant under the L tracks on South Wabash. We talked about the old neighborhood until after midnight. The next day I put the trailer up for sale. Parliament fired Juan one last time.

The Man In the White Jaguar

One Chicago horror story I never told anyone happened when my 10 year old automobile broke down in front of a housing project on Division Street during a torrid summer afternoon. It's the same Division Street that Studs Terkel wrote about, with the Gold Coast and its wealthy denizens located just blocks away from the wretched of the earth, Chicago's lumpenproletariat. Anyway, my timing chain broke at an intersection just south of the massive housing project. I walked into a nearby liquor store and called for a tow. I stood out by my rusting car, hood propped open, steam pouring out of my radiator. A couple of teenagers stood around on the corner directly behind me. Two boys, they looked to be about 16. They were wearing gang colors, black, white and red. I didn't pay much attention to them, and they studiously ignored me. I must have looked like one more broken down, middle-aged white guy wearing work boots, jeans, and a t-shirt.

It was a Tuesday afternoon, and the traffic was light. Occasionally, I caught a whiff of a lake breeze. I could smell the pungent cheap beer the two kids were drinking. Then an old white guy pulled up to the intersection in a shiny new white Jaguar with Florida license plates. He stopped for the red light. He obviously had just left the expressway and was headed eastbound for the Gold Coast neighborhood nestled along Lake Michigan. As I wiped the sweat out of my eyes, it crossed my mind to ask him for a ride to the service station which I had just phoned. It made sense to wait in an air conditioned service station rather than continuing to bake under the Midwestern summer sun in the middle of Division Street.

I knocked on his driver side window. Reluctantly, he pressed the electric motor button to lower the window just a crack.

"Yes?" He sounded crisp and perfunctory, as he sat in air conditioned comfort. I noticed his white hair barely concealed a big bald spot.

"Hi. My name is Peter MacNaughton. My car broke down." I pointed to my dented rusting car. "How about a lift down to Wells Street?" I pointed in the direction he was headed.

"You should buy a reliable car. Then you wouldn't have these problems."

"Yeah, well, I can't afford one. I'm a machinist."

"Why don't you walk? You look like you need to lose some weight. It will do you good."

As I stood back contemplating an obscene riposte, I felt somebody stick a piece of metal in my back. It was one of the kids. In hardly a whisper he said, "Get the fuck outta here." As I turned, very slowly, the kid brushed past me and stuck the gun barrel into the tiny open space that the old man had used to address me.

It was a very big handgun, a .357 magnum with a 12 inch barrel. All the old guy had to do at that point was floor it, blow the light, and escape. But he apparently was too addicted to following the rules.

"Open this window, old motherfucker," the kid yelled.

The light changed, but the Jaguar remained stationary. The window came down a bit. I backpedaled toward my car, glad to be out of it. When I felt my front fender behind me, I turned and got around to the other side of car, putting it between me and that big magnum.

"I said open this window, motherfucker," the kid yelled again. This time the window came down. Across the street, I could watch and hear the entire scene unfold.

"What do you want?" the old man asked, sounding calm.

"I want you out that car, man" the kid replied. "I'm taking that car."

"No, you're not. What are you, a damn thief?"

"Who you callin' thief, old motherfucker? Shut the fuck up and get out that car."

"No." The old man yelled. "I'm not going to give you my car."

At which point the kid pistol whipped the old guy through the open window. The car lurched forward a couple of times, but the kid had his hand around the old guy's throat now and the barrel of the gun right in his face. I could see the blood running over his face.

"Put that motherfucker in park," the kid yelled, as the two of them continued to struggle. The old guy wisely complied.

"Now get the fuck out that car," and the kid bodily yanked the old guy right through the open window and unceremoniously dumped him into the middle of Division Street. Then I could see the guy was wearing golf shoes and some very expensive casual clothing.

The kid jumped into the car, and as he took a few minutes to familiarize himself with the controls, the old guy got back to his feet.

"Go ahead, you black bastard, steal my damn car. You know what? You're worthless. You're a worthless human being. Always have been, always will be. You're nothing but a common thief."

I couldn't believe the old guy's audacity and stupidity. From across the street, I yelled, "Hey, man. Get out of there." I waved frantically at him to move away from his car. He glanced at me, gave me a contemptuous look, then continued his tirade.

"The police are going to catch you. You won't get ten blocks. You dumb ass."

The "p" word finally got the kid's attention. He quit fiddling with the old guy's car phone and leaned out the window. I distinctly heard the ominous back click of that big handgun hammer. It was a double action gun. You could pull the hammer back half way, then pull the trigger, or you could pull the trigger clean through to get off a shot. "How the police gonna know who I am?" the kid demanded.

"I'm going to tell them who you are, that's how."

In one athletic move the kid effortlessly pointed the big gun out the window and shot the blaspheming old man right in the mouth. The bullet blew off most of the back of his head and spun the already dead torso around a full 360 degrees. "Fuck you," the kid yelled at the corpse and burned rubber through the red light torquing down Division Street.

I ducked behind my car in case he decided to shoot the witnesses, too. But I bobbed back up as soon as I heard him peel out. The other kid had disappeared. A middle aged woman scurried out of the liquor store and waddled back to the projects as fast as her flip flops permitted. Alone with the body, I felt horrified. Then a sense of weird gratification took over. I laughed. Then speaking in the direction of the corpse I said, "You should have given me that ride, you dumb motherfucker." I laughed again. I couldn't help it. I thought it was funny. The class war that everybody likes to deny exists had taken yet another victim. The lumpenproletariat had plucked a member of the upper middle class. Then the cops would probably, as predicted by the old asshole, pluck the lumpenproletarian.

As a representative of the working class, I had duly tried to warn the dumb asshole, but he insisted on getting himself killed. Now, instead of feeling remorse over his death, I was laughing. I knew when the cops arrived, they'd wipe the smile off my face, but until that moment arrived, my subconscious kept bubbling up tidbits of black humor. "Your money didn't help you, huh?" I yelled. "That's what you get when you call a murderer a thief," I yelled. "That's what you get when you bring a golf club to a gun fight," I yelled. I found myself laughing my ass off. It occurred to me, the blatant bloody murder had caused my psyche to go into shock.

I thought about writing up the episode into an account I could sell to the newspapers. Then I paused to wonder, what kind of story would that make? One human being murdering another for a luxury automobile. A great writer would have compassion for the wealthy man, and his heart would bleed a little, too, for a sixteen year old boy who was capable of murder.

Then I thought, who's grieving for all the people the old man probably screwed over. After all, if you have great wealth, it means you vacuumed the money out of other people's pockets. He may have supported evil governments or they supported him in order to amass the kind of wealth necessary to purchase a Jaguar. He probably fired people from their jobs or caused them to be fired. He may have evicted people from their domiciles or caused them to be evicted. He probably owned stock in the vast multinational corporations that manufacture the weapons of mass destruction. So who's zooming who? Maybe the planet is a better place for the rest of us with the pompous old man dead.

The tow truck arrived and the driver walked over and examined the corpse. I made a deliberate attempt to sober up and pull myself out of my manic state. Then the driver set to work rigging the tow bar. Just another day at the office for him. I struggled to get my story straight.

After all, I didn't want that kid roaming the neighborhood, murdering more people. He needed to be rounded up and jailed. He could have stuck that gun in my face instead of the old guy. I angrily chided myself again for failing to feel any remorse. I told myself, for all you know, he sold roses for a living, and paid his workers well. Maybe he inherited all his wealth and had spent his entire life as a scientific researcher trying to rid humanity of deadly diseases.

I forced myself to look at the lifeless body again and vast blood spill along the curb littered with broken beer glass. "Where's your compassion?" I mumbled under my breath so the tow driver couldn't hear me. Such is daily life in the Psychotic Atomik Empire I told myself.

When the cops finally arrived, they asked me what had happened. I told them I had been in the liquor store making the phone call for the tow truck when it all went down.

"I didn't see anything."

The Hacker

"Art, I want that Webmaster job. I've worked at Imperial for two years now doing that job. It's only fair that they give me that job full time. Are you going to back me up or not? You're a manager there. Why don't you help me?" Christine Dalton banged two frozen dinners into their microwave oven and stabbed the start button. She duly noted the empty ice cream carton sitting on the kitchen counter top, an ice tea spoon left in it, the remains of Art Lunacharsky's late night snack from the previous evening. She removed the spoon, and dunked the sour smelling box into the trash. She snatched the kitchen wash cloth and energetically burnished the counter top free of ice cream smudges.

Satisfied the counter top had been restored to sanitary order, she removed her work shoes, pulled her blouse out of her skirt, then reached under and yanked off her panty hose. Relieved to be shedding her office clothes, she turned the corner of their small apartment and found her boyfriend, Art, fiddling with the stereo. Despite the fact that they had barely arrived at their apartment on Chicago's North Side after a frantic, Friday evening rush hour L ride from the Loop, he had already managed to strip down to his boxer shorts and a t-shirt. His sports coat, slacks, dress shirt and tie lay rumpled on the living room floor where he had tossed them. The cluttered room reeked of various fetid odors from piles of clothing that were overdo for the cleaners. Half empty bags of potato chips and empty pizza boxes littered the coffee table and the floor next to the sofa. Stacks of Imperial technical manuals sagged next to Art's favorite easy chair.

"Did you hear me?"

"Sweetie, I can't make Audrey hire you. I'm in sales and applications. She's in human resources." He finally dialed-in his favorite radio station, a smooth jazz format, on their music system. Art stood about five feet eight inches and could be described as pudgy. His black hair was rapidly thinning despite the fact that he was only 25 years old. His wire rim glasses added to the older appearance. He moved to embrace Christine. She dodged the on-coming bear-hug. And even more artfully, she dodged an emotion she felt welling up. She knew all his moves. In the background, Ramsey Lewis worked through some elaborate piano riffs.

"You're never there for me. You never back me up. You always take sides against me."

"Be reasonable, Christine, they've got valid reasons for not giving you the job. I'm making good money with the company. Let me make the bucks. Go back to school and get your computer degree. We can get married. When we have enough money, we can retire to the country. You look so cute with your panty hose in your hands."

"I'm getting that damn job, whether you help me or not. That old bitch is interviewing three men for the job this week. I'm going to get on the interview list."

"Sweetie, you have to loosen up. You're developing a monomaniacal thing over this job."

"Because it's my job. I've been doing the damn job for two years. They're just not paying me for it. They're getting away with murder paying me minimum wage as a temp and getting a professional level job done. It's not fair."

"Sweetie," Art approached her again.

"Goddamn it, don't treat me like a child." She backpedaled again out of reach of his embrace. "I need you to respect me. And I need you to go in there and talk with Audrey, or with Brantley, if necessary."

Art finally stopped trying to close-in on her. She could tell she had finally hurt his typically over sensitized feelings by the look on his face. "Don't take this to Brantley. He's not going to fool around with you. He'll fire you in a heartbeat. Don't let the Hawaiian shirts and his hippie-days photographs fool you. That guy is a shark. He'll eat you."

Abruptly, the microwave signaled their dinner was ready. They sat on the sofa eating their steaming entrees directly out of the plastic packaging and watched the evening TV news. Afterwards Christine retreated to "her" room, a neatly organized tiny bedroom where she kept her powerful computer and books. Art had been forbidden to bring anything into the room and had to formally knock and announce himself when the door was closed. That night she closed the door. She focused her concentration on her resume, then picked up Imperial's web site and added a few enhancements and embellishments to an already elaborate web site that contained hundreds of computer screens describing in detail all of Imperial Dog Food Corporation's vast array of flavors and types of dog food.

Frustration had always been Christine's lot in life. She felt nullified from day one because she was short, barely five feet tall. She received no respect because she was a woman, and that was compounded because she was so petite. People frequently mistook her for a child. She was constantly "carded" despite the fact she was 25 years old and realized that would go on into her 30s or beyond. She had lifted weights in college to try to bulk up, but her efforts had been a failure. She kept her flaming red hair very short in spite of Art's pleas to let it grow out. He hated it short.

In a final act of treachery, nature gifted her with a very deep voice. She constantly startled strangers when she initiated conversations. In college, her friends called her "Froggy." They also told her she was the only redhead they knew who wasn't "fiery." What they didn't tell her was that her blue eyes always seemed to have the clairvoyant capacity to see into people. What she didn't tell them, was that their worst fears were well grounded.

She had met Art in college - the University of Illinois at Chicago, an urban campus just west of the Loop. Her father drove a bread truck and her mother worked at K-Mart as a sales clerk. Her parents raised her uneventfully until she was 14, then suddenly decided to have a big family. Now she had brothers who were 11, 10, and 9 years old. She felt like an orphan. She felt completely left out of the "second" family. Her contribution to the family had been extensive babysitting while she attended high school and college, while her parents never seemed to have money to help her pay off her sizable student loans.

Secretly, she liked to look on the positive aspect of her childhood and adolescence. As Nietzsche had said, "That which doesn't kill us, makes us stronger." She thought she had handled the ordeal well and learned to develop her interior muscles. Her deepest secret was that she had self-developed into a "power personality" capable of rigorous functional analysis and planning. Her secret fantasy consisted of starting her own computer consulting company. Her next thought was always, "Yeah, who's gonna do business with a 25 year old chick who looks like a fucking pixie?"

She had moved in with Art during their sophomore year, because there was chemistry, although not much in the way of shared interests. Chiefly she did it because it made financial sense. Now she put up with the jumble and mess and the nearly constant parade of friends and acquaintances who Art invited over to their apartment on a nearly 24 hour basis. Only her computer room remained sacrosanct from the chaos.

Once Art remarked, "How come you never have any of your college friends over?"

"I don't collect friends like you."

"I get the feeling that people aren't that important to you. Ideas, systems, software, computer languages are what's important to you."

"Yeah. You're probably right. So what?"

Christine had majored in business instead of computer science, which gave Audrey Patton, the human resource manager, her reason for not hiring her for the Webmaster job. She had worked in a pizza joint in a working class neighborhood on Diversey Avenue all through high school and college. She had worked part time during the school years and full time during the summers. After she had met Art, she used to make love to him standing up in a broom closet of the pizza place. She could never figure out why Art was so embarrassed about it when her co-workers poked fun at them. She found it mildly amusing, but nevertheless, pragmatic and convenient. Art's face bloomed bright red, if they unlocked the door and found fellow pizza workers laughing about it.

Opposites do attract. She had always respected Art's intellect even if she couldn't really understand a lot of the impetus behind it. When they first met, they had stayed up all night arguing over Art's favorite existentialists like Sartre, and her favorite author, William S. Burroughs. They both still conducted secretive readings to accumulate intellectual ammunition for the occasional pseudo-scholarly conflagrations in which they still engaged. One of her favorite occupations involved catching his warm brown eyes in an intellectual contradiction, then listening as his voice slowly turned soprano in spirited defense of an indefensible position.

Art's family was related to Anton Lunacharsky, first Commisar of Education in the Soviet Union under Lenin. Christine thought Art probably had inherited a solid block of DNA from his socialist ancestor because he, too, was a socialist, of the armchair variety. He had been active in the 1980s in street demonstrations for the people of Central America. His family came from the South Side, Hyde Park. His father was a physician and his mother taught at the University of Chicago. Art was the baby of the family. He had two older sisters, Alexis, and Andrea. He still paid dues to a democratic socialist organization, but he never attended meetings or street demonstrations. The most difficult thing for Christine to understand was Art's concern for people thousands of miles away whom he had never met. Nevertheless, something about his oceanic concern for humanity did impress and move her. Art liked to talk about "the magic feeling he had for her." She simply didn't trust her feelings, magic or otherwise.

One evening, after work, after pizza in the joint where she had once worked, and after three bottles of wine the conversation had drifted to;

"What's your favorite color, Art?"

"Red."

"Give me a break. You're an applications manager with a capitalist firm."

"I'm still working class."

"Please. That insults everyone who works here. You've never done a day's work in your life."

"Ok, what's your favorite color, sweetie?"

"Black."

"Because it's so trendy right now, right?" She felt sad because black had become so trendy. She didn't like being considered one more brainless member of the herd who followed trendy. But she couldn't help it. She liked black. She bought charcoal grey jackets and white blouses just to make her black jeans and her black leather coat stand out.

"Maybe, alternative trendy."

"I see."

"Maybe you're right."

"At least you're honest."

"Yeah, I'm honest."

Monday morning Christine steamed into Audrey Patton's office with a fresh resume. She secretly hated Audrey, a 45 year-old, divorced woman with over processed, dyed hair, who liked to leave one button too many unbuttoned on her blouse. Whenever she countered Audrey, she detected the strong scent of unfiltered cigarettes on her breath and on her clothes. It nauseated Christine. After Albert Brantley had commented on the aroma at an office Christmas party, Audrey had taken to wearing a particularly odiferous perfume with a very musky smell.

"I'm applying for the Webmaster job." Christine placed her resume on Audrey's austere looking desk. The sole ornament consisted of one discrete photograph of her grandson. Otherwise, the desktop included an appointment calendar, a telephone, and computer terminal. No extraneous papers were ever evident.

"And we earned a degree in computer science over the weekend did we?" Audrey chirped in the cracked voice of a committed smoker.

"You know I don't have a computer science degree, Audrey."

"Well, I'm sorry then, Christine. This job requires a computer science degree."

"But I've been doing the job for two years."

"I'm sorry. The requirements are the requirements."

"And who determines the requirements Audrey?"

"I do."

"So, how about changing the requirements to two years of experience putting a web site together for Imperial Dog Food Corporation and a degree in business administration?"

"I'm sorry, honey, we've been over this many times. I'm following standard personnel practices. You should have a computer science degree for this position. All the best practices manuals agree on it."

"I'm not taking no for an answer. You should at least interview me. I'm the only person who knows what direction corporate wants to take with the web page. How is some newcomer to the company going to know everything I do. I'm the one who put the whole thing up on the web. I created the architecture for the site. Anybody else would take weeks or months to come up to speed on the project.

"Sorry."

"So you're not going to interview me?"

Audrey just smiled.

"And you're interviewing people this week?"

"We have three very strong candidates coming in this week to interview. They all have experience. They all have computer science degrees."

"And they're all men."

Audrey leaned back in her high backed chair and tapped her short nails on her desk top. "Maybe one of them would consider hiring you as his assistant." The unspoken addendum to her remark was; "if you behave yourself, child."

"This sucks."

Christine thought about going over Audrey's bony head and talking to Blayne Whitless, Audrey's boss and Vice President of Human Resources. But Art's warnings deterred her. After all, she didn't want to lose her temp job, not after all the work she had put into the company. She continued to wrestle with the idea, but the fear paralyzed her. And, Art continued his campaign of dissuasion. Although she remained silent about the issue, Art knew she had it up on her internal anvil, banging on it, night after night.

Then, in the middle of the week, she spotted Duane Didley, a distant relative of Audrey's, show up for an interview for the Webmaster's job. Duane had interned at the company for two summers in a row. According to Art, he had earned a solid nickname for himself in the sales department - "the village idiot."

That afternoon Christine made an appointment to see Blayne Whitless. His office was located five stories above her office and the main administration floor, on the 32nd floor of the Loop skyscraper. Her previous encounters with Blayne had consisted of watching him golf, play volleyball, and play softball at company sponsored charity benefits around the city. He had played for some professional sports team, she forgot which, and his chief contribution to the company seemed to be the ease with which he could get publicity for the company.

When she entered his private office, she was struck by the awesome stretch of expensive carpet she had to cross after entering the door in order to each the side chair near his desk. The view outside of his window, which overlooked Grant Park and Lake Michigan, could only be described as breathtaking. She did detect the faint odor of ozone from a copy machine.

Blayne, who was about 10 years older than her, graciously welcomed her. He probably stood six feet three inches, with an athletic build, and short blonde hair. His desk was devoid of everything except a telephone. She received an intuitive flash that he probably kept sports magazines in his desk drawer. Blayne was the only senior exec besides Brantley himself, who dressed in "business casual" apparel instead of the "haute couture" of charcoal-grey pin stripes, pleated trousers, and red suspenders.

"And what can I do for you today, little lady? How's our web site doing? I told Brantley we've had almost a hundred thousand hits already."

"That's what I wanted to talk to you about. Audrey is interviewing three people for the job full time. And she refuses to interview me."

"So, you want to interview?"

"Blayne, I want the job. Yeah, I wanna get interviewed. Then I want to get hired, full time. It's only fair. I've earned it, don't you think?"

"Ok, I'll ask her to interview you. Anything else? How about those Cubs?"

"Yeah, there's something else. Audrey keeps telling me I'm unqualified because I don't have a computer science degree. She'll interview me, alright, then she will tell me I'm unqualified."

"I can't touch that. I can promise you a fair interview, but Audrey is the keeper of the qualifications."

"Great. That helps a lot." She watched a sailboat, far below, drift across the deep mysterious lake.

"I'll look into it, OK?"

Sensing that his capacity for conflict had already been stretched to the maximum, Christine said, "OK," and left.

That night she laid her plans for conquest. She brought up the web site from her home computer then spent eight hours reconstructing, reconfiguring, and remolding. Like Eisenhower planning the D-Day Invasion, she methodically elaborated a strategy replete with various options, back-ups, fall-backs, and possibilities.

By the time Audrey got around to interviewing her, Imperial Dog Food's website not only belonged to Christine, it was Christine. Of course, after her perfunctory interview, Audrey uttered the characteristic, "We'll let you know."

And, of course, the new Webmaster was hired and on board, before Audrey formally acknowledged, via letter, that Christine had not made the cut. That day Christine pulled the plug on the Website. After the crash, the Webmaster, Duane Didley, who still had fresh ink on his college diploma, politely, but firmly requested Christine's assistance in getting the Imperial message out to millions of internet subscribers. Christine laughed in his face.

"Hey, man, if you're so brilliant, why can't you boot it up?"

After being summoned down to Audrey's office, Christine relished the ensuing discussion.

"Honey, you really can't do this. I know you're angry about not getting the Webmaster job. But you simply can't do this. You're only hurting your career. This looks childish to the rest of us."

"Audrey, did you know that they call you a 'power skirt' behind your back?"

At first Audrey didn't respond. First she stubbed out her cigarette. Then she lit another one. "Honey, did you know they call you Mrs. Data or Mrs. Spock behind your back?"

"What?"

"Sometimes they just call you 'the Machine,' honey. People think you're over-focused. Driven."

"Bullshit."

"Honey, you have to unlock the website."

"Or what?"

"Or else."

"Or else what?"

"You're fired."

"You'll never get your website back, then."

Audrey forcibly expelled the cigarette smoke from her lungs. "Christine, be reasonable."

After they fired her, Christine took a long walk along the lake shore. The late Spring breeze ruffled her hair and despite facing the biggest challenge of her life, she felt free, liberated, a free woman in Chicago. She listened to the traffic forming a distant roar at her back on Lake Shore Drive.

Art threw a monumental shit-fit when he arrived at their apartment uncharacteristically early. "What the hell are you thinking about?" She thought he sounded more concerned than angry.

"I'm thinking its totally unfair. That's what I'm thinking about." She answered quietly.

"They're going to fire both of us. Do you realize that?"

"I've got it under control."

"Under control? Are you kidding me? They already fired you, and now they're threatening to fire me. You call that 'under control?'"

Standing in them middle of their jumbled living room, she folded her arms and stared at him. "I said, it's under control. Brantley will call me next."

"Listen," he approached her cautiously, "They told me you had until tomorrow morning or they are going to call the cops. They're not bluffing. So give them back their website, will you? Please?"

"I've got more than their website in my pocket. I've got their whole system rigged for demolition. If Brantley doesn't deal with me, I'm sending all the companies data bases to hell. If the cops bust me, the systems will flash warnings before they go, and then flash "Free Christine" screens afterwards. I got some other goodies loaded in there, too."

Art warily placed his hand on her shoulder. Facing her he said, "You've got to back off of this. They aren't fooling. What about us? I always wanted us to quit after a few years and buy a farm. We could have a bunch of kids and animals. Don't you want to do that with me?"

"Why don't you ever back me up? I want a life, too. I want a job where I can demonstrate my competence. This is the job, if they'd just admit I'm the best person for it and give it to me."

"They're not going to do that. They just want their website back. If they don't get it, they're going to come down on you big time. Just give it back to them. And don't even think about doing anything else to their computer."

"Come on. Loosen up. Join the Dalton gang."

Art turned away and flopped into his easy chair. Mentally, Christine wrote him off at the moment. No courage. She stalked into her room and went over her "Santa Fe" plan in her mind again. Christine heard the phone ring, and Art answer it. He curtly rapped on her closed door.

"Brantley?" she yelled through the door.

"Yeah."

Albert Brantley looked like the best preserved 55 year old man Christine had ever beheld. She realized never having to do a day's work in his life had done wonders for his health. Brantley came from money. Big time Barrington Hills money. If she remembered correctly, his father owned at least one Chicago area steel mill and a chunk of the stockyards. Brantley had enjoyed playing the role of black sheep as an adolescent and a young man. He had served in the national leadership of more than one left-wing organization. Christine had always wondered how people in left-wing organizations could be stupid enough to elect guys like Brantley into national leadership. In the mid-1970s Brantley had corrected course, gone to law school and then on to an Ivy League graduate business school.

Surprised that Brantley had suggested meeting at his exclusive greystone home on north State Parkway on the Gold Coast, Christine had confidently dressed casually: black jeans, grey pullover blouse, black leather coat, no purse. The cool Spring evening had brought a faint mist off the lake. She found the address and was greeted by tall iron gates and a buzz box. After getting buzzed-in by person's unknown - she couldn't even identify the gender for certain - she found herself in very luxurious home. Brantley, of course, a grey, balding six footer, greeted her wearing one of his legendary Hawaiian shirts. Very cordially, he directed her to a large, yellow-leather sofa. The floors were burnished hardwood, the walls brick or white stucco, and modern artwork, metal sculpture and paintings, adorned the walls and floor. She realized an interior decorator had done the room in a powerful primary color motif.

She felt very nervous. The colors seemed to swirl and blend into a psychedelic spider's web with her in the epicenter.

"Can I get you anything to drink, my dear?"

"No thanks."

Brantley sat across from her in a matching leather chair. He took the last sip from his mixed drink then placed it in front of him on his massive glass and metal coffee table. "Well, you certainly did a bang up job on the system, Christine. I'm told by everyone, our own people as well as outside consultants, that it's a work of genius. You can be proud of yourself."

"I'm not a genius, Mr. Brantley. Just an overworked temp who deserves to get the full time Webmaster job."

"Of course. You've earned it. Anyone who can tie a computer into knots as you have should be at the head of our information technology department."

"I just want the Webmaster job."

"You got it. You start tomorrow."

"Honest?"

"You have my word on it." Brantley arose and formally shook her hand. "Deal," he added.

"What's the pay?" Christine stood up, too.

"Whatever we're paying the guy we just brought in plus a dollar?"

"Ok," She laughed. She realized she sounded nervous. "Oh, yeah. What about the new guy?"

"You want him as your assistant?"

"Ok."

"Done. Check-in with Audrey in the morning. I'll phone her and let her know that we need to find you an office. I want you up on the 32nd floor with me, where I can watch you." He laughed heartily.

"Ok. I'll see you in the morning then." She started for the front door.

"Sure. Sure. Just one thing before you go, my dear."

"Yeah? What?"

"Can you put the system back before you leave? I'd very much appreciate it."

"Oh, yeah. Sure. No problem." Christine followed Brantley up a set of hardwood stairs to a loft overlooking the grand living room. From somewhere the faint smell of gardenias wafted. He pointed out his personal computer to her. She quickly took up her station in front of the machine and focused on digging out the system.

In the morning, Christine listened as her cellmate repeated, over and over again, "I didn't mean to shoot him." The inflections in her tone informed Christine that her cellmate was Hispanic, probably with roots in Mexico. She had hardly slept that night. Doors clanked all through the night. Occasionally drunken women's voices echoed into her cell. She had no blanket, and she wondered when they would permit her to use the washroom. The forces of oppression had unceremoniously dumped her into the tight, two bunk cell. The cops had busted her the previous evening as she walked up the sidewalk to her apartment. She had to admit to herself that Brantley had fooled her completely. His loss. His total loss, she kept telling herself.

She had never imagined, in her entire life, that she would ever wind up in Cook County Jail. Through the bars and down the corridor she heard someone vomiting. Later she could smell it.

When the guard came for her later in the morning, she was very surprised. She assumed a public defender had come to visit. When they cashed in her bright, fluorescent orange jail suit, and returned her clothes she knew something was up. Maybe Brantley had some second thoughts.

When Art greeted her in the lobby of the big jail complex at 26th Street and California Avenue, she was astonished.

"Why did you bail me?"

"Why? Are you kidding?" He hugged her despite her resistance. She wanted to tell him that she had already cashed him out of her life. She didn't like false pretenses.

"Why did you bail me?" She pulled away from his embrace. He looked like hell, tired, with his hair in knots. Then she realized she probably looked just as disheveled. Dozens of police cars wheeled past in both directions. In the still, early morning air bunches of police jostled past them on the sidewalk. "You're going to be in as much trouble as me, now. They're going to say we planned it together. That it was a conspiracy. I can't believe you're that dumb."

Art didn't answer. She realized that for once he was speechless. Speechless with emotion. Maybe rage.

"Don't get all emotional. Not now. I can't take it. I'm under a lot of stress."

Art shook his head sadly. Then he seemed to catch his breath all at once and said, "Because I love you. Don't you get it?" She noticed he was crying.

And then, all at once, she finally did get it. Her long orphaned emotions, put away into a dark box in the middle of her psyche, burst out. First, she cried. Then she hugged Art. She felt Art's hot tears on her neck. A long time elapsed before she managed to calm herself. She felt embarrassed over her sudden volcanic outburst. Art, of course, wallowed in the eruption and its aftermath, bubbling away with endearments and encouragement. She still didn't quite trust her emotions despite the wisdom they had offered up. And she ardently wished she had better control over them. The cops studiously ignored them and kept marching past in all directions, to court, from court, and back to the streets for more court fodder.

When her 24 hour fail-safe rigging exploded, they were already in New Mexico. She collected her $100,000 Imperial Dog Food check in Albuquerque, then wired it to her Mexico City bank account. By the time they arrived in Santa Fe, Albert Brantley couldn't access his computers anymore. And even if he had, the data bases had all been sent to hell, but only after every temp worker in the company had received a hefty hacker bonus deposited directly into their bank accounts by the Imperial computer.

Chicago Story

When I tackled the skinny kid on the bicycle, I didn't realize how much power and force still resided in my middle-aged body. I was 50. I was fat, but I could still tackle like linebacker. Actually, better. Because when I played high school football, I never had to bring down anybody on a bike.

Anyway, the little thief looked surprised when I bushwhacked him. I came flying out of a North Side Chicago alley and smashed into him with all my 250 pounds.

As we skidded over the broken glass and potholes in the cracked cement street I noted the terror in the kid's eyes, then felt an odd satisfaction; I was going bald, and I looked soft, but 30 years of chucking steel as a machinist had bestowed unnatural strength to my sagging body.

I had anticipated a vicious, animal fightback from the kid. Instead I witnessed fright. He screamed when we banged into the rough pavement then skidded ten feet across the ragged street, him on the bottom, shredding clothing and skin, me on top, weighing him down like a lead shroud. The little cookie jar filled with change shattered when it blasted into the curb, showering me and the kid with quarters, dimes and nickels.

The whole fucking thing started one hot day in July when I was late returning to the factory from lunch. The shop, a tired brick building, was located next to the North Branch of the Chicago River in an area where one small factory after another was getting bulldozed to make way for middle-class people from the suburbs to move into the city. I didn't know why I was so uptight about being two minutes late in returning from lunch - Midwestern work ethic, I guess. The hot dog joint on Western Avenue had been crowded, the cooking crew appeared to be understaffed, and it just plain took forever to get my cheesedogs and fries. When I caught a powerful whiff of perfume, I tried to occupy myself in line by staring at the lovely legs of the young women, but felt guilty about it when one of them turned around and eyeballed me.

I started eating one of the cheesedogs in my car, as I drove back to work. Those cheesedogs had an exotic taste about them. I couldn't decide if it was special spices in the meat, the cheese, or what appeared to be home made buns. Some of the smartasses in the shop said the unique taste was due to the use of horsemeat.

I hated rushing through lunch in the 20 minutes allotted to us. And, like I say, I don't know what my concern was, because they were going to shut the place down at the end of the summer anyway. By Spring, the place would be one more condominium development for the college educated types from the suburbs.

I hated working as a machinist, too. I was sick of the constant pressure to get the parts out. I was sick of the bosses. And I was sick of being treated like I was a moron. But, I was afraid to quit because I couldn't imagine what I'd do for a living.

When I pulled into the factory parkinglot, I was met by the lead man, a professional asshole. "Hey, we ain't payin' you to watch the parkinglot." So, I was frazzled, thinking about the spicy smelling mustard and melted cheese I had spilled down the front of my blue work shirt, and I did the dumbest thing you can do in Chicago. I forgot to lock my car door.

About an hour later, as I was putting in a tricky set-up in a horizontal milling machine, this little Polish guy comes running up to me, all excited. I didn't know this guy very well, in fact, I had only said "hi" to him a couple of times as we passed in the corridors between rows of ancient, oily machines. He worked out on the shipping dock. He seemed like a calm guy, so when he came bouncing up to me, I knew something major was up.

After listening to him spout broken English at me for about a minute, another Polish guy came up, a pal of mine, Al, who happened to be a lathe operator. Al asked him in Polish what the problem was. The guy yelled something back, all the time jumping up and down, while he pointed out the back door.

Al yelled to me as he charged out the back door, "Some fuckin' kid is breaking into your car."

A whole stampede of us ran down the crowded aisle, freaking out the lead man and the owner. The owner was a peckerhead who always wore a suit and tie and liked to watch us through the glass in his air-conditioned blockhouse which was situated in the middle of the shop floor. As we ran out on the loading dock, I saw guys older than myself vaulting over bulky boxes of parts and running down the alley like they were teenagers. Across the parkinglot, we could see this dumb ass kid, maybe 14 years old, maybe 90 pounds, exiting my car and jumping onto a beat-to-shit, red bike. Guys were yelling, and throwing nuts and bolts at him, but the kid, who was wearing Puerto Rican gang colors, calmly mounted the bike and sped off. He was carrying my steering wheel locking device with him.

He went whipping down our little industrial street, then peeled out onto Irving Park Road. He sailed into the afternoon traffic with a breeze from Lake Michigan at his back.

I checked the car. He hadn't done any damage, which was more than I could say for the wrecking crew who had chased him. I found half a dozen dents in my paintjob from nuts and bolts. He had riffled through the glove box. That's when I noticed he had ripped off my flashlight, too. And, I discovered he had ripped off a small steel box that contained an old fashioned drafting compass which had belonged to my father and been passed down to the new generation of machinists. The antique wasn't worth spit, but it had meaning for me. I had forgotten that I had left it in the backseat. I had planned on buffing the piece up, then putting some lacquer on it to preserve it from rust, then mounting it or putting it on display somehow. I went back inside the plant, got my keys, and locked the car.

For the balance of that hot, humid afternoon I could feel my blood boil. If there was anything I hated, it was a fucking petty thief. Its ok to steal from the rich bastards, or the big companies, or the government because they steal from us. Worse, they pretend like it ain't stealing. But stealing from other people, regular people, man, that was conduct unbecoming a human being. I started to hate that fuckin' kid.

The following week the little asshole broke into Al's car. He tried to steal his radio, but the little Polish guy on the dock had been watching extra careful. His vigilance paid off. We nearly caught the little prick that time, but we weren't quite fast enough. The kid infuriated everybody when he gave us the high sign with his middle finger as he glided out onto Irving Park Road. We watched him soar down the crowded boulevard uninhibited by traffic regulations. Talk about adding insult to injury. That's when I resolved to catch him.

I decided to keep it simple. We set the bait, an unlocked car with a small cookie jar of change on the front seat. We parked the car close to the loading dock. Al went up on the roof of the factory and took a cell phone with him. We had a hard time keeping the little Polish guy off the loading dock. Then we stationed the big, mean machinist in the alley next to the escape route.

I had intended to beat the little asshole into unconsciousness - then drop a dime on him and have the Chicago cops shovel him into an ambulance. But, standing on top of him with my pants leg torn and my bloody knee sticking out, I wondered about all that.

I could tell the kid was dizzy from the crash. He couldn't get oriented and his limbs were pulling in different directions. I was wired from the exhilaration of victory. I had nailed him, but good.

"Get your foot off me, cocksucker."

"What?"

"I SAY, get your motherfuckin' foot off me, man."

I was standing with my steel toed boot on his chest. I moved it to his throat and put on a little extra pressure. He wiggled fiercely. He looked pretty well lacerated from the crash followed by the slide over the jagged pavement.

"Mighty bold words for somebody who's about to have their throat crushed."

He wiggled. I shifted even more weight on him until he held still, then I let up a notch, and he gasped for air. Blood was seeping through his white t-shirt. I felt sorry for the little asshole despite myself. I admired his fighting spirit.

"What's your name, Puerto Rican boy?" I let up another notch enabling him to draw enough air to speak.

"Fuck you."

"Wrong answer." I shifted weight back on him. He waved his hands in surrender after a moment. I let off again.

"Hector."

"Hector what?"

"Who the fuck are you, man. The fuckin' police? Fuck you. I don't tell you my fuckin' name." I shifted my weight back on him to shut him up, while I decided what I was going to do - stomp him into jelly, or pick him up and dust him off. The guys from the shop had gathered around by then, and were yelling for me to vaporize him.

"Oh, man, you wrecked my bike." And indeed, I had wrecked Hector's bike big time. Both wheels had been bent into an "S" shape. The chain had broken and dangled from the wreck, and one of the pedals had broken off. Clearly, the mangled bike was finished.

Finally, I decided to give the dumb fucker a break. I yanked him up onto his feet. He faltered and fell right back down again. I realized I had already knocked the crap out of him. He tried to get up under his own power, but fell back onto his already bloody knees.

Across the street the lead man yelled out one of the windows, "What the fuck are you guys doing? Are you on strike or what?" The crowd broke up immediately. Everyone started shuffling back across the street. "How about it, mill hand? We got fucking work to do here."

"Fuck you, I'm on strike," I yelled back.

Of course, they fired me. They had to make an example of somebody who said, "Fuck you, I'm on strike." I didn't give a fuck, I was sick of production machining. 30 years was enough for anybody. I had money in the bank, I could afford to take some time off and think things through.

Hector started hangin' with me at my cousin's garage under the Ravenswood L tracks, while I tried to repair his bike. Of course, that was after he returned my compass, and agreed that he was done ripping off people. After a half dozen repair sessions, I thought the thing was coming around, but Hector announced that it would never be the same. Too many repair parts - it just wasn't his bike anymore. But my buddies marveled at my repairs. Maybe it didn't look like Hector's bike anymore, but it sure looked good, and I was damn proud of it.

I found that I liked working alone, no boss, just me and the metal.

So, I bought him a new bike. One like the people from the suburbs were using. The fucking thing cost me nearly two weeks of skilled metalworker pay. I tried talking him into working in a machine shop with some of my buddies. But he only lasted a couple of days, then he was out racing around on his bike again.

I opened a one-man bicycle repair shop.

The last time I saw Hector, he was flying underneath the L tracks racing the train above.

The Crab Box

Lakeysha felt proud as she drove a battered, used automobile off a tiny used car-lot on Chicago's West Side. She had managed to work her way off welfare, quit drugs, regain custody of her three children, and move out of the housing project.

Now, finally, she owned a car and could drive to a bank branch in the distant suburbs where she had been promoted. Although her new job site was far beyond the reach of public transportation, she would no longer have to worry about fellow West Siders sticking her up at gun point. In her six months on the job at her West Side city site, she had already looked down the barrels of .357 magnums, a 9 millimeter, and one 12 gauge shotgun.

She drove directly to her aunt's house to show off her new automobile. Her aunt had raised her after her mother had passed from severe diabetes. Unfortunately, when she arrived, she found her uncle, a confirmed alcoholic, beating her aunt with an umbrella. After considerable difficulty, she broke up the beating. Still raging, her uncle departed for the local tavern. Unbeknownst to Lakeysha, he liberally poured the contents of an entire box of sugar cubes into her gas tank, as thanks for breaking up a perfectly enjoyable beating.

A week later, when her car mysteriously quit running, she lost her job because she no longer had the means of getting to the suburbs. Her old bank branch had already filled her old position. And, in short order, she lost her new apartment because she couldn't pay the rent without a job, and then her children, because she had become homeless. Naturally, her uncle wouldn't permit her to return to aunt's apartment.

In the homeless shelter, they assigned Lakeysha duties helping the old cook, an ancient woman was full of stories of New Orleans and endless seafood recipes. The old woman kept a large box of live, donated crabs on one end of the kitchen counter.

To dull the pain of her recent setbacks, Lakeysha resumed her old habit of smoking marijuana. If she permitted the food delivery man to feel her up, she could always persuade him to leave her a joint. She didn't care if she couldn't pass a pre-employment drug test anymore.

Curious why the old woman never put a cover on the teeming mass of live crabs, Lakeysha asked, "Why don't you cover them crabs? Ain't you afraid one of them is gonna get out and escape?"

"No, honey. I knows my crabs. Every time one of them fixes to climb out the box, the other ones grab it by the foot and pulls it back. Uh, huh. That's a well known fact. I been cookin' seafood for 60 years. Ain't none of them crabs goin' nowheres."

Greg Norton Meets Paul Auster

First there was Greg, then Auster showed up, then Pink showed up. Last there was Brown. But Greg wasn't Gregory Alan Norton, the psychosocial author, and Paul Auster wasn't the famous bourgeois author. Greg actually had a dream that he met Paul in the Heartland Cafe, in Chicago's far North Side neighborhood of Rogers Park. Greg was sitting outside on the patio on a warm September afternoon enjoying a sandwich when Paul suddenly manifested himself and asked if he could join him.

At first, Greg, who is straight, thought his might be a homosexual come-on, but he noticed Paul was eyeballing the women in the cafe, even as he asked to sit at the table. Greg, being a communist type, believed in sharing all public conveyances, including cafe tables, so he said, "Yeah, sure, why not?"

"Sorry to inconvenience you, but I'm from New York. I'm in town for a book signing party, and I think somebody has put a private detective on me. " I watched Paul glance across the street in the direction of a massive railroad embankment that split the neighborhood. As I looked along the same vector as Paul, I noticed a brunette woman, maybe in her 30s, with a notebook, slip back into the shadows of the road underpass beneath the tracks. In the distance she looked tall, and was wearing white pants and a wheat colored blouse.

"Didja see that?"

"Yeah. She saw us looking and disappeared herself."

Paul turned and faced me. "I'm truly sorry about this. Let me introduce myself, I'm Paul Auster."

After a perfunctory handshake we both involuntarily shifted our gazes toward the underpass and the woman lurking in it. "Why don't you just go and confront her?"

Auster glanced at me, frowned, and lowered his chin, his face plainly communicating the thought, "Now, there's a dumbass idea." "Think she's going to be forthcoming about the reason for following me, do you?"

"Probably not, but it would probably discourage her, and she'd break it off."

"Yes, but that wouldn't give me very much information would it? Who ever is paying for her services would simply hire another person who would simply be a bit more discrete, more professional in disguising themselves. Then I would be followed and wouldn't be aware of it. This way, I know to look out."

"I'm Greg Norton by the way." I decided to complete the introductions. "I'm a writer, too."

Auster suddenly stopped surveilling the underpass. "Really? What have you written?"

"*There Ain't No Justice, Just Us,*" a novel.

"Sorry, I'm not familiar with your work." A troubled look crossed his face, and he changed his chair position so he could look past me and survey the underpass while appearing to be in conversation with me. "Excuse me. You were saying... about your novel."

"Yeah, its about a wildcat strike on the South Side of Chicago that occurred in 1979."

"Oh...?"

I had read Auster's essays and knew he tried to stay current with as much contemporary writing as he could. "You know you could lead her into a blind alley somewhere, loop around behind her, then confront her. It would take a little planning, put you could do it. If you got her frightened enough, she'd spill the beans."

Auster's face beamed an indignant look in my direction. "I'd sooner invite her to lunch than pull something like that. I'm not a thug."

"Want me to go invite her?"

Auster paused. "I actually wrote about a situation like this in one of my novels, where a character breaks bread with his shadow."

"So, life imitates art. I'll go get her and invite her to lunch."

"No rough stuff."

I got up and headed out of the cafe. As soon as I turned down the sidewalk, I could see the woman on the other side of the underpass, jotting down notes. She didn't seem to notice me, and I was upon her in less than a minute.

"Hey, why don't you join me and a friend for lunch? "

She looked up in astonishment from her non-descript, red, spiral notebook. She obviously hadn't seen me coming. She was a beautiful young woman with brown eyes, curly, shoulder length hair, and a great figure. Stunned by my presence she stood there speechless.

I gently guided her elbow toward the cafe, "Comon, free lunch. What do you have to loose? I've got a great friend, I want you to meet. He's a famous author."

Some people can be psychologically dominated, and this woman was one of them. She pulled her elbow free of my grip, but she did follow me. "I don't even know you. Why should I have lunch with you?"

"Because my buddy is a famous author."

"Famous author? Who?"

"Paul Auster." I glanced over my shoulder and noted that she was following me, however reluctantly.

"Paul this is ...."

"Jennifer."

"Jennifer this is Paul Auster, author of the *New York Trilogy*, *Mr. Vertico*, *Moon Palace*, and a bunch of other stuff, too.

"Well, hello," said Auster.

Looking embarrassed, Jennifer sat down at our table. She kept her notebook in her lap. Wanting to take full advantage of her discomfiture and mental disarray, I tried to keep up the banter. "So, it looks like you're a writer, too, Jennifer." I pointed to her notebook.

"Yes, that's why we thought we'd invite you, " said Auster. "Greg here is an author, too. We were discussing writing techniques."

She nodded absently at Auster. "So, what are you writing?" I asked.

"Oh, I'm not a writer. I was just taking some... real estate notes about houses in the neighborhood."

"So, you're a real estate agent. Give me your card, I'm looking to buy a place in the neighborhood."

"Well, I'm not a real estate agent, I'm just a researcher."

"Ah ha. Taking notes about the conditions of the houses I take it." I said.

"Yes. That's right."

"Bullshit. You're following Auster and writing down notes about his activities." I was growing tired of all the crap. I'm not a middle class person. I'm industrial working class, and where I come from, you get all the cards on the table. Jennifer, if that was her real name, looked even more stunned than she did when I first confronted her in the underpass.

"I..."

"Lets just fucking see your notebook." I extended my hand.

"Please," said Auster. "No need to be rude to the young lady."

But as he apologized, she passed the red notebook over to me.

"Look, Jennifer, I want to apologize to you for Greg's behavior."

"Yeah, you were right Auster. She's been following you since you landed at O'Hare Airport. Says here you flew in on a United flight last night at 11:30 PM. You had a limo waiting that took you to the Allegro Hotel. You stayed in room 423. And you had room service bring you a bottle of red wine at 1 A.M.

You clocked out of the hotel this morning at 10 AM and took the L to the Morse Station. You took a cab to a bookstore on Sheridan Road. You walked over to the Lake Michigan beach. You played with somebody's yellow dog. Then a blonde woman picked you up and drove you to another book store on Clark Street. You did a book signing for a couple of hours. Then you walked to an outdoor cafe... No notes after that. I guess that brings us up to date, except for who's paying you to follow Paul?"

They both sat there looking dumbfounded. Auster, apparently because his prognostication about being followed had been correct. And "Jennifer," because she had been publicly caught out. I broke the silence. "I swear to God, I'm gonna write a short story about this, Paul. This shit is too much like your books."

"All art is infested by other art, according to Leo Steinberg, the art historian," said Auster as he carefully examined the red notebook.

"So, what gives, Jennifer. Who you working for?" I asked, not wanting to give her time to invent a story.

"A guy in Florida named Brown. My code name is Pink."

Auster and I exchanged meaningful glances. "Brown" was one of his fictional characters who had retired to Florida.

I smiled at Auster, "Think of the history of art as a supermarket of ideas. I think Anna Held Audette said that.

Jennifer stared at us blankly, "Huh?" was her response. The lake breeze briefly flapped open the top of purse, and in the owner's patch I clearly saw the name "Lillian."

"Brown never mentioned why he wanted you to follow me?"

"No. I just pick up the money in a lock box once a week down at Union Station."

"Once a week? How long have you been doing this?" I asked.

"Oh, I just started yesterday, but Brown said this would be a long term assignment." A waitress arrived and distributed new menus. Jennifer started looking hers over mumbling something about "using an ice tea." Auster simply sat there looking stunned while a cool lake breeze bathed the neighborhood with fresh air. Overhead a screeching lake gull wheeled in the air.

"How did you meet Brown," I asked.

"Well, I'm in grad school, so I work at an escort service, and my boss asked me last week if I wanted some private detective work. I'm not very good at the escort work, so I don't get many calls back, I need the money, so I said, OK."

"I'd call you back." This slipped out of my mouth without prior mental monitoring. Something unusual for me. This was only the third woman I had ever met who admitted working as a hooker.

Pink smiled faintly in my direction.

Auster said, "So, your boss knows Brown?"

"Yeah, I guess."

"What's his name?" Auster and I asked in unison.

"Mr. Blue."

Again, another "fictional" character from the Auster cannon. "Well, I think you can handle this from this point forward, Paul. You're familiar with Brown and Blue. You can figure out how to locate them. Write your address down on the napkin, and I'll send you a copy of my novel for review and promotion."

"Wait a minute..."

"Yeah, I know. You only promote work you believe in. You actually do have morals and principals and live up to them. I understand. I'll mail you the book."

"As long as that is understood..."

"Yeah, yeah, I've read your stuff."

"You're right, of course, I know about Blue and Brown. I thought that was all over with."

I turned to Jennifer. "How about a date this afternoon? We can take the L downtown, and I'll show you Buckingham Fountain this evening."

"I can't. I'm on the job. I have to follow Paul around."

"I'll pay if you give me a discount on the standard rate. After all, Blue doesn't get his cut of this one."

"I'll take the L back downtown with you," said Auster. "I can meet you guys at Buckingham Fountain. I'm tired, I'm just going to take a nap in my hotel room. Nothing worth noting in this," he waved the red notebook as he handed it back to her.

"Ok, then." Jennifer cheerfully agreed. Turning to Auster she said, "Did you want to get in..."

"No, no, no. I'm happily married."

I shrugged a big "so what" in Auster's direction. He gently waved his hands back and forth, "no way."

Greg Norton proceeded to write down the story of that dream encounter in the red notebook after he enjoyed the delights of Jennifer. Later, Blue would find him in a parked car in Humboldt Park, and thought he would have an easy job of murdering him. Probably as easy as Grey-Green had it up in Vermont that time with the kid, only this time, he was the one with the bat. Consequently he didn't bother concealing his baseball bat as he crossed the street. Norton spotted him through the windshield. Blue was very surprised when Norton neatly put one round into each of his knees using a .38 caliber pistol, one of a matching brace once owned by Gray-Green and his son Di Maggio. And so it goes in the self-referencing meta-literature of postmodernism.

Wildcat

When the strike at our factory finally erupted, it tore through ties of friendship and family and produced the entire zodiac of emotions from elation of the strikers to fear of job loss by all.

Of course, I didn't know it then, back in my high school days in the 1960s, but I was a sensitive artistic type. However, when I looked in the mirror, I saw a hulking young man over six feet tall and 200 pounds who maintained a permanent scowl that frightened everybody. I scowled because I hated school, I hated the factory, and I hated my life.

Our shop, Bastard and Blessing, sat directly on the east bank of the north branch of the Chicago River just north of Irving Park Road in a working class neighborhood of diverse European and Latin nationalities. When I walked in the door in the morning, the stench of machine oils, solvents, and metal cutting fluids struck my nose with its sour bouquet. In the afternoons, when all the machines were singing their daily, atonal satanic symphony, the air turned blue with burning oil. Behind the factory, down the steep river bank, houseboats had sunk in the narrow river. Older folks told me that families had to live on the boats during the great depression of the 1930s.

I worked in the burr room, an area of the factory fenced off by chicken wire from the rest of the shop. I worked there because that's where the 16 and 17 year old rookies always started out. We were drenched in the pungent stink from the carbon tetrachloride tanks. We all worked for BB Brain, the six foot four inch tall Irish foreman, or B squared as the young guys called him. Our job consisted of hand filing sharp edges and cleaning cutting oil off parts.

And, at the age of 17, my fate had already been sealed. When I graduated high school, I was supposed to follow my father's career path and become a precision machinist. I hated that idea, too.

Christine Croce, my Italian girlfriend with jet black hair and blue eyes, worked in the shipping and receiving department. Many days, the only reason I came to work, was to see her. We were making plans to get married after we graduated and were working on saving up enough money to put a down payment on a small house. My buddies, who were all on the same mission, to date every girl in Chicago, respected our relationship. Maybe they just respected my permanent scowl, but instead of poking us with annoying jokes, they spoke in the same tones about Christine and I as they did about their religion or parents.

Like a lot of people, I had other family members working in the shop, too. My father, who had gotten me the job, worked in the tool room as a tool and die maker. My crazy French great-uncle, Etienne, worked as a fork lift driver. And, of course, everybody had a plan for me: Christine wanted me to get a tool and die apprenticeship to stay out of the military draft for the Vietnam War, my father wanted me to get a tool and die apprenticeship so I would be in the skilled trades and earn enough money to support my future family, and Etienne wanted me to get a job as a union organizer so I could organize the shop and get a living wage for the unskilled people and address Bastard and Blessing regarding all the hazardous conditions in the factory.

Etienne, a tall old man with a white beard, had to endure the calumny of racial epithets every day. The bosses called him, "Frenchy, French Fry, Froggy," or just plain "Frog." "Frenchy" was supposed to be the friendly version and "Frog" is what they called him after he had annoyed them, which was frequently. Etienne had grown up in Europe as an anarcho-syndicalist. He had deserted the French army in 1915 during World War I because, like the Bolsheviks, he refused to kill working class soldiers of other countries. When he got to the United States, according to the old hands in my mother's family, he had gone through a brief period of prideful patriotism in his adopted country and worked overtime at becoming a U.S. citizen.

Unfortunately, once he had succeeded in 1917, his grateful new government promptly drafted him and sent him in a different uniform to within one and a half miles of the location he had deserted two years previously. This unexpected turn of events only fanned the flames of his fiery, idealistic revolutionary temperament. At break times in the factory, he sat on a 55 gallon drum out on the loading dock wearing his burgundy beret, and speaking with a strong French accent, urged people to demonstrate against the Vietnam War or bring a union into the shop.

My father, a confirmed Anglo-Saxon, hated it whenever my mother's family members, the Lissagarays, visited and the old folks started speaking in French. Whenever I started spouting it, I'd get the evil eye, and I knew I had better get back to English. After all, my last name was MacNaughton. My father had gotten Etienne his job, as well, to his eternal regret. He was constantly telling the old man to keep his mouth shut, because the bosses knew he was back there spouting off about the union.

One winter's afternoon we heard a siren approach the factory. Then it cut off. Then, after a long pause, it resumed. We assumed there had been another traffic accident on the icy Irving Park Road bridge over the river. Then I saw my co-workers in the deburring room leaping off their shop stools and clustering by the doorway leading to the main aisle. I followed them to the doorway where we were treated to the sight of Etienne leading a fairly large group of women down the aisle toward the front office.

"Come on, don't be afraid. We must raise this issue with the manager. If we don't, more people will be injured." Etienne shouted.

Christine had apparently joined the agitated group as it left her department. I asked her, "What's going on?"

"Yolanda Cruz cut off part of her finger in the automatic broaching machine. We've been asking the foreman for guards on those machines for over a year. They keep telling us, they're going to get to it, but they never do."

I recognized Yolanda's name. She was a middle-aged Puerto Rican woman who kept chickens in her dilapidated garage. Sometimes my father bought eggs from her. Her husband had been killed in the Korean War, and she had three kids about my age.

"We're going up front to complain. They took Yolanda in an ambulance."

Etienne spotted me, "This is your big chance. Help these people. Explain to the bosses what are the problems here."

"Me? No way. My father would kill me." I was already scanning the growing crowd for my father's face but the tool room was on the other side of the building. It would take some time for the news to reach them.

"Come on, Peter. You must help. My English is not good enough for this." Etienne had grasped me by the elbow. Meanwhile, the deafening clatter of the machinery slowly ceased, replaced by the wild shouting of the ever growing mob. I saw BB Brain hustling up to the front office ahead of us.

Christine edged in next to us, "Are you coming with us, or what?"

"What the hell, we're all gonna get fired if we go up there."

"Oh, man, what's with you?" asked Christine.

I managed to squirm out of Etienne's grasp. "Peter, we cannot wait."

Someone yelled, "Here they come." Everyone looked up toward the front office and beheld the young man who ran the personnel department purposefully striding down the aisle in our direction. He was followed by

BB Brain and another department boss. The young guy, Hess, was wearing a dark suit, white shirt and tie. BB Brain and friend were wearing their usual rolled up white shirts and black ties. The group of managers stopped in front of the assembled workers. Etienne and Christine stood in the front row. I back peddled toward the burr room.

Hess yelled, "Alright, everyone. I understand everybody is upset. We are going to get guards put on those machines today. Please return to your work stations. We're losing a lot of production. Everybody needs to return to work."

People shouted back "Where's the guarantee you're gonna get it done?" and "That ain't the only thing that needs fixin'."

"I personally guarantee all the broachers will have guards on them as soon as possible." Hess shouted.

"My ass." An unknown man from the rear of the crowd shouted back.

"I understand you're upset. But losing a lot of money for the company isn't going to help the situation. You all need to be working so we can afford to put guards on the machines."

And that was the exact wrong thing for Hess to say.

"Who you trying to kid? You guys are making a fortune with this company. You ain't paying us nothin'," an unknown woman shouted from the rear ranks. The crowd roared approval. People were shaking their fists in the air.

BB Brain stepped forward and acted like he was going to say something. Hess said something to him which I couldn't hear over all the yelling from the workers, and BB Brain crisply stepped back. Hess held his arms up and fluttered his hands to signal the crowd to quiet down. Surprisingly, it worked.

"Look, I'm just as upset about this as you all are. I would like to get over to the hospital to visit her to see how she's doing, but I can't until you all go back to work."

"Worried about your insurance premiums are you?" someone shouted.

"I'm as concerned about her as you are."

"Bullshit."

"Please." He fluttered them down again. And people were finally beginning to quiet down. It looked like the energy was dissipating from the group. Force of habit was calling them back to the machines.

"What about medical insurance? And what about a raise for everybody?" Etienne shouted.

"Yeah!" Christine shouted. And turning to the women in the front, got them all yelling again, too.

"This is not the time for all that. If you all want to discuss that, we can arrange a round table discussion after work. Now everybody needs to get back to work, damnit."

"There will be no work without a negotiation," Etienne yelled. The roar of approval behind that formulation was heard in the front office.

"Look are you people going to follow a troublemaker? Let's get back to work. We can discuss the rest of this some other time."

No one made a move toward dispersing. "Would you two like to discuss this up front? If everyone else goes back to work, I'd be happy to go over things with you two."

Etienne said, "No, you discuss with everybody right now."

"Be reasonable. We can't do that. Come on. Let's talk." Hess turned around and beckoned Christine and Etienne. Christine and another woman followed immediately.

"No, wait. This is a trick," said Etienne.

"Oh, come on. Do you want to talk or not?" said Hess.

"Comon, Etienne," said Christine. "This is our chance. They want to talk."

"This is not correct," said Etienne following the two women who were having difficulty keeping up with Hess as he strode back to the front office.

At first the group attempted to stay put while the leaders discussed things in the front office. But BB Brain and the other boss worked on convincing people, one on one, to return to work while they waited, and in short order they had everybody, including me, back in their harness. The commotion had gone on during afternoon break, so there was no chance for people to socialize across departments until quitting time. But small groups gathered and talked until managers walked over and dissipated them.

I watched the listless people from second shift line up by the time clocks as usual. BB Brain stood as a guardian by the clock. Something unusual for him. At the end of the shift he was generally in the front office filling out his production report. Then I watched an older Polish man from the loading dock going down the line saying something to the people in the line. Most of the second shift was Polish. Whatever he was saying was causing an instantaneous commotion. BB Brain strode over to the line, but instead of staying in line, most of them walked out with the old guy.

Then, about five minutes before quitting time, I heard all the women from Christine's department yelling as they headed out the door with their coats, tool boxes, and other belongings. I didn't see Christine in the group. Someone yelled, "They fired them!"

Then, my father, who I hadn't seen all day, appeared at my side. "I'm glad to see you didn't caught up in this bullshit." He took off his blue shop apron. Then he pulled off his thick eyeglasses and methodically cleaned each lens with a special lens cleaning paper.

"What's going on?"

"Whatta think? They fired those guys."

"Who?"

"Your idiot uncle and your girlfriend." My father casually lit his Lucky Strike. He had his coat and cap, and as usual, had come by to pick me up. We would wait in the burr room until punch out time.

"Why is everybody leaving? They're all gonna get docked for leaving early."

"Those guys? They think they're on strike. Only problem is, we ain't got a union. So they're all fired, but they don't realize it yet. You should see the front of the factory. Cops got 'em on the other side of the street."

Sure enough, after we punched and walked to the parking lot, we could see the majority of the people on the other side of Irving Park Road, in a park, yelling and holding up "On Strike" signs.

"What are we gonna do?" I asked.

"Whatta think? Make the best of it. I can't quit workin'. How the hell do I pay the bills, if I ain't workin'?

I tried to ignore the yelling from across the street, as we walked through the black slush in the parking lot to get to my father's Cadillac. Then I heard my name called, looked up, and saw Christine beckoning me across the street to the mass picket line.

My life took an interesting turn during the strike. Of course Christine didn't like what my father and I were doing, and every night she either phoned or came over to our apartment to try to talk me into striking. Etienne quit talking to me. So did my mother, both my sisters, and everybody else who spoke French in the family. My father got the same treatment, but he didn't seem to care. As long as he was working, he was happy.

I didn't like walking from the parking lot to the back factory entrance because everybody was yelling shit at us, like "Scab" and worse. But the strike did bring some fresh attractions. First, BB Brain suggested that I could start an apprenticeship because both apprentices had been fired. Second, Linda Choate, daughter of the big boss, Charles Choate, had come to work in the factory. Their family was from the wealthy North Shore suburb of Wilmette.

What I liked about Linda was that she didn't wear jeans and t-shirts all the time like Christine. She dressed like a woman in dresses, blouses, nylons, nail polish and make-up. I had seen Christine dressed like a man so often that I found myself talking to her like she was a man. With Linda I had a man to woman relationship, like its supposed to be, one where you can get that magic feeling about somebody.

And I felt like I had become somebody who counted, too. The company had put me into a "junior managerial training program." They assured me that if the government attempted to draft me they would write a letter and get that canceled.

But the strike, in its second week, wasn't going good for the company. At first they got some black people from the South Side to cross the picket lines to run some of the machines that could be learned in a couple of hours. They brought them in via a temp agency and crossed the lines in school busses with the windows painted over. But when those people realized they had been brought in as strike breakers, they all left. They tried to recruit some more, but the word was out on the South Side.

Then they tried a group from the West Side, mainly young people. They brought them in the same way, but got a slightly different result. After they figured out what was going on, they joined the picket line for the balance of the day. The temp agency refused to pick them up, and the strikers took a collection for bus fare back home for them.

My father told me that a "real" union was helping, now, The United Steelworkers. He said it was impossible for a wildcat strike to last that long.

Anyway, I liked the leadership role the company had begun to assign me. On Tuesdays and Wednesdays I got to put on a suit and tie (the company paid for it) and after work, I would call on people at their apartments and try to talk them into coming back to work. Mostly people were polite and told me I was mislead, or too young to realize what was going on. Sometimes they suggested I might be stupid or that the company was pumping me up.

And the company was hurting, those of us in the shop could see that. Two thirds of the people were on strike. And instead of them dribbling back like Mr. Tully (BB Brain's real name I discovered) had suggested, the drain was going the other way. People were hammering on their friends or relatives at night until they joined the walk-out. Bringing in the strike breakers accelerated that process.

One night Christine caught me and Linda Choate in front of the house of one of the women who worked in her department. Linda and I were supposed to be talking the woman into returning to work. Instead, we decided to kiss and make out in her car, parked directly in front of the brick apartment building. Christine had come for the same purpose, to make sure the woman stayed on strike.

She banged on the driver side window where Linda was sitting. Linda didn't see her because she was kissing me while I worked my hands down the front of her dress. Linda twisted around and in one fluid motion pulled down her dress and adjusted her bra. Christine was rapping on the window so hard I thought she was going to break it. Linda rolled down the window.

"I just wanted to let you two know there's no need to make a visit here. Everybody here is union. We're not going back until we get a contract."

That was the first time I had heard the word "contract." I knew they were talking to a regular union.

"Well, I wouldn't expect you people to understand what's best anyway. You're all going to lose your jobs if the company goes bankrupt. None of our competitors have unions. You're going to organize yourselves right out of a job." Linda started rolling the window back up.

"You people? Who's you people?" Christine looked at me.

"You uneducated people who follow communists."

"She's talking about your uncle, Peter. " Christine spoke through the rapidly disappearing gap between window and car frame, "We can't afford to keep your damn jobs anyway, unless they start paying more."

"Let's leave," Linda said to me as she started the car.

Christine waved to me.

Inside the shop we were down to the skilled trades men, machinists, die makers, electricians, and some set-up men and group leaders from different departments. And a curious process was unfolding for me and them. The bosses, like BB Brain, were having to spend a lot of their time at customer's factories doing public relations work in order to keep some contracts. Especially one big outfit, Blue Sky, a wholly owned subsidiary of Pumping Sunshine, because there was talk they might buy the company. Because I could do trigonometry and could see the big production picture that the bosses had to explain to me, I had slowly become the chief shop floor manufacturing guy. Even my father had to bring me prints and discuss how they had to be modified in order to get production out. Of course, he remained master in his tiny area, but I had the handle on the big picture.

Then one night they had assigned me to visit Yolanda Cruz. I didn't think much about it. Linda didn't accompany me because she was preparing for her debutante dance and party that they were planning to hold at the Conrad Hilton Hotel downtown. She had informed me that I couldn't go, it was only for people from her community. That didn't really bother me, either. I didn't want to go. I never really felt right around so many wealthy people. I didn't understand the social conventions from the chit-chat to the table settings.

Anyway, I tramped up six flights of stairs to get to Yolanda's apartment which was located near Humboldt Park. The building was located next to a parallel alley just north of North Avenue. I got a funny feeling when I walked up to the building. When I was a kid in the 1950s, the L had run through that alley. Now, nobody even realized that the alley had once been filled with steel superstructure and trains taking people to and fro. I stopped for a minute and looked down the alley toward the east where the L had joined up with the still existing Logan Square line. I had always seen the L as a ticket out of town, a conveyance of liberation from the fucked-up lives we had to live. When we were kids, hanging out the windows, watching the neighborhoods whiz by, it was a way to forget all your troubles.

Now, in the alley, I felt like I had some secret, ancient knowledge that others in the neighborhood were not privy too. And because the train didn't come there anymore, I felt abandoned.

I waited in the fetid hallway after pounding on Yolanda's door. It smelled like somebody had pissed on the tattered rug.

Yolanda answered the door. "Yes? Oh, its you. They told me to look out for you." Yolanda was a beautiful woman despite being middle-aged. "Come in."

Most people didn't let me in. They usually just politely talked to me through the half opened door. Inside her apartment, everything was a mess, the TV and radio were both blaring, and she was attending to a child around the age of five or so who was seated at the kitchen table. She was wearing a low-cut blouse and her hair had been recklessly piled and pinned. "What can I do for you? Do you want some coffee? I have good coffee." I noticed the stub of her finger was still bandaged. The broacher had cut off half her finger.

"No, this is a business call, Yolanda. I'm here to ask you to return to work."

"Why should I go back to work? I can't feed my children on the wages Bastard and Blessing pays. I might as well stay home and starve instead of going down there and working all day, then starving."

She said that in such a honest, matter-of-fact way that I couldn't answer her. While I sat there speechless at the end of the table, she coaxed the child, a little girl, to eat what looked like pieces of fried banana. Eventually, after a long silence on my part, she turned to face me. "Yeah?" she asked.

"Uh…"

"All I get there is minimum wage. I cannot support my granddaughter, here. Or myself. Or my children. I should be packing my stuff in boxes, because I am not going to be able to pay the rent this month. And where am I going to go? I don't have a deposit for another apartment. So then what happens to us? We go out and live in the snow?" She started crying. "My oldest son delivers newspapers, shovels snow, but it ain't enough. He's gonna have to drop out of school and get a full time job to support us. Then he's gonna get drafted because they take the Puerto Ricans before they take you white boys."

I didn't know what to say because she was right. I was used to living with my father's skilled wages and my semi-skilled wages. We never had to worry about the rent, and we always had food and gasoline for the car.

"I don't know about all this stuff. But I think you're wrong. If the Steelworkers didn't give me twenty bucks in strike pay this week, we'd be starving, man."

The next morning, instead of going to work, I stopped at my uncle's apartment in Uptown. With unconcealed delight he handed me a Steelworker card to sign. I got my pink slip in the mail from Bastard and Blessing the next day. When the remaining guys in the shop heard about me getting fired, they all walked too, including my old man. At the next

Organizing Committee meeting which was held in a church by the lake on Lawrence Avenue, I got elected to the organizing committee.

A week later we walked into the corporate offices of one of the biggest customers, Blue Sky, located in a fancy "corporate campus" in the northwest suburbs. The buildings had been newly constructed and looked lavish with landscaping on the exterior, and fountains, art work, and miles of expensive carpet in the interior. Bastard and Blessing had asked to hold the meeting at a "neutral location."

Our advisor from the Steelworkers, Karl, a big guy who always needed a shave, and who liked to constantly crack jokes, told us to look out, Blue Sky wasn't neutral. But after five weeks of striking, people were running out of money and were willing to agree to meet just about anywhere. The company could see that, too. The picket line was down to a half-dozen per shift, people who had to show up to get their strike pay.

I could tell from the start that Hess and Choate had no intention of settling with us. They provoked everybody on the committee and wouldn't budge and inch on our requests for medical insurance, a safety committee, a safety budget, modest raises, and recognition of the Steelworkers. They wouldn't even allow Karl into the meeting because he didn't work there.

One thing led to another. We started arguing. It got hot when Hess called Etienne, "Froggy." Hess worked out on in Lincoln Park health club on a regular basis, but I had been chucking steel. So, when I sucker punched him with an upper cut, his feet probably came three inches off the floor.

Long story short, Hess had a busted jaw. Hess was in Ravenswood Hospital and the cops transferred me from the nice suburban lock up to the Cook County Jail at 26th and California. I phoned Linda from the jail, but her comment was "Are you kidding?" Then Karlny showed up and said they were raising bail. Karl said the newspapers had run the story and now there were reporters and photographers out on the picket line which had been growing. He said neighborhood people were out there, now, too. He estimated five or six hundred people were milling around on the sidewalks in front of the plant. Only two hundred people worked there. After Karl and I split a big Hershey bar, the cops told him to move on.

Christine and Etienne showed up later and bailed me. She had feared the cops would beat the hell out of me. So she was uncharacteristically emotional when we met up. We wound up kissing in the car, as Etienne drove home.

The next morning Blue Sky phoned the Steelworkers and said they were ready to settle. They had bought out Bastard and Blessing. Blue Sky asked the suburban cops to drop the charges on me. The Steelworkers said they would handle Hess's lawsuit against me.

Etienne declined to run for union office, and I got elected president of the local. They elected Yolanda Vice President. Old Etienne made sure he came to every union meeting to raise hell about why the union wasn't doing more on various grievances. After Christine and I got married, we finally negotiated for health insurance. Linda graduated from Yale and got a job as an intern in the Nixon administration. The Steelworkers made the law suit go away. And BB Brain, he just kept on being BB Brain.

The Terrorist

I was trying to surreptitiously smoke a joint the July day Dick Richhead barged into my tiny private investigator's office. I hadn't lit the roach from the night before yet, so the sweet, ubiquitous odor of marijuana had not yet blanketed the room. I palmed the roach. I thought the smoke tended to mask the other rancid smells in the hermetically sealed space.

The office was located near northwest of Chicago's Loop in an ancient industrial area. The factories had moved out, and wealthy suburbanites were moving into the area, cutting the massive brick buildings into lofts. Of course, after dark, the legions of homeless returned from their daytime sojourns around the city and filled the neighborhood.

"You're MacNaughton, right?"

I pointed to the wall in back of him where my state license hung, proclaiming Peter MacNaughton had the right to do private investigations. During that diversion I managed to pocket the joint in my sports coat.

I looked up from my office chair into the eyes of a older, blonde man, maybe six feet tall. He was wearing an expensive pin stripped charcoal grey suit.

"Yeah," I stood up and shook hands, aware of the social divide between my jeans, casual shirt, work boots and seedy corduroy coat and the obvious full corporate citizen in front of me.

I never came into contact with guys like this. I tracked down missing persons for a fee. I did a lot of it on the Internet, then once I had some leads, I made phone calls, or last resort, visited places. Sometimes when I found people, I discovered they were a lot happier in their new surroundings, no harm had been done other than leaving a broken heart or two in their wake, and I didn't rat them out. I'd refund the seeker's money and move on to a serious case where a child or adolescent had gone missing. So, when Richhead came calling, I encountered an event that was definitely out of the ordinary.

"I want you to find my son, Nathan."

"Ok."

He handed me a copy of the morning's newspaper. The headlines read, "RICH KID KIDNAPPED IN SHOOT OUT." The event had been all over the radio and TV all morning. Richhead's college aged son had been kidnapped by leftist terrorists or more specifically, "black nationalists" led by a white woman. Apparently they had raided Richhead's mansion compound up in Highland Park, Illinois, a wealthy North Shore suburb. Gunfire had erupted when the army of security guards around the house woke up, and Richhead's son, Nathan, had disappeared with the raiders, along with a fair amount of loot, including cash, jewelry, and even a couple of valuable paintings. Apparently, the raiders had returned fire on the security guards.

"Uh, you know what, Mr. Richhead. I don't take cases involving violence. I'm not armed. I'm not licensed to be armed. And these guys are obviously armed. I don't think you really need me. The police have to be involved in this in a major way, right? Hell, my guess would be the FBI is on this. And now that I think about it, they probably have declared these guys "internal terrorists" under the Patriot Act and they'll have the CIA and the entire force of the Federal Government on this. You definitely don't need me."

I can't get involved in this case even if this asshole pays me a million bucks, because all the Feds are gonna be involved, and the first thing they would do is investigate me and dig up all my old radical, revolutionary background. Next thing I'd know, they'd have me in the slammer saying I was involved in this bullshit. No fucking way can you take this fucking case, man. This dude is bad fucking news.

"I was told your usual retainer in cases of this nature is ten thousand dollars up front, two thousand in expense money up front, and two thousand a week thereafter. Here's your first check. But I want results when you phone me one week from today." He handed me a business card containing two lines of text, his name, and a phone number with the tag "private." He also handed me several photos of Nathan, some large, some small. "Do you burn incense in here?"

"Yeah."

After a modest amount of research, I discovered Richhead was on the Board of Directors of Push Electronics, Blue Sky Industries, and Screwyablue. He had been a CEO of two of the companies.

Two things bothered me. Where did he get my name as a referral? And where did he get the payment scheme? I usually asked for a hundred bucks up front, started doing research, and if it didn't look promising, I refunded the money. On the promising cases I kept the money, then sold information to the customer as I acquired it for costs plus a modest hourly fee.

Actually, a third thing bothered me. The fucking case itself. I knew I would come to grief with it. Before it was over, the Feds would have me in an interrogation room and have my ass indicted for a bunch of shit I hadn't done.

By middle age I had joined and departed three national organizations, one with unofficial international ties, all of which advocated the revolutionary overthrow of all the capitalist governments in the world. Two of the groups had simply melted away in interminable sectarian bickering, and I had been expelled from the other for "bourgeois deviations" - or in other words, too much original thinking along Marxist lines.

Curiously, I did have one lead in the case. I had mentioned Nathan's name while discussing the news and sports with one of my West Side dope contacts, John Black. John and I had been in two of the groups together. A long time factory worker, he had come via a Maoist split in the Communist Party, and I had joined via a Maoist student group that was absorbed by the national organization. After the organization hit the reefs of sectarianism, John and I remained buddies, but we were both lapsed revolutionaries. Now, I bought my dope from him.

"You know that college boy has been coming down to this neighborhood and buying dope?"

"Really?"

"Oh, yeah. Well known fact. That boy has been driving down to Independence Avenue and buying up all the dope. Don't even haggle on the price. Just pays whatever they asks."

"What's he been buying?"

"Everything. Mostly hard stuff like rock and heroine."

"You're kidding. "

"No, I am not. That boy is a hype." That was the local street lingo for an addict who was using needles.

"I wonder how the kid got mixed up with politics?"

"The usual, I expect. You know, dope, money, politics?"

"Narco-terrorism?"

John shrugged his shoulders. It was dawning on me John knew or suspected a lot more than he was saying.

"Who did the action, John? What group was it? What kind of black nationalists are lead by a white woman?"

John weighed out my baggie in his West Side garage. The place was hot and stuffy and looked like a motorcycle museum. It reeked of motor oil, and various automotive fluids. John was a Harley man. "I don't know, man. You should ask Dave." I could feel sweat running down my forehead. I took off my sportscoat.

He was referring to a former mutual friend, Dave Morrison. John worked for Dave as a delivery man and furniture repair man. Dave, our former comrade, had managed to establish and grow a fairly successful antique furniture restoration business on the near West Side.

"Dave, he'd know."

"Why Dave? He's been out of politics forever."

"Yeah, but his old lady ain't."

"Marilynn? She's in Cuba, man."

"Not anymore."

Marilynn Morrison, or Marilynn Coolidge as I had known her when she was my college sweetheart, had disappeared into Cuba after several "bank appropriations" (left speak for bank robberies) on the East Coast. Marilynn, of course, was the reason for my falling out with Dave. We had a brief fling after her separation from Dave. When I found out she was wanted, I asked her to find new quarters as soon as possible.

"What are telling me, man, she's back in town?"

"I don't know nothin' man. Here's your shit." John tossed me my baggie.

"When are you going to fire that lazy, black, alcoholic, con-man, worthless piece of shit, Dave?" asked Mary Morris.

Dave Morrison, a forty year old Yuppie entrepreneur, who lived and worked on Chicago's near West Side, only half listened to his girlfriend, Mary Morris, prattle on about his employee, Mr. John Black. Simultaneously, he stirred the mornings' first cup of coffee, listened to the cable TV news, noted an advertisement for Buddy Guy at a North Side blues club, and wondered how he would make a promised furniture delivery that afternoon without John's help.

John Black, a sixty something African American who lived at a variety of addresses on Chicago's far west side, was absent without leave, once again, from his post as a master craftsman at Dave Morrison's antique furniture refinishing operation. Despite the fact that the old fuck was unreliable, irresponsible, undependable, unpredictable and alcoholic, Dave still liked the old guy could not bring himself to fire the old man, no matter how much he fucked up. The bottom line on John was that he was a remarkable craftsman.

"He's capricious, impulsive, and doesn't show up for work at his slightest whim. What did he tell you last Monday?"

Dave Morrison picked up his cue although his consciousness was slowly being absorbed by a television news story about "black terrorism." "He told me that he wanted to ride his motorcycle around the 'hood before he came to work."

"There you go. It's time to fire him, Dave. You're running a business there. You're not running a charity operation for minority senior citizens."

"Yeah, I know."

"Shit, Dave. You have to learn to make decision. You have to learn to treat your business like a business. That black sonofabitch is taking advantage of your benevolence."

"Yeah. You're right."

Mary Morris paused, suspected that perhaps she had been coming on too strong, and changed tack. "Give any more thought to meeting my venture capital connection on LaSalle Street? You're going to need capital to expand your operation, and this guy, Shapiro, has financed lots of start-ups, mergers, and expansions. He could be your ticket to the big time."

Mary had worked her way into a partnership in a Loop law firm by age 35 by running her competitors for the position out of the firm. Mary didn't put up with any bullshit, and although her boyfriend, Dave, often frustrated her, she felt a curious attraction to the man. He seemed to possess the feeling and warmth which she thought she personally lacked. She found his tendency toward procrastination upsetting, and found it difficult to understand why it took him so long to make up his mind about everything from making a selection off a restaurant menu to firing obviously unproductive employees.

Mary had come to a grudging acceptance that the two of them were opposite on nearly every count. She was a Republican who had voted for Ronald Reagan in both elections, while Dave said he was a "radical" or an "environmentalist." She dismissed his politics as warmed over hippie-dippy, rad-liberal bullshit from the 1960s. Mary remembered that Dave's ex-wife had been a "heavy" in the radical student and women's movements. She knew that he had encountered some trouble with the authorities over his politics when he was a young man, but she considered that episode behind him, and the authorities were there to be fucked with anyway - right?

"So... what should I tell Shapiro? Want me to set something up?"

Dave, mentally adrift in the TV news report about a recent police shoot-out with black "terrorists" on the North Shore, couldn't refocus in time to save the conversational thread. He gathered that at least one black "terrorist" was on the loose in the Chicago metropolitan area before the video faded out into a kitchen cleanser commercial. "Say what?"

"Shit. You say you're not sexist, but you don't listen to a fucking thing I say. I said, DO YOU WANT ME TO SET UP A MEETING WITH SHAPIRO, THE VENTURE CAPITAL MAN?"

"I need to think about that, Mary, I don't want to rush into any deal."

"Your business is going to fall apart. If you're not growing, then you're losing ground. You have a lot of customers waiting in line for their deliveries. You're hot in Lincoln Park right now, Dave, but you can't treat your customers like that forever. They will get tired and go to the competition. Better believe it. Strike while the iron is hot."

"I'm getting the work out. Lucinda will help me get this stuff out today."

"Your part time Mexican helper. Your sometime, once-a-month, if she gets around to it, Mexican token female employee. Is this the person to whom you are referring?"

"Alright. Cut the shit, Mary. I'11 give her a call, and she'll come and help me."

"If she's not producing Mexican nationalist community plays, or manning a rape crisis line, or busy with one of her other harebrained schemes."

Dave did not want to discuss the merits of yet another of his employees, Lucinda Martinez, a Mexican American college student who had worked for him on and off for years. Lucinda seemed flighty or even fickle to others with the plethora of unfinished projects that she left in her wake, but Dave knew she was visionary, and he wanted it to go down in the books that should she ever find fame, that he had been one of her early mentors. He regarded her as well worth his nurturing efforts. "Wanna go see Buddy Guy play on Friday night?"

"Your livelihood is going down the drain, and you want to go see another tired old blues guy."

"Hey, we're talking about Buddy Guy."

"I know, 'our own national treasure in Chicago.' No, I do not want to sit around in another smoky blues dive. I do want to go to the fundraiser for historic building preservation. The governor of Illinois might show up there."

"Another cocktail party in a loft with a bunch of pretentious, wealthy north shore suburbanites?"

"You live in a loft, sweetie." Mary referred to his semi-glitzy digs located just west of Haymarket Square, just north of the Randolph Street market, and just south of the Lake Street elevated line. He had rented the dilapidated building years ago, when the neighborhood had simply been one more rotting rustbelt industrial district. As his business prospered, he had upgraded the building, bought it, then upgraded anew. Now he worked out of a fairly spacious former factory on the first floor and maintained a loft apartment above. He was constantly involved in carpentry projects, farming out only the most complicated work that was beyond his craft expertise. The loft was now furnished in the latest fashion. John Black thought that the placed looked faddish when he occasionally stopped in to pick up his paycheck or drop off customer collections.

"Well?" She asked.

"Well what?"

"Are you going with me?"

Before he could respond, Dave heard the characteristic buzz tone on his telephone that told him he had another incoming call. "I got another call."

"Well, see who it is, then get back to me. Hurry up, I can't fuck around all day."

"Ok." Dave answered his other call assuming it was another irate customer from Lincoln Park demanding to know if he had finished refinishing their furniture. He had originally met Mary that way. He wound up redoing most of her furniture. "Hello, Dave Morrison here."

"Dave, this is Marilynn." Long pause. "Remember me?" she added hopefully.

He had recognized his ex-wife's voice at once, although it had been more than ten years since he had last heard it. "Of course. I thought you were in Cuba."

"I need a favor."

"Wait a minute, I'm on another call. Let me get back to you." With that he switched the line back to Mary. "It's my ex-wife. Let me call you back."

"Your ex-wife? What the hell does she want?"

"Probably everything."

I didn't like the idea of having to approach Dave. He had been furious when he had learned that Marilynn had stayed with me. And Dave wasn't the type who got worked up very often. All that had gone down more than ten years in the past but I was still leery of approaching Dave to ask questions.

I also didn't like the idea of having to turn over information to Richhead about Marilynn's involvement in the kidnapping. That info would go right to the cops and the Feds. I didn't want any part of that.

On the other hand, if you don't have the information, then you can't betray anybody. Maybe you can string this guy out for a couple of more checks then walk away. You stay clean and you've managed to vacuum a few bucks back from the rich guys.

"What do you have for me, MacNaughton?"

"I've made some progress on the case Mr. Richhead. I've discovered your son was involved in the drug scene. Apparently, he was a heavy buyer out on the West Side."

"Nathan? I don't believe it."

"Believe it."

"Do you have proof?"

"That's not the kind of business where they give receipts. I developed this information from an unimpeachable source. Better believe it, because its true."

"Who kidnapped him, then? This was drug related?"

"I don't have the answer to that. I'm working on some interesting leads."

"What your hypothesis then?"

"I don't deal in guessing. I sell facts. I do have a question for you, however."

"Yes?"

"How is it that you picked me for this case? And where did you get the information about my fee structure? Somebody sent you? Because you coming here does not add up. I don't get clients like you."

"I have to confess, Mr. MacNaughton. Actually, I made a mistake. I was recommended to use the MacNaughton agency on the other side of town. I simply mistook your agency for another. However, since you seem to be doing well on the case, lets stay with it." He peeled off two grand in hundreds and handed it to me. I figured that covered the cost of the two cans of air freshener I had pumped into the office.

I thought surprise would probably be the best strategy in dealing with Dave Morrison. I couldn't see him slamming the door in my face, so I drove over to his loft located next to the Lake Street elevated tracks. He lived in a building that used to be a bicycle factory. I think they had a showroom downstairs, and the workshops on the other two floors. The building was located where another set of elevated tracks had once crossed over the Lake Street line. They tore that line down when I was a kid in the 1950s, and today nobody realizes the snaky old steel superstructure used to wend its way through the neighborhood. But Chicago was like that - big chunks of the environment would change on you or simply vanish.

I was surprised when the Yuppie woman opened the door. At first I thought I went to the wrong address, because this woman did not look like she belonged in Dave's life. She was wearing a slinky and expensive black "business" dress, heels, nylons, and a some expertly applied makeup. She smelled like high priced perfume. And she had weird eyes. Grey eyes.

"Yes?"

"Uh, I was looking for Dave Morrison..."

"And you are?"

"Oh, sorry. Pete MacNaughton, his old buddy from college."

"You'll have to excuse me, but he's never mentioned a MacNaughton to me."

"You're his... wife?"

"Fiancée. Would you care to tell me what you'd like to see Dave about?"

"Well, its pretty personal."

"Dave isn't loaning money to his old hippy friends anymore."

"No. No. Nothing like that. But, I do need to talk to him."

"And you haven't seen Dave in how many years?"

"Ten. Listen, its important."

She just looked at me with those grey eyes, her chin pointing ever higher with each exchange.

"It's about his ex-wife, Marilynn. I gotta talk to him. Tell him that. He'll talk to me."

"Come right in, please. Dave isn't here but please make yourself comfortable. I'm Marry Morris. Would you like some coffee, Pete?"

I checked the phone books and the Internet, and then I went to the central library branch and checked the business directories. There was only one MacNaughton listed in Illinois as a private investigator and that was me. So, the story about the wrong agency was definitely bullshit. But, I knew a detective on the police force who owed me big time. I decided I'd ask him what was up, because the cops had to know I was working the case.

Several years previously the cops had been investigating a murder in the Gold Coast neighborhood. I was working for a woman whose husband had disappeared. Long story short, the address book belonging to a Gold Coast call girl, a Puerto Rican woman named Irma Maldonado, wound up in my possession. The cops came looking for me or rather the address book for evidence in a murder trial, but before they officially arrived, a Detective Soto found me first. He asked for the page with his name on it to be removed. I didn't see how it could affect the murder trial one way or another so I obliged the guy, and turned down the grand he had offered me. I figured it was bad business taking money from cops.

"What made you think I was involved in that crap, Dave?" Marilynn Morrison asked her ex-husband.

"Well, shooting, terrorism, you know..."

"Look all that is in the past, man. I just need some help getting a good criminal lawyer. I want to settle up on the past. We did two banks. We never injured anyone. We never fired our weapons. "

"Who kidnapped the college kid? They said it was African Americans and a white woman. When I found out you were in town, I assumed it was you."

"I don't even know this fucking kid. I've been in Cuba for a decade, man. I'm not part of any armed unit anymore. I just want to get a lawyer, get things cleaned up, and get on with my fucking life."

"Ok. I'll start looking for a lawyer."

"Don't start looking for a fucking lawyer. Find a fucking lawyer. And find somebody who can conduct the surrender. Somebody we can trust."

"I've been out of politics, too. I don't know anybody anymore."

"What about Pete? Call him. He's a rent-a-pig now. Get him."

"That asshole?"

"Who else knows both sides?"

"So Pete, what do you know about Marilynn?" I thought Mary looked like one of those slinky fashion models. We were sitting in Dave's plush living room drinking lemonades provided by Mary. I kept tinkling my ice to melt it into the drink to make it less acidic.

"I know she's in town."

"Oh. I thought she was in Cuba?"

"Past tense."

"What do you think she's doing here? Trying to get back together with Dave?"

"I doubt that."

"Why?"

"I don't think Dave wants to get back on that roller coaster ride. Listen, where is Dave? I really gotta talk to him."

"He's making a delivery run. He should be back any minute. Do you think Marilynn has anything to do with this?" She held up the morning newspaper. The headlines read; COPS SEARCH FOR RICHHEAD.

"Uh, I wouldn't know about that."

"But she belonged to a radical group that robbed banks, right?"

"That was a long time ago."

"But that is true, isn't it?"

"Yeah. I guess. Again, a long time ago."

"Right, so she must be running out of money by now, right?"

"She's been employed as a writer and a journalist in Cuba. She doesn't need money."

"You like her, don't you?"

"We're old college buddies."

"I see. Maybe more like sweethearts?"

"You know, I seen that rich white boy is everybody is looking for," said John Black. He was smoking a joint and sitting on a yet to be restored antique couch covered in layers of thick plastic sheeting. He was sweating from moving furniture. He was dressed in black jeans, workboots, and a black, red, and green t-shirt. Despite his age, big muscles rippled under his dark skin pushing up the shirt around the bulges. On the other side of the small storage shed, Lucinda Martinez sat on a empty shipping crate that had contained an antique end table. She was wearing cut off jeans, and a blouse tied off above her navel. She looked sweaty with her long black hair tied back with a colorful handkerchief.

"Are you shitting me? Where?"

"Down on Independence Avenue. On the other side of the expressway. He's down there with his buddies in a boarded up place."

"South of the expressway? In a house?"

"Yep."

"You sure, man? Every fucking body is looking for that kid."

"Yeah, its him alright. I seen him good about midnight out in the alley in back of the place. Got his little white girlfriend with him and his gang. She's always waving a big handgun around."

"Gang?"

"Yeah, he's running a gang of kids he recruited. I think they went up there to the mansion that day and was robbing it when they got caught. So, they started shooting at the police. I think that crazy girl probably started doing the shooting."

"You don't think he was kidnapped?"

"Hell no. He done kidnapped himself. They's down there on Independence Avenue doing dope like its goin' out of style. They be buying up all the dope in the neighborhood. They be buying so much its running up the prices on everything. I had to pay damn near double for this weed." John passed the joint to Lucinda.

"Tell MacNaughton, so you guys can split the reward money." She exhaled a lung full of sweet smelling smoke, and passed back the joint.

"I already told old Petey, but I don't want no part of that money or the situation. That's nothing but trouble."

"Yeah, the cops are gonna be all over the neighborhood when they find out."

"You can take that to the bank."

Detective Soto agreed to meet me under the L tracks in Wicker Park where North, Milwaukee, and Damen Avenues met at a six corners intersection. While I waited, I realized this elevated line had been part of the same one that used to pass near Dave Morris' house. And another ghost line had spiraled out from where I stood and ran parallel to North Avenue out to Humboldt Park.

I was lost in a reverie of thoughts about taking no longer existing Ls out to the city limits when Detective Soto whispered in my ear, "Hey, asshole, I coulda shot you in the back and you would have never known who did it."

I spun around in the gloom under the superstructure of the elevated while the midnight glare of streetlights cast an eerie reverse glow of lattice work light patterns on us. "We're even after this MacNaughton. And we don't never meet again. I appreciate what you done for me last time. But that was then, and this is now."

"Ok, I'm cool with that. I want to know why Richhead picked me to do the work."

"That's all? Man, you missed the train on this one, if that's all you're gonna ask me."

"Whatta talkin' about?"

"Ok. Richhead picked you because the FBI told him to pick you. They picked you because of your rich knowledge of radical left fringe scene, and they knew you would be happy to take money for information. You being a known communist and all, they figured you knew all the players."

"Oh, shit."

"I'm gonna give you a real piece of information, because you obviously need it and don't got it. A real favor, like you done for me. So that we're really even and I don't gotta look at your face no more."

"What's that?" I stiffened for a minute when I heard sirens. We both fell silent as we watched an ambulance shoot down North Avenue westbound toward Humboldt Park.

"Your old girlfriend didn't pull the job. The rich guy's kid is a crack addict and pulled the job himself. The woman they seen - that was his addict girlfriend. The blacks he had with him - that's his drug gang. Wasn't no black nationalist action. He's holed up blowin' all the money on drugs. But the FBI is gonna pin the rap on your old girlfriend and get her for internal terrorism. Maybe you too, if you get involved. Maybe help her out. Help her escape."

"How did the Feds know Marilynn was in town?"

"Think about it."

I remained silent.

"Man, you are the worst PI I ever heard of. You can't figure out anything. Who has the most to gain by letting Marilynn catch a case?"

"The new girlfriend?"

"Hey, you ain't as dumb as you look."

"Thanks, man." But Soto had already turned around and was stalking down the alley away from me.

Dave Morris had agreed to meet me at a restaurant with an outdoor cafe across the street from the Art Institute on Michigan Avenue. I recognized him right away with his long ponytail of white and blonde hair and his trademark tie-dyed t-shirt, jeans and sandals. His attire hadn't changed in over 30 years. He ordered some fancy salad and a diet soda. I ordered a cheeseburger, fries and black coffee. It was a beautiful breezy summer day with a lake breeze.

"Listen, I got some iron clad information, and I need you to pass it on to Marilynn."

"Take off your sportscoat and hand it to me. Then open up your shirt."

"I'm not wired Dave. I had to do this in person because they got ways to listen to any phone call. We had to do it in public, so they couldn't say we were sneaking around." Dave just eyeballed me showing no emotion.

"Ok." I wrestled off the sportscoat and handed it to him. I unbuttoned my dress shirt and revealed my hirsute torso.

Methodically, he went through all my pockets, read all the little notes, like "get gasoline" and "Buddy Guy, Live..." When he was satisfied, he handed the coat back to me.

"Dave, I'm trying to help. I'm trying to avoid..."

"Just state your case. I'm listening."

"No, you listen you fucking hippie relic. I don't know where you get off thinking you're morally superior to me. Your moral vanity act is sickening, man. Where the fuck were you in the old days, when we had organizations and tried to make an impact on society. I never fucking saw you on any picket lines or in the bus afterwards getting carted to jail. "

"You're dirty Peter. And everybody fucking knows it. Nobody trusts you any more, and nobody is going to tell you shit about anything."

"That's just fine, Dave. Because nobody needs to tell me shit. You're the dumbfuck who needs some information, not me. And if you shut-the-fuck-up, I'll give it to you. Not that I'd ever try to bail your sorry ass out of anything but because you just happen to be the middle man."

"Right. This is coming from the sell out, the liar, and the traitor."

"Everybody had to sell out Dave. You included. If you didn't sell out, you perished. I see you running a capitalist enterprise complete with exploited third world workers."

"Yeah, and you're working for the police."

"No, Dave, from time to time I work with selected policemen to return runaway teenagers to their homes. What you don't understand is that social revolution is not a morality play. Everybody is dirty. Everybody is mentally sick from living in this system. Its only a question of how dirty and how sick."

"You're the dirtiest then. You're a fucking liar and a traitor."

"Dave, I lied to you about Marilynn to try to spare your feelings. You're right. I'm busted, I fucking lied to you about Marilynn. But if you call me a fucking traitor to the revolution one more time, I'm gonna bust you up, man. Right fuckin' here. Right on Michigan Avenue."

After a long pause, Dave said, "So, what's this important news?"

"Don't know if you know it or not, but Marilynn didn't do that action up at the Richhead mansion."

"I know that."

"Good, so you are talking with her. Tell her the Feds are going to frame her for it anyway. "

"Bullshit."

"This goes down every few years, Dave. Think about the Haymarket martyrs, Joe Hill, Sacco and Vanzetti, the Conspiracy-8, Hurricane Carter. Its a long sad list."

"Bullshit. You're a traitor because you told the Feds Marilynn was in town."

"No, Dave. You got your new girlfriend to thank for that."

"Bullshit."

"Bye, Dave. I'll see you in hell." I got up and left.

During the last meeting I had with Richhead in my hermetically sealed air conditioned room I related his son's long slow descent into drugs and his growing alienation with both his father and his decadent position as a parasite in the social order. Letting the kid major in liberal arts instead of business had been a major mistake. All kinds of funny ideas about social justice and a economic fairness had crept into the kids consciousness and began to psychically torture him with the contradictions.

"You know, when your son asked to go to counseling when he was a freshman, you should have sent him."

"How do you know about that? "

"You paid me to know about that. I know lots of stuff. Like it was your son, his girlfriend, and his gang who robbed your house, not black nationalists and a radical white woman. I also know you're paying or pressuring the Feds or some Feds to make this look like something it isn't.

And, by the way, if the Feds pick me up, I have a friend who's going to deliver this entire story and a hundred pages of research notes complete with signed affidavits from witnesses to all the major newspapers." That was total bullshit, but I had seen that move in the movies and had read it in mystery novels. It always worked on paper, so I thought I'd try it.

"Where's my son, now?"

"I don't know where your son is, and I ain't gonna look. Fuck you, and get out of my fucking office."

John told me later that Lucinda took Marilynn down to El Paso in a car, then Lucinda's friends reverse smuggled Marilynn over the border to Mexico City. Last I heard, she was back in Cuba teaching 5 year olds. John told me that Dave was out looking for a new girlfriend. Such is life in the Psychotic Atomik Empire.

Factory

"MacNaughton."

"What?" I shouted over the din of the dog food factory. I hadn't seen my machine shop foreman sneak up behind me. I lurched out off my shop stool and stood between my machine and the boss, effectively blocking a close-up inspection of what I was doing. It was about 7:30 PM, and I was working second shift as usual. It was a hot summer night but I was wearing my sand colored khaki uniform complete with a shirt with a big name tag that read "Pete."

I hope to hell this dumb fucker doesn't see that my boring bar isn't cutting steel.

I had set the bar to cut air for the last half hour before lunch time. The cutting tool would inextricably advance on automatic feed toward the headstock of the lathe until it hit a stop. I would then manually back the apron of the lathe back to the starting position, then resume operations. From a distance or to untrained eyes, I looked busy, boring out a fixture for large dog food containers. In actuality, I was fucking the dog.

"I want to see you in the office." He yelled in my ear.

"Why?" I yelled back, trying to make myself heard over the roar of the nearby punch press department.

"Because I said so, that's why."

"Is this a disciplinary session?"

The foreman, a young man, not yet 30, stared at me with an exasperated look on his face, "Yes, as a matter of fact it is." He was wearing a spotless white shirt and plain black tie which was complemented by his bright red face.

"I'll need my union committeeman, then."

"He's working up front on an important project. What's the matter, can't do your own talking? Why do you have to stand behind the union every time I have to talk to you?"

"Because I have a civil right to have my union committeeman present. That right is backed by the full weight of federal labor law."

This time, they intended to fire me.

"Ok, have it your way." He threw up his hands then waved me off the way people do to street peddlers. He strode off toward his block house office in the front of the machine shop.

I shut down my lathe, cranked the cutting tool to within a few thousands of an inch of the interior steel wall I had been boring to get rid of the evidence of my malingering on the job, then set off to find my union committeeman who was wandering around somewhere beneath the roof of the 20 acre factory.

I loathed the union committeeman, "Doc," a short, fat hillbilly because I was convinced that he had been bought out by the company. With conspicuous slowness, I carefully removed and folded my shop apron on top of my tool box, then leisurely cleaned and put away my precision measuring tools, and finally locked the boxes. I noted that Attila the Douchebag, my pet name for our new boss, seemed to be watching me from his desk. He looked more agitated than usual. I strolled over to the drinking fountain and took a long drink before I ambled out of the department on my quest for my union representative.

They're going to fire you this time, man. I got 250 bucks in the bank. I'll get one more check to pay the rent and utilities. I can apply for unemployment, but these motherfuckers are going to challenge that. Man, what kind of job can I apply for? I've got a degree in history and twenty years of work history as a machinist.

I started wending my way through the punch press department looking for "Doc." The women operators each waved to me as I passed their massive, rapidly stoking machines.

It's the petition, man. You're gonna get fired for passing around that petition. You had to do it. If that's what it's about, then this is worth it. You had no choice. They cut down the first flag bearer, so you stepped up. Be proud, man. You don't want to live like a himp. Don't be afraid. Be angry. Act like a fucking communist.

The company had recently fired a woman, Linda, who they claimed had taken too much sick leave collecting "workman's compensation." Nothing existed in writing contractually or in law regarding the amount of time anyone could take. The basic reasoning had been, if you're hurt, you're hurt. When you're better, come back to work. Work paid a lot more than compensation, so there was no incentive to stay on it.

When they announced Linda's firing at the union meeting, people were very upset with the company for doing it, and with the union for permitting it. The union, the IBU, (nobody knew what the letters stood for - we called it the International Bureaucrats Union or alternatively the International Bullshit Union) claimed they had filed a grievance on her behalf.

The following Monday on first shift, her long time friend, Carmen, started passing around a petition protesting the firing. She did it legally, moving it around during breaks and lunch. The company promptly fired her. We wouldn't know the official reason for that for another month at the next union meeting. But her friends were saying she was fired for passing the petition.

So after Carmen went down, I retrieved the petition from a fork-lift driver and started it back around the factory. I redid it, demanding reinstatement for both women. But that caused double work, and I had to get the thing re-signed by everybody. I did have one helper, Vicky, a middle aged woman a couple of years younger than me whom I suspected was both alcoholic and a coke addict. But she was the party type and had lots of friends so I handed her another copy to pass out. Naturally, word got out immediately from the snitches that I was doing it.

You know the way it probably leaked out? People were probably discussing it in the lunchroom and a supervisor overheard it and asked a few questions. One of the dummies probably just flat out gave up the information. No concept of the importance of the information or how it could be used. And now it's my ass.

For some reason, images from a Hollywood "B" movie that they had aired on a cable TV the night before kept cropping up in my conscious-ness. Cops and robbers, totally boring and repetitive. Superheros who fight off super vicious bad guys.

Why couldn't they just make one movie true-to-life where somebody gets pissed off at their moronic boss then blows them away? Just once I'd like to see a movie about a punch press operator who loses her cool after her boss unjustly chastises her, and she calls in a bomb threat to the factory, or comes to work after a three day disciplinary vacation and blows her boss away with a 45 caliber automatic. Then I realized you do see that movie from time to time. On the nightly news.

Of course, I'm your basic, marginalized, underemployed lunatic-fringe type who's been overeducated for manual work. A monster lurking in the social fabric, I'm the type the corporations and government dread: educated and working class. Educated and working class equals totally alienated, the kind of people who join the socialist parties, and the forces of oppression understand that.

So, as a classic misfit in the Psychotic Atomik Empire, I yearn for insurrection, sabotage and disrespect for all forms of authority. When I hear about a guy packing bearings full of lapping compound, I laugh. When I learn one of friends has called in bomb threats, I'm delighted.

Most people are fried by the time they hack their way through the traffic congestion to get to their work place. Then they have to survive 8 to 12 hours of alienating work. The only thing I can't figure out is why the majority never seems to catch on and overthrows the government to put an end to the fucking bullshit. Probably because there is no convincing alternate.

Everybody in the punch press department waved to me as I passed. Some of the set-up men tried to duck me. *Chickenshits don't want to sign the petition. Afraid of me because I'm trouble. Man, they're afraid of losing their jobs. They don't have a college degree. As if the fucking degree was anything anybody could fall back on anyhow. The Fourth International did a paper one time that mentioned the acute anxiety most people experienced in daily life.* I remembered a book from distant college days, a survey course on existential philosophy. The title of that book was <u>The Age of Anxiety</u>. And that's what the class war boiled down to in the factories and offices of the Psychotic Atomik Empire. You never knew when you were going to lose your job due to the economy, company consolidations and buyouts, or when some asshole will simply decide to fire you on a whim.

I found one of the set-up men skulking back in the poorly lit area where they stored steel coils. "Charlie" was smoking inside the building, a major offense against the corporation. Clouds of blue smoke boiling out of the screw machine department made smoking in the building into a joke. The burning cutting oil they used could be smelled in the parking lot.

"Hey, Charlie. Got the new petition for you to sign." I handed it to him. A skinny, middle-aged white guy, Charlie or whatever his real name was, never had much to say. He never went to union meetings.

He slowly wiped the machine oil off his hands onto his pants. He removed the cigarette from his mouth and studied the petition.

Comon chickenshit. Just fucking sign it.

"Its the same one you signed last time, man. Only difference we added Carmen's name."

He took a greasy pen from his chest pocket and signed.

"Thanks Charlie."

"You think this is going to do any good?"

"Can't hurt."

"Yeah, I guess. " He turned his back and resumed looking at the tags on the coils, presumably looking for the next roll to mount on his punch press.

Our organization, unofficially linked to the Fourth International (because it is illegal in the United States for workers to form organizational combinations with workers from other countries, but legal for corporations to go multi-national), once participated in a peace march in the Chicago suburb of Rolling Meadows. The object of the march was to reach the gates of the U.S. Army Psychological Operations unit. Helicopters flew overhead from the start of the march in a forest preserve all the way to the base. When we arrived, dozens of civilians and soldiers pointed video cameras, film cameras, and regular cameras at us. They pointed more surveillance devices at us than firearms. In the past I had been accosted by the Chicago Police going berserk, the National Guard with bayonets and teargas, and even police on horses. But that demonstration remains in my mind as one of the creepiest things I had ever witnessed. I'm sure some of those cameras weren't loaded, but they were more effective than firearms.

I carefully wiped off the grease that Charlie had inadvertently smeared on the margin of the petition, then refolded it, and placed it back inside my shirt. *There's not much difference between the way factory workers had to do things back when Gorky wrote* The Mother *and today. We still have to smuggle in socialist literature. We still have to pass petitions like the country was occupied by Nazis, and we still have to live in fear over every move we make. Then, we had no civil rights to be violated. Now, they give us civil rights on paper, then take them away on the shop floor.*

Curiously, the United States is the only country in the world with a left without working class representation. In the United States, the left is composed largely of middle class intellectuals. Certainly the leadership of the left is mainly middle class intellectuals. So, working class socialists wind up fighting the corporations and the government, their own bureaucratized unions, and their own middle class dominated sectarian left.

Why do you do this shit, man? The only rewards are getting fired, having the police hassle you, having the FBI create files and maybe a case against you, or maybe just plain get shot and thrown into one of the swampy ponds in the industrial districts around Chicago.

I paused at an open door that lead to the shipping dock and the August night over the Illinois prairie. I glanced to see if anyone was looking, then slipped through the door. Outside, I found a woman press operator and a mechanic quietly smoking on the cracked cement steps. I knew their faces from passing them in the factory for years, but not their names. The outside air felt cool on my face. A vast orchestra of crickets chirped away in concert under the stars.

"You guys want to sign the petition protesting the two firings?"

"Sure." They said in unison. I carefully unfolded the petition and handed it to the woman first. I knew from long experience women were quicker to sign than men. If I handed it to the skilled mechanic, he might start raising issues over it, then find a reason not to sign. Of course, he would never admit he wasn't signing out of fear. But fear was contagious and then the woman wouldn't sign either.

After she signed, she handed it to him, and I realized these two were lovers in their late 30s. I wanted to remain outside with the chirping crickets and the fresh air, but I thanked them, and returned to the rancid odors, dust, and noise of the factory.

You do it because of the indestructible streak of idealism in your wretched personality. You do it because your genes are programmed to do it. Just like carpenter genes are programmed to produce beautiful cabinets. They create cabinets because that's what they do. You raise hell because you've been programmed to be part of the conscience of a race of hairless, tailless monkeys.

I crossed a main aisle between the presses and the dog food can machines. When I did, the straw boss, a guy in his sixties, spotted me. He nonchalantly approached me.

"Hi, what are you doing up here? We don't have any machines down."

"I'm looking for the union steward."

"Doc? He's in the cafeteria up front."

"Thanks." I walked on.

That fucker was one of the most effective bosses the company had on the shop floor. He never started any shit, but he knew everything that was going on. And he wrote out so much disciplinary paperwork that the workers called him Shakespeare. I didn't bother stopping to hand the petition around even though a couple of people were trying to flag me from their machines, because I knew Shakespeare was probably prowling somewhere in the shadows taking notes. He wouldn't stop tracking me until I was out of his department.

Instead of going directly to the grungy cafeteria with its fluorescent lights, I stopped off in the men's washroom by the time clocks. I found a variety of Puerto Rican forklift drivers and Mexican machine operators holding an animated conversation. Mainly young guys, they were formed in a large semi-circle around one of the wash basins talking about women.

One of the guys, Rico, a tall handsome man with raven hair and light skin, had been in the Puerto Rican Socialist Party. He asked the others in Spanish to sign the petition. They all did. And then they resumed the conversation like I wasn't there.

I'm in a dream. Didn't William S. Burroughs say that in one of his interviews or books? Your life is a series of encounters with others, punctuated by daydreams, reveries, memories, sleep, and dreams. But when they haul you in the office in front of several ugly faces, that's no dream. You're fired and you can have your next daydream at the unemployment office where you have to fight to try to get your unemployment turned on. Or when you're standing in front of the lathe trying to figure out how in the hell to make a part, with sweat pouring down your face, that's not a dream either.

In the cafeteria, I found Doc sitting at one of the long, dirty lunch tables having coffee with the second shift supervisor. They were sharing mutual laughter over a joke when I walked in.

"I need to talk to you."

"Ok. What's it about?"

"Attila the Douchebag wants to talk to me."

"So? I'm busy. Go talk to him."

"He says its disciplinary, Stewart." He hated his own name, Stewart.

"Well, find out what he wants, and then I'll come down if necessary."

"I'm officially asking for union representation in front of a witness, Stewart." The manager made a face and looked down at his coffee.

"Ok. Go back down there, and wait outside his office. I'll be down directly, and we can go in together."

"Right." I swiveled around and left. *My ass. Motherfucker is going to call down first and see what's up. Then he's coming down and both those assholes are going to pile on me.* I decided to take another route back.

I found a pack of electricians working on the main slitter for the factory. The machine was down, but no bosses were in sight. I walked up to the group and asked the lead guy, Roy, a former local president to sign the petition. I didn't show it to him, because I didn't want him to see the names on it.

"I can't sign that, Pete. That's up to the local officers to decide what to do. Bring it up at a union meeting. That petition isn't going to have any weight."

"If the whole factory signs it, they gotta know its trouble if they don't hire them back."

"Yeah? Who's gonna cause that trouble? You?"

"Me and everybody else."

He turned back to the panel board in the machine. "I'm not signing it." The others kept working and acted like I wasn't there. I knew it was useless to approach them in that situation. I might get a couple of the younger guys to sign if I caught them alone, away from Roy.

Skilled trades make more money than some "professionals." Of course they have to work 60 hours a week, week after week, year after year, but they make a lot more money than a forklift driver or a machine operator. Lots of these guys have part time businesses on the side, too. They own nice houses in middle class subdivisions. They own nice cars and big toys like motor homes, boats, snowmobiles, jet skis, and vacation homes. They like the union because they get big pay. And the US left worships them because they think they're going to lead a working class revolution some day. What the US left has yet to figure out is that the non-union workers are the ones who may lead a social revolution some day. Those are the sans coulettes of our time. Not the big pay union workers.

People asked me why I volunteered to help organize more locals of the IBU. I told them belonging to a bureaucratic union was better than no union.

Besides, then you get to fight both the company and the union for your rights and decent pay. But at least with a bureaucratic union you had the opportunity to fight. It's a step by step process.

I found a Mexican janitor next, and he signed. He had been demoted to janitor while the union stood by, as usual, and did nothing. Then I passed two white millwrights in their 60s in the aisle. They were filthy from crawling under a strapping machine. Neither one had a high school education and neither had been through an apprenticeship. They were "shade tree mechanics." They both signed.

The last time I had volunteered for an organizing drive at a small factory up in Woodstock, Illinois, where they had imprisoned Debs in the county jail after the Great Railroad Pullman Strike of 1893, I had encountered white and Mexican workers who were renters, drove battered automobiles, and accepted revolutionary ideas as readily as the morning weather forecast.

Of course, there was no welcome mat placed out for them in the U.S. left, so the United States remains the only country in the world where there is no discernible working class presence in the left.

I strolled through the forklift repair shop, but nobody was home. Before heading down the aisle, I peered around the corner looking for Shakespeare or Attila, but didn't see anyone, so I headed back to the machine shop.

In the can test shop I found three women water testing the dog food cans to make sure they didn't leak. All three had signed Vicky's petition, or at least they said so. As I passed through the truck driver's waiting room, I placed the rank and file bulletin from our organization on the table. With great difficulty, our grouping had made progress organizing drivers and other Teamsters over the years in the battle against that union bureaucracy.

I handed out our organization's rank and file union newsletter at union meetings, then fought to have a motion passed to get the local to buy it and distribute it. I won the vote by a margin of four votes. I had to go to every single union meeting to keep the IBU from rescinding it because the bureaucrats hated it. It linked our shop's battles to the national and international ones. And it showcased the bureaucratic problem in every issue. That was not the kind of labor journalism the big shots or the little shots wanted in the union hall.

As I passed by the Quality Control bulletin board on my way to the shop, I noticed someone had left the dry erase marker in the little tray beneath the board. I looked both ways down the aisle, then carefully erased the daily safety slogan and number of days since the last industrial accident. In big black letters I printed, GIVE LINDA AND CARMEN THEIR JOBS BACK.

As I finished, I turned around to find an African American machine operator, a taciturn man in his 40s, had watched my propaganda efforts. His name was Ted.

"They said I would find you over here. I want to sign the petition. But not here. Let's go over by the welding shop." He nodded at the bulletin board.

"Yeah, I hear you." We moved quickly to an empty welding booth about 100 yards away from the board. Before we could finish, I noticed Shakespeare walk past the board toward the QC department. Either he hadn't seen the new safety slogan or he didn't care. What really concerned me was that he might have been tailing me, and I hadn't noticed.

A couple of the evening welders signed the petition. Several others said they had signed Vicky's. The evening boss in the welding area, a guy in his mid-60s, waved me out of the area. A short guy with a grey crew cut and standard black pants and white shirt, he was a good guy who had come up through the ranks. He never reported anybody. He just didn't want any trouble. And I was definitely trouble.

I wasn't passing a petition around. Do you have a witness saying I was passing a petition around? I walked up front to see my union committeeman. He sent me back here to wait. I don't know anything about the bulletin board. Do you have a witness who says I wrote that on the bulletin board?

When I reached the shop, I was pleasantly surprised when the die makers said they had signed Vicky's petition. That made it a lot easier for me. Arguing with those boneheads, skilled labor, was a pain in the ass. As I made the rounds, tool box to tool box, I realized she must of come through at the start of the shift and signed them all up. They all wanted to get into her pants, so they signed. They'd probably remind her, too, when they met up with her again at the tavern down the road from the factory.

There's a swamp on one side of that road where people dump stuff they don't want. And there's an abandoned gravel pit filled with deep water back in the woods on the other side. Make sure you don't wind up there instead of the tavern.

I folded the petition back into the safe spot between my khaki shirt and t-shirt. I would compare notes with Vicky the next morning. I would drive down to the tavern to meet her about six A.M. before she started her shift. Sometimes when we met, I realized she had never gone home.

I meandered up to the blockhouse and peered inside. No Attila. I leaned against the block wall with all the indifference I could muster. Shortly, Doc appeared.

"Hi, Stewart."

"What's this all about? What did you do? And call me Doc like everybody else would you?"

"I didn't do anything, Doc. I don't know what his fuckin' problem is."

"Well, maybe that's the problem. You didn't do anything. Maybe he wants you to do some work."

"I work as hard as you do, Doc." That was a reference to the vast amounts of time he spent either up in the front office enjoying air-conditioned hospitality all summer shooting the shit with the big shots or sitting the cafeteria with one department boss or another discussing baseball scores or where the best fishing existed in the area.

"I spent my time productively taking care of y'all. If you'ns didn't get into so much trouble, I'd be out on my machine more."

"Is that right?"

"I know you been pushing that petition around again. You're asking for it, you know. They're gonna fire anybody has anything to do with passing that thing around."

"What petition?"

"Yeah, right. You're gonna get it one of these days MacNaughton. And there ain't nothing the union is gonna be able to do about it, neither."

"I heard that song before."

"And you're gonna hear it again, before it's over with, goddamnit."

"Yeah, I'm sure."

"Some people never learn."

"You got that right."

Attila came storming up to the blockhouse with an engineer. They were holding a big assembly print for the main coil cutter. The engineer must have stayed overtime. The big boys wanted that machine running. Attila glared at me as he slammed open the door to the blockhouse. Doc and I followed in their wake.

Attila turned to us right away. I noted the bright red hue of his face. "What do you guys want? I'm busy. Can't you see that? What's the problem now?"

"You told me you wanted to see me." I said.

"For what?" Attila demanded.

"For how-the-hell do I know?"

"I want you to get to work. Get some goddamn work done."

"I was working when you interrupted me."

"Well... work faster."

"Is this a verbal warning?" I asked. Doc stood by completely ignorant of the rules of engagement or grievance writing. I realized as I stood there, the dumb fuck had probably never written a single grievance in his two years on the job as a committeeman.

"Yes."

"Then, I'm going to file a grievance."

"You'll have to do that on your own, partner," said Doc.

"Well, if you refuse, then I'll take the day off tomorrow to go down to the labor board, and file on you, too, Doc." That was complete bullshit, but neither one of those two turds knew it. "And, you can't charge me for the day off either, because it's against federal law."

"Can he do that?" asked my boss. Doc looked at my boss with a blank expression.

"OK, then this is not a verbal warning."

"Then what the fuck is it?"

"I don't know. Just quit fucking around so much and do some work for a change."

"That's it?"

"Yeah."

Then, my boss made an elaborate show of ignoring me. I walked out and left Doc behind. I heard some yelling inside the blockhouse, and as Doc exited I could distinctly hear the words, "Get out!" all the way from my toolbox. Doc didn't bother to debrief me.

I put a little notebook on top of my tool box. I kept notes of all the transactions between myself and the union and company. I always put the thing on display so news of the little book would get back to both management and the union hacks. I boxed each entry against the others to prevent any future tampering and ensure the thing could be used in any legal procedures.

I missed my meeting with Vicky in the morning because I couldn't get to sleep until 4 A.M. I generally got off at Midnight, but I had to pound down several beers before I could relax and sleep.

I did meet her the next day when I pulled into the parking lot around 3:30 P.M. Vicky came running out on the hot asphalt to greet me, her long unkempt blonde hair trailing behind her.

"Did you hear what happened?"

"I just got here." I made sure my windows were left open a crack before I got out of the car.

"Carmen got her job back!"

"Really? What about Linda?"

"The union says they're working on that."

"How did Carmen get her job back? We didn't even turn this in, yet." I handed her my section of the petition.

"Well, after you wrote that on the board, everybody took out markers and wrote it all over the factory all morning. Everywhere you looked GIVE LINDA AND CARMEN THEIR JOBS BACK."

"I wrote on the board?"

"Oh, bullshit. Everybody knows you did it. Anyway, at noon they posted an announcement on the union bulletin board that Carmen was coming back to work next Monday - they reduced it from firing to a week off."

"Hear anything regarding me?"

"No. What?"

"Just curious," I said.

"Meet me after work at the tavern so we can celebrate."

"Sure." I walked into the factory for another shift in an infinity of factory shifts in the Psychotic Atomik Empire.

About the Author

Gregory Alan Norton's short story publication credits include *The Princeton Arts Review, George and Mertie's Place, Tarpaulin Sky, whimperbang, Rockford Review, Nebo, Missing Spoke Press Anthology, Struggle, Writer's Corner, Oyez Review, Short Story Bimonthly, Slugfest, Jack the Daw, Mobius, Thunder Sandwich, Cooweescoowee,* and *Plum Biscuit.*

His novel, *There Ain't No Justice, Just Us* (ISBN 0-7388-0004-X) is available at Amazon. com.

Norton, a Chicago writer, has served as an activist in the civil rights, peace, and labor movements. He served as an organizer and newspaper editor for the United Steelworkers and has participated in other unions as well.   www.gregoryalannorton.com

9 781891 386589